Toehold in Europe

Book 5 in the

Combined Operations Series

By

Griff Hosker

Published by Sword Books Ltd 2016
Copyright © Griff Hosker First Edition

A CIP catalogue record for this title is available from the British Library.

Cover by Design for Writers

Dedicated to my little sister, Barb, and in memory of my dad who served in Combined Operations from 1941-1945

Prologue

January 1943

We had been on the island of Malta since the Torch landings in North Africa. With the Americans now in the war we had almost driven the Germans and Italian from Africa. Malta was now safer and meant we had a shorter journey for our raids. Lieutenant Ferguson, our new liaison officer, had been shipped over from Gibraltar and was now at our new base. We were not on the main island but the northern island of Ghawdex. Officially we were in the port of Marsalaforn but we had found an uninhabited bay just north of Marsalaforn called Qbajjar Bay. As soon as we had found it we had moved there. Sergeant Poulson and Petty Officer Bill Leslie had managed to erect shelters which would be invisible from the air and we didn't mind roughing it. We were Commandos! Lieutenant Ferguson found it hard to adjust, at first, and then he acquired two generators and became as happy as a sand boy! We were a community who lived apart. We could train and practise our skills unobserved using the nearby army base as our Quarter Master.

Major Fleming, our new and thankfully distant commanding officer, knew nothing about the move. As far as he was concerned we were in the port of Marsalaforn. What he didn't know would not hurt us. We chose our new base as we were free from the attentions of the German and Italian air forces. They came each day from Sicily and bombed anything which looked military and anything else which took their fancy. From the air we were invisible. We knew this as the Captain of our captured E-Boat, Lieutenant Alan Jorgenson, had managed to wangle a flight on a

Lysander and he had flown over our bay. He saw nothing and he knew what he was looking for. The pilot who took him in was known to us as he was part of Major Fleming's network. He took agents into Sicily and Italy and picked them up. He was happy to have a peaceful mission for once. Our work was dangerous enough but his was positively suicidal.

We had been allowed a few weeks to recover from our operation in North Africa but, as the new year arrived, so did the orders. Our little clandestine unit was rejoining the war. The quiet days of just training were ending and we were given our first orders.

Part 1

Malta

Chapter 1

The main problem with our new base was supplies. We had become adept at scavenging. I suspect some might have called it stealing. The problem with the army was that they liked to hoard things which they would never use. Every time *'Lady Luck'* went to Valetta for the supplies we could not get in Marsalaforn Bill Hay or Polly Poulson would accompany the ship and liberate that which the Army did not keep a close watch on. Thankfully we had no problem with ammunition since the Americans had joined the war. .45 ammunition was plentiful now.

We three Lieutenants had taken to eating breakfast together in or outside Lieutenant Hugo Ferguson's hut. As he rarely left out new base it was the best apportioned. Alan slept on *'Lady Luck'* and, more often than not, I slept in the open. Hugo flourished a piece of paper as we entered. He was eating a slightly burnt slice of toast. "Orders! From the Major!" We were both showered in toast crumbs.

Alan rolled his eyes and lit another cheroot. I smiled, it was Hugo's way. He was like an enthusiastic schoolboy. "It was inevitable. I mean we have had almost two months without firing a shot in anger. They couldn't leave us here forever."

Hugo wiped his mouth with the back of his hand, "Quite!" He swallowed a mouthful of tea and continued, "Major Fleming wants us to have a look see at a little place in Sicily; Agrigento."

Alan held up his hand and disappeared. Hugo cocked a quizzical eye. "Maps and charts. You know Alan, he can't think until he has a map in his hand."

The Royal Naval Lieutenant returned clutching maps. Not all were official. Every time we raided anywhere we liberated as many maps as we could. These were annotated and guarded as jealously as any plans for war. He unfolded one and, after peering closely at it for a moment, jabbed a stained finger at it. "There, on the south coast. I reckon about a hundred miles from here." He looked at Hugo expectantly.

"Right! That looks like the place. The Major wants us to go over and assess the defences there."

"Invasion!" Alan was right. It was obvious to all of us that with North Africa almost secure they would soon be looking to getting a toe hold in Europe and Sicily was a prime candidate. "I hope the Major realises that they do have aeroplanes which can do reconnaissance!"

"I believe he does, dear boy, but the problem with an aeroplane is that the Eyeties and Jerry know that we are up to something. Besides I think that they are still needed to either protect Malta or to finish off Jerry in the desert. I think the little Major likes the fact that we are invisible."

I smiled at his use of 'we'. He felt part of the team even though he never left the safety of the base. He had not been our liaison for long but he was as much part of the unit as any of us. "We will have to play the German card, Alan. We can repaint another number on the side and use those German caps we took last time."

"I suppose. The problem is, Tom, that if you and your lads get stuck there is no British army unit close by. If you are left there you are on your own."

"I know. But we are Commandos after all. Right then, Hugo, is it just this Agrigento we are looking at?"

Hugo smiled, "The Major would like you to assess as much of the coastline for defences as possible."

I laughed, "And that is verbatim eh? It sounds just like Major Fleming." I turned to Alan. "What time do we leave?"

"We will have to leave in daylight. It is a hundred miles to Sicily. I am guessing that Valetta will have no idea what we are up to?" He meant did our friends in the navy and the air force know what we were up to. If they did there would be no problem.

Hugo grinned, "Of course not."

"That means the white ensign until dark and then the swastika. Right I will go and plot the course."

"And I will sort my lads out."

We were Commandos and we were never idle. Sergeant Poulson and Corporal Hay had the men practising cliff climbs on the nearby rocky walls which towered over the bay. I stood and watched. They were not the highest cliffs and probably did not need ropes. It was the technique which was important. We had to know how to work as a team. My non-commissioned officers were ensuring that even the least experienced had the opportunity to take command on the short climb. Who knew when the officers and sergeants might be incapacitated?

"Right lads, over here! We have orders."

There were grins and smiles all around.

"Thank the Lord for that!"

"I am fed up of training!"

Polly Poulson shouted, "Shut it! You sound like a bunch of raw recruits!"

They squatted down around me. "Smoke if you like."

As they lit up and I looked around their faces I knew that I had been extremely lucky. There were bad apples in all walks of life but I appeared to have none in my section. I would trust any one of them with my life. Come to think of it I had!

"We are going over to Sicily for a look see at a little place on the south coast called Agrigento. Now this means we will be in enemy territory and behind enemy lines. Nothing new there I know. The difference here is that they speak Italian and we don't.

We are going to have to learn about Sicily and the Sicilians. We will be going in under German colours and the deck crew will have German uniforms. Our job is to test the defences. I intend to operate in three groups. That way we can cover more ground but it also increases our chances of getting caught. You lads know the rules, if you get left behind you are on your own. We don't come back for you."

They nodded and Bill Hay said, "Sir, remember that Hitler order we saw. If we get left behind and caught then we will be shot."

George Lowe tapped out his pipe, "Then make sure you don't get caught. I thought Hitler was daft before but now..." he shook his head, "he's not a full shilling. No Commando is going to surrender now and it takes a lot to kill a Commando. He will just lose more men trying to take us."

George spoke for all of us. We would try to escape but if that failed then we would take as many Germans or Italians as we could.

"Good! That is the spirit. Lieutenant Jorgenson is working out the route." I looked at my watch. "If he has enough fuel then I think he might choose to go later on this afternoon if not it will be tomorrow. Either way you know what to do. Scouse, check the radio. Bill, George make up some charges. Sergeant do a Bergen check in an hour."

There was a chorus of 'Sirs!" and the whole section disappeared.

Once in my hut I grabbed my own Bergen and emptied it on to my camp bed. It was always better to pack and check each item as it was stored. I put in my wire cutters, toggle rope and cosh first. Then I put in my camouflage net. We all had them and they were cut down from larger sheets. I coiled some parachute cord. It was tough and it was light. I put in some C rations. They were the one thing we all packed that we hoped we would not need. If we had to open them it meant we were stuck behind the lines. I put in shoe polish; who knew if we might need to black up. I put in my binoculars. I took the silencer for the Colt and put it in one of the side pockets. Then I began to pack the ammunition I would need. There were five spare magazines for the Thomson and three for the Colt. I had managed to acquire six for the Luger but I was always on the lookout for more. I had six Mills bombs and one German potato masher. That done I laid the bag to one side. Sergeant Poulson would check mine along with the others.

I laid my weapons out on the bed. A Thompson, a Colt, a Luger and a Commando dagger. I stripped down and cleaned the three guns and then reassembled them. I had managed to get a holster for the Luger and I put both pistols in their holsters and secured them. I laid the Thompson on the Bergen.

I turned my attention to my battledress. I emptied everything from the pockets and then chose what I would put back in. I had a lighter, even though I did not smoke. I also took matches and a flint. I had a compass. I put in my penknife. I took my notebook and tore out all the pages with writing on them and then replaced the notebook and pencil in my battledress. All the other items which lay on my bed I put in my chest. We took nothing which might give us away. I knew that all my men would do the same thing.

Sergeant Poulson appeared in the entrance to the hut. Doorway was too grand a word for a curtain. I stood, "Carry on Sergeant. I'll go and see navy!"

The E-Boat was a hive of activity. "Come on lads, get those drums of fuel emptied."

The Engineer, Jock Campbell, was calmly standing, cigarette dangling from his mouth, as the huge fuel tanks were filled. I admired the Chief. During action he was in the bowels of the ship and if anything happened he would know nothing. There would be no escape for him. Yet he was always there no matter how fierce the gun battle above him.

Petty Officer Leslie shouted, "Are you looking for the Skipper, sir?" I nodded, "Bridge."

I went up to the bridge. I could have found him by following the smell of his cheroot! He was poring over a map.

"Our Major Fleming has a sense of humour Tom. This Agrigento is less than twenty miles from an Italian Naval base at Licata. I will bet a month's pay that there are more anti aircraft guns there than you can shake a stick at! If that is your idea of fun! That will be why we are being sent in. The RAF probably can't get close enough for decent photographs. It will be down to you poor sods and boots on the ground."

"If the RAF could do anything, believe me, they would."

"Sorry, chum. I keep forgetting that your dad is a big wig in Whitehall!"

I ignored the jibe. "So when do we go?"

"We have enough fuel and ammo. I reckon if we leave at four and dawdle our way across we should be at the coast just after dark and then you and your lads can get ashore."

I nodded, "I am landing as three separate groups. That way we can cover more ground."

"Listen, Tom. We will be doing more of this I can tell. Just get in like Flynn eh? We are just putting our toe in the water so to speak. We need to find our way around the coast. This time the Italians are not fighting for Il Duce's African Empire, this is their back yard. They will be more territorial."

"There is no point in leaving a job half done though is there? Fleming will only send us back in."

Alan threw the stub of his cheroot to hiss into the blue waters. "You are right! I hate that about you!" He laughed, "Are your lads ready?"

"We could board now."

He nodded, "Sixteen hundred hours we push off. Better get some hot food if you can." He handed me my copy of the map and some blank paper. "If you are splitting up you have best give them maps. I have marked the pickup point and reserve pickup points on the map.

As I passed Bill Leslie I said, "Will you be at the wheel tonight?"

"Reckon so sir. Skipper and me have an understanding."

"Good. I always feel better knowing that I have a mate at the wheel." He grinned. We had known each other back in the day when I had been a sergeant and he had been an able seaman.

I jumped into the water and waded back to the beach. The section was taking it easy. They knew that we might well go hours without sleep. "Three hours until we push off. Better get some food if you can."

Ken Shepherd jumped up. The scar from his recent brush with death was still vivid above his eye, "I'll check the lines then eh Sarge? A bit of fresh fish will go down a treat!"

Sergeant 'Polly' Poulson said, "Emerson, Fletcher, go and give him a hand. Scouse, stop fiddling with that radio we both know it works. Get a fire going. Give him a hand, Crowe."

I smiled. Scouse was an old hand now. He had been pretending that he needed to work on the radio to avoid another job. Sergeant Poulson was an even older hand. We had made a circle of some driftwood logs and I sat there with my sergeants and corporal while our men did their assigned tasks.

"Sergeant Poulson you take Shepherd and Hewitt with you. George you take Emerson and Crowe with you. Corporal Hay I will take you and Scouse. We could really do with another couple of men if we are going to be doing much of this. Still we should manage eh?" They nodded. I laid my map out. "Here is the landing site. Poulson you go along the coast, west, George take the east. Bill, we will go through the town. It doesn't look that big. The two pick up points are in red. Red One and Red Two. If you don't make Red One then head for Red Two. You had better copy the maps. Bill, make a copy for us. We will leave the original here."

We had learned to make our own maps because it gave less information to the enemy if we were captured. We had not lost a map yet but Bill and I had been captured in North Africa and I had been glad that we had nothing with us which the Germans could use. I watched as our three erstwhile fishermen returned with their catch. We left rods out with lines and bait. The results were erratic. Sometimes we caught nothing and at others, like now, we had six fish. We had no idea of their names but beggars could not be choosers. They would be gutted and cooked by the three fishermen. We could all cook. It was a vital skill for men who had to live on their wits and that was what a Commando did. The rest of the army had a cookhouse. We had ourselves. We preferred it that way.

The maps were ready at about the same time as the fish. Another reason we had chosen this secluded cove was that we could make our own rules up. Here there was no officer and other ranks; we all messed together. When we had finished we all washed out our own dixies and cleared away our own rubbish. We were a team.

The only problem we had with our new home was the lack of a jetty. We had to wade out to the E-Boat and climb up scrambling nets hung along the hull. It was a small price to pay for the security of knowing that we were invisible. Hugo waded out too, "Good luck, chaps."

Alan pointed a finger at him, "Do not tell the little general that we have left tonight. Tell him we leave tomorrow!"

Hugo laughed, "Of course!"

My men disappeared below decks as we headed north west. We flew the White Ensign but, once it was dark, we would become an E-Boat again. We stored out Bergens in the mess. I saw Bill Leslie. He was in the Petty Officer's mess and he was pouring rum from his tin mug over what looked to be a piece of wood.

"What on earth are you doing?"

He put a finger to his lips. "Breaking King's Regulations, so keep stuhm eh sir? We aren't supposed to save any of our daily rum ration but I pour half a tot on this bar of baccy. It soaks in and keeps it fresh. It also makes a nice rum flavoured pipe full." We had a choice of bar tobacco or cigarettes if we smoked. Bill was a pipe smoker.

"Very resourceful. I will keep quiet although I doubt that you would be reprimanded by the lieutenant."

He shook his head, "I lost a stripe once. I am not risking it again." He ran his finger around the inside of the mug, licked it and then returned the bar of tobacco to his pouch. "I'd best be on deck. Captain will want me soon."

When I returned to the mess the men had stowed the Bergens neatly around the side and were applying stain to their faces. We still had some way to go but it helped to prepare us mentally. It felt like putting on war paint. I took out the map after I had applied my own war face. We were landing to the west of Agrigento. Sergeant Poulson would have the easiest time and it would be up to him to secure the beach for our extraction.

"What do we know about this place, sir?"

"It is an old hill city. There look to be ancient ruins on the top but the photographs we have are from before the war. We have to find what the RAF couldn't."

Emerson said, "Suppose there's nowt there sir?"

I smiled, "Then we will have an easy time and a leisurely voyage back."

Emerson was one of the new members of the section. I did not mind his questions. They showed he was interested.

"We will be landing about a thousand yards west of the little fishing port, Porto Empedecole. Sergeant Poulson's section will check the port out and then secure the beach four hundred yards to the west of it. I will lead my merry troop up the hill to the old town and, if we can, the temple. George, your section will look to the east. According to the pre-war maps and photographs it should be empty. You need to confirm that." I left the map on the mess table. "Study the map in case we get separated. If there are no questions then get some shut eye. I am off to the bridge."

When I moved the blackout curtain I saw that night had fallen. Alan had his German cap at a rakish angle and above us fluttered the German flag. I jammed the field cap on my head and joined him and Bill Leslie on the bridge. The lookout, Bert Jones, obligingly moved over.

"How is it looking, Alan?"

"All quiet although we have no radar. The array would give us away. We are relying on Jones' eyes."

"Don't worry Mr Harsker, if there's owt out there I'll see it."

I nodded. Alan was not hurtling across the sea. To all the world we would look like a returning patrol. E-Boats constantly prowled the waters north of Malta looking for isolated ships they could attack.

"When I drop you off I will head west and do a recce there. The more information we can gather the less likely Major Fleming will send us back. I'll turn around and pick you chaps up four hundred yards from the Porto Empedecole. You have three hours."

"It will be tight but we should manage it."

"Aeroplane sir, nine o'clock." We turned to our left. Bert had good eyes. It was a dot and it was high up.

"Can you make it out Jones?"

"Looks like a twin engined job. Probably a Junkers 88."

"Well if we can see him then he can see us. Better get your chaps ready in case Jerry decides to crash this party. Keep the same course and speed Chief. After all we are Germans tonight eh?"

"Jawohl sir." Bill's accent was awful and Alan and I smiled. It was lucky that we had more German speakers on board. The problem was we had no Italian speakers and I wondered if that would come back to haunt us.

I returned to the mess. "Right lads, Jerry has spotted us so get your guns in case we are rumbled. This could be a short little excursion."

We had discovered that the firepower of our nine Thompsons could augment the boat's armament well. I did not take my Thompson back on deck. We were still German and I lifted the flap on my Luger. I thought we had escaped scrutiny. Sicily was a thin line in the distance when we heard the throb of a patrol boat. Bert said nothing but pointed to the east.

Bill Leslie said, under his breath, "That's a big bugger!"

Alan said, "German only." As if to make the point he shouted, in German, "Wacker, on deck, relieve Jones. We need German speakers now."

It looked like an Italian corvette. It had a three or four-inch gun forrard and a handful of anti aircraft guns. We could have outrun it and, probably out gunned it but we were clandestine and we had to try to fool them. As the corvette closed with us I saw that they had their gun crews closed up. They were suspicious.

"How do we play this, Alan?"

"Arrogant Germans. We know that Jerry has a low opinion of his ally. You back me up."

The Italian captain used his loud hailer to shout something at us. I assumed it was an order to slow down but we didn't understand it and we ignored it. When it was repeated Alan took his own loud hailer and snapped back in German, "Speak in German if you wish to talk with me!"

When the voice changed we knew that the Italian captain could not speak German. "Captain Baggio wishes you to slow down. We have some questions for you."

"Then he should have spoken in German." He put his hand on Bill's shoulder and we began to slow.

"What ship are you?"

"We are S-159 from Tunis. Who are you?" There was a delay while the German speaker translated.

"We are the Regia Marina vessel Persefone out of Licata. What are you doing here?"

Alan was a fine actor. He snapped, "We are on a special mission for Admiral Doenitz. Do not interfere. You have already slowed us down. We have a schedule to keep. The Kriegsmarine are efficient unlike some other navies!"

"My captain reminds you that you are a guest in our waters."

"And I would remind your captain that is was only the German Army which saved you in Greece and North Africa. Now let us be on our way!"

"Captain Baggio says he will report you to the authorities on Sicily."

"Good and then he will enjoy a new career as a ferry captain in Naples harbour. Good night!" He said, quietly in English, "Now Chief let us show them a clean pair of heels eh?"

The E-Boat had far more power than the corvette and we sped away towards Sicily. Wacker said, "She's turning around, sir. Looks like she is going back on patrol."

"Good. Although we may have to take a different course on our way back."

"What do you think she was doing here?"

"Anti submarine patrol. Did you not see the depth charges?" Alan grinned, "Just think you could be going in by sub. I know how much you like that!"

"Don't even joke about subs! They are floating coffins!"

I had been in a submarine and suffered depth charges. I did not like the confined spaces.

Alan kept up the speed a little longer to make up for the time we had lost. "Better get your lads on deck. We will try to get you as close in as we can."

"Right lads, on deck. Remember we are ashore for just three hours and then we rendezvous at Red One." They nodded.

"What was all that about, sir?"

"A nosey Italian. Lieutenant Jorgenson was a little rude about the Italian navy but it seemed to work. Remember either hand signals or speak German when you are ashore." They nodded. In our off-duty times I was teaching them French and German. They had awful accents but it was better than nothing.

I left my Thompson in the mess. I fitted the silencer to the Colt. I was not taking my Bergen. I wanted my hands free. This was a three-hour recce. We would not even take the radio. If we needed the radio then it meant the operation had gone badly wrong. When I returned on deck I saw that the island was much closer now. I suppose before the war there would have been dots of lights. It would have been a lively place full of visitors and locals making money. Now there was a black out. Bill slowed the boat down to lessen the white bow wave and reduce the engine noise.

The engineer had worked hard to muffle the engines so that we were more silent than most E-Boats.

The crew of the *'Lucky Lady'* had the three rubber boats ready. With five in each boat we would be a little overcrowded. It was another reason I was not taking my Bergen and machine gun. Alan pointed to starboard. I could see the entrance to the fishing harbour. That was Red Two. As he headed up the beach he pointed again. That was Red One. Soon he slowed until we were barely making way. The shore was just forty yards away. We were well practised at this and we quickly embarked and were paddling away from the E-Boat in an instant. My men used the spare paddles and I held the fifth as a rudder. As Bill Hay leapt ashore I dropped the paddle in the bottom of the dingy and hurried up the sand to join him. Scouse followed us.

We ignored the other two patrols. We all had our own job to do. We left the beach and crossed the promenade. We were heading inland. Up ahead I saw the citadel on top of the hill. It was more than a mile away. We had no time to waste. The night and the dark were our friends and we had to use them.

Chapter 2

There was a time when the new smells of Sicily would have seemed alien to us but we had been in the Mediterranean long enough now to be used to it. The lemon and olive trees augmented the smell of the unusual flora which covered this most southern part of Italy. It was almost midnight and although the locals would have only recently retired the streets were empty. Perhaps they had had a curfew. I had the map in my head. The road we ran along was a quiet one and it ran parallel to the promenade and coast road. It was residential. I had chosen it because it headed towards the citadel. As it ascended we were afforded a view south when the buildings became sparser. I saw a half dozen boats in the harbour. None were military.

Suddenly I held my hand up and drew my Luger. Hay and Fletcher looked at me. I pointed to my nose and mimed smoking. I could smell pipe tobacco. I waved them left and right. Crouching I headed up the track to the left where the smell seemed to be coming from. I heard voices and they were speaking in Italian. I dropped to all fours and crept towards the wall of the building ahead. As I reached it I looked up and saw the barrel of a 75 cm gun. I looked to the east and saw that there was a line of guns every fifty yards. I began to back away. When I was far enough from the wall I looked west and saw more guns. I could now see them clearer. They had camouflage nets over the top. They would have been invisible from the air. This was the line of batteries for the defence of this coast. We would not be able to get by them and up to the temple.

I led the other two and we retraced our steps to the road. I waved them east. Now that I had seen the artillery I was more alert. It was fortunate that I did so for had I not I would have stumbled into the machine gun pits. None were manned but there was a line of them. I looked to my left and saw the hill city was just half a mile away. They had ringed this ancient walled city with guns. I would have loved to go further into the city to see just what other defences they had but we had been ashore for an hour and a half. We had to return to the rendezvous. However, we had discovered enough to satisfy the Major's curiosity. They were ready for an invasion. If we tried to take Agrigento it would be like Dieppe all over again; a disaster.

As I turned to head back to the rendezvous, a piece of paper in the bottom of the nearest emplacement caught my eye. I grabbed it and stuffed it inside my battledress. I waved my two companions towards to the harbour. There were more buildings close to the fishing port. We had to move carefully and slowly. I was acutely aware of the passage of time but to rush would have risked discovery. Our rubber soled shoes saved us for we heard the sound of boots ahead. We ducked behind a wall. I prayed that the occupants of the small house would not emerge or we would be spotted. I did not raise my head as the patrol marched towards Red One. From their footsteps I estimated that there were five men in the patrol. Suddenly I heard a voice and it spoke German!

"Halt. Ten minutes rest only!"

They were less than twenty yards from us. We could not move. We would have to wait. I glanced at the fluorescent dial of my watch. *'Lady Luck'* would be at the rendezvous in half an hour.

"Why do we have to guard this harbour? What is wrong with the lazy Italians?"

"Franz if you want a job doing properly then you give it to a German. The Italians are cannon fodder that is all. I have heard that their tanks have eight gears, three forward and five back!" They all laughed at the common perception of Italians. They surrendered too easily.

Another voice said, "The Fuhrer should do what he did to Austria in thirty-six and annex it. Send the Italians to the eastern front."

Just then the first voice we heard snapped, "Quiet! I can hear a boat. Quickly! To the beach!"

Their boots sounded inordinately loud on the stones. I took out my Colt and tapped the other two on the shoulders. I led them after the Germans. Thanks to our rubber soled shoes we were making no noise and we kept to the shadows. I could hear the E-Boat too. I had to hope that the German patrol would recognise the ship as an E-Boat and stop their search. Those hopes were dashed as I heard them shout, "Halt! Hands up!"

They had spotted some of our men. I was the only one with a silencer and I pointed to the daggers the other two carried. I saw the five Germans in a semi circle and George and his men had their hands up. Beyond them I could see, in the distance, the dark shape that was *'Lady Luck'*. Where was Sergeant Poulson?

The German sergeant shouted, in English, "Commandos! Gangsters! The Fuhrer has told us what to do with you!" I heard him slide his bolt back and his men copied him. We did not have long. My men all knew what was going to happen. I took aim and nodded. The sergeant might fire first but there would be a slight delay from the others. It is hard to shoot a man in cold blood. My Colt spat out and the sergeant pitched forward. The other Germans hesitated. Bill and Scouse had their hands around the necks of two others as another silenced Colt spat a bullet at a fourth. The fifth died when George Lowe rammed his dagger up into the throat of the last German.

"Pick up the bodies! We can't leave them here. Hay, Fletcher, hide the signs of the blood."

Sergeant Poulson and his patrol rose from their place of concealment. "Sergeant get the bodies to the boat. We will watch here until you come back for us."

"Sir."

George Lowe wiped his dagger on the body of a dead German before hefting it on to his shoulder, "Sorry sir."

"Post mortems later. Get the bodies to the boat. Move!"

I turned to face the town. Had any one heard us? It all seemed quiet. I looked at my watch. It was two thirty. The patrol might not be missed until dawn. They would search for them. I looked at the sand. Hay and Fletcher had done a good job. I knelt down and smoothed out the sand as I backed towards the sea. The other two copied me. If this was France then the tide would have covered all traces of the attack but the bone-dry side was testament to the lack of tides. By the time my feet touched the water the three dinghies had picked up the Germans and my men and were heading back to the boat. It would not be a swift journey. To our right, and on the other side of the harbour wall, I heard Italian being spoken. Had we been spotted? Then I heard laughter. It was the Italian fishermen. They were preparing to go to sea. We would have to give them a wide berth and that might make our journey a little riskier.

When I saw the two dinghies returning to us I breathed a sigh of relief. We all paddled as hard as we could. I was the first on deck and I said, "Alan, the Italian fishing boats are about to set sail."

"Bugger! Right we will head west. As soon as we are far enough away I will open her up." He gestured to the dead Germans. "What will you do with them?"

"Strip them and take off their identity tags. We will drop them over the side between here and Malta. The fishes and the gulls will do the rest." I shrugged, "There was nothing else that we could do."

"I know."

My men had laid the five Germans out on the aft deck. The crew were unused to seeing death so close to them. "Right lads, we have an unpleasant job ahead of us. Strip the Germans of everything and I mean everything. These five Jerries are just going to disappear. Let them wonder what happened to them. We keep everything that they have with them. Watches, papers, love letters, uniforms, the lot. They will come in handy. Then tie one of the rocks Lance Sergeant Lowe brought aboard to each body. We want them to sink without trace."

"Right, you heard Lieutenant Harsker, get to it."

"Sorry we were late getting to you, sir. There was an Italian foot patrol further north. We had to lie up too."

"We were just lucky that we were able to follow them or George and the others would have been shot."

It took some time; bodies are not very cooperative but eventually we had them all stripped. I looked aft and could no longer see Sicily. "Right George, first body."

He and Groves hurled the body far enough astern to clear the propellers. I was not worried what the blades would do to the bodies but I didn't want the ship harming. I waited until we had travelled a mile and shouted, "Next!" When all the bodies had been thrown overboard I said, "Below decks. Debrief time."

We always had an immediate debrief just in case something happened on the journey home. At least that way the foray into foreign fields would not have been in vain.

I allowed the men to smoke as the sergeants made their reports. It was soon obvious to me that they had made Agrigento into a strongpoint. The natural defensive site had been improved. There were guns everywhere. I finished writing it down and then said, "I see German hands all over this. They know that the allies will be reluctant to bomb such a historical site. We gave them Paris in nineteen forty just so that they would not destroy it. They are relying on us doing the honourable thing."

Private Emerson said, "That's not right sir. Lads could get killed if they attacked here. It's only an old building. That isn't worth men's lives is it?"

"No Freddie but the war will end one day and you don't want your children asking why you destroyed so much history do you?"

"No sir but what about those poor sods who won't have any kids to ask that?"

He was right but we had to concentrate on doing our job. "Sergeant Poulson, make a copy of my report. I will be on deck with the captain."

Bill Leslie was on the wheel and I could smell aromatic tobacco as I came on deck. Alan had to know that he was using his rum ration. Obviously, he was doing a Nelson and turning a blind eye. "Bodies all gone."

Allan shuddered, " A gory little job. Necessary though. Was the recce worth it?"

"I should say so. They have made Agrigento into a fortress. They have the harbour covered and the guns are well hidden. It would have to be carpet bombing to get rid of them."

"And with the ancient buildings up in the hill that is not going to happen." He looked at the sky and then his watch, "Right lads, it's time to get back to being navy again. Switch flags and caps." He pointed aft, "Those German helmets will come in handy."

"I thought so and the ammunition too. There were twenty potato mashers amongst the Germans. They always have a use."

By the time dawn broke we were back to being a Royal Navy vessel. We might have raised eyebrows but we were flying under our true colours. Symons had rigged the radar array so that we had eyes in the sky once more. We were almost home when he said, "Sir, three aircraft coming from the north."

"Friendlies?"

"Can't tell, sir, but I doubt it. We would have heard them flying north and we heard bugger all sir. If I was a betting man I would say single seat fighters."

"One nineties then?"

"That would be my guess."

"Action stations. Full speed Chief." He turned to me. "If your lads could add their firepower I would appreciate it, Tom."

"Righto! Commandos on deck!"

Sergeant Poulson must have anticipated my command for the eight of them sprang from the hatch like greyhounds from a starting gate. The men went to their stations with practised familiarity. Polly handed me my Tommy gun and I leaned with my back against the radar hut.

Able Seaman Jones pointed aft, "Three one nineties. And they have seen us."

The crew all wore tin lids. My Commandos did not. I heard the sound of nine Thompsons being cocked. The **'Lady Luck'** had more guns than was normal. We had fitted extra Lewis guns as we had acquired them. We would throw up a wall of steel and Lieutenant Jorgenson would make us a hard target to hit.

"I will throw her to port as they attack and then bring her to starboard. It might throw their aim."

We knew that they had a limited amount of ammunition. The Focke Wulf, however, carried bombs and they were the danger. Even a bomb forty yards away could hurt us. They came in line astern. "Don't open fire until I give the command!"

This was Alan's show. We were just the passengers. There was a faint hope that they might take us for an E-Boat. The White Ensign was sometimes hard to identify. When the leading aircraft opened fire, I knew that they had not been fooled.

"Coming about! Turn! Fire!"

As Bill Leslie threw the E-Boat to port the guns on the E-Boat opened up. We held our fire. The leading one ninety was committed to the attack and we saw the single bomb as it was released at the place we had just vacated. The second and third aeroplanes had the time to adjust their angle of attack but they were being fired upon. I saw forty-millimetre shells striking the leading aeroplane.

"Turn, now!"

As the boat was thrown to starboard my Commandos fired at the second German as he roared over us. He was so low we could see the bomb still attached to his fuselage. Nine Thompsons can do a great deal of damage and our bullets must have penetrated the cockpit from below for it continued to rise in a great loop, smoke pouring from it.

"Come about!"

Bill brought us back on our original course. As the aircraft we had seen plunged into the sea and exploded, half a mile astern, the last two fighters reformed for a beam attack. My men all changed magazines. Their first had not been emptied but we had a few moments to reload and a full magazine was always preferable.

Only one fighter had a bomb and he was the more dangerous adversary. The two came in low with wing tips just feet apart. These were good pilots and they were brave. This time Alan could not avoid them and their shells poured into the hull. He had Bill spin the wheel as they opened fire and the bomb from the last Focke Wulf exploded astern of us. I emptied my magazine at the two of them as did the rest of my men. Smoke came from one of them as they banked and headed north.

Alan had a concerned look on his face, "They walloped us pretty well then. Middy, take the helm. I am going to check below decks. Petty Officer Leslie, head for home but take it steady until I find out the damage."

The Midshipman was a new one. We did not merit two lieutenants and when the opportunity came for promotion he had taken it. Midshipman Higgins had not conned the ship before and I knew why Alan had given Petty Officer Leslie the last instruction.

I saw the fearful expression on the young officer's face, "Don't worry Middy, Petty Officer Leslie has done this before."

He coloured, "I know, sir and I'm not worried, it's just that it is a German boat!"

Bill Leslie shook his head, "The engines make her go and the wheel makes her turn. Ships are ships, sir and the '*Lady*' is a little belter." The way he referred to the ship made it sound like a woman. Sailors were unique. Pilots did not get so attached to their aeroplanes although Dad had told me that Spitfires came close.

When Alan returned his face told me that the news was not good. "The Chief Engineer is dead. He was torn in two by the cannons. He knew nothing about it but..."

Bill Leslie nodded, "If you have to go then that is the way. Jock Campbell was a granddad you know, sir? His daughter in law gave birth just before Christmas. You know what they say, one comes in to the world as one is taken away. He never got to see him though. A shame, that."

"What about the rest of the engine room crew?"

"It's a mess. They are all wounded. SBA Johnson has his hands full. It's a good job Hewitt was on board." He nodded to the Midshipman. "Get some stoker's cocoa organized will you Middy? I think we all need one." As the shaken Midshipman went to the galley Alan said, "I am afraid this scuppers Major Fleming's plans. We will be out of action for a couple of weeks and that is if we get replacements."

"I am fairly certain that Major Fleming will strive to get another boat for us.

"I know Tom but we are a team."

"It is just temporary and besides I will use the opportunity to get more men. Nine of us aren't enough for some jobs. Let's look at this positively."

"Ever the optimist. How you can see anything behind this black cloud I have no idea."

I shrugged, "The dark days for me were in Belgium when we were retreating and all my pals were either captured or killed. If you come through that then everything else seems a bonus."

Wacker got on the radio to tell Lieutenant Ferguson what had happened. He was a powerhouse and he assured us that he would have everything sorted out by the time we reached Valetta. We went directly to that battle-scarred port. We would need the dockyard there. It was almost dark when we arrived. An irritated harbour master sent us to Marsaxlokk. Our draught meant that we could be repaired there and it would not take away a larger dock for a more valuable ship.

As we edged our way in I saw an old dilapidated two masted island schooner and a couple of naval officers. I wondered if the schooner was being repaired or broken up. It seemed to me that the latter would be the best option. There were also three army ambulances. It was a reminder of the losses we had suffered. We tied up to the side. "Well Tom, I am not certain how you will get back to the base."

"Don't worry about that. I take it that you and the crew will stay here?"

"Too right. I want this repaired and crewed sooner rather than later. When you do get back then badger old Hugo eh? You had better get your lads ashore."

We had already packed the Bergens with everything we needed form the E-Boat. It felt quite sad to be leaving her. I almost felt as though I was being unfaithful. I shook my head, I was becoming a sailor!

As I stepped ashore the two Naval officers approached me. As they did I saw that one looked to be little older than Midshipman Higgins while the other was older than my dad and yet they were both lieutenants.

"Lieutenant Harsker?"

"That's me."

He saluted, "Sub-lieutenant Davis and this is Sub-lieutenant Magee. He is the commander of your new ship, *'H.M.S. Dragonfly'*. Temporary, of course. He will take you back to your base. Major Fleming has asked that you use this until Lieutenant Jorgenson's ship is repaired."

I nodded and looked around, "Good. Where is she then?"

The grizzled old sub-lieutenant took his pipe from his mouth and gestured, with the stem, at the schooner. "There she is sir, *'H.M.S. Dragonfly'*." My face must have fallen for he laughed, "Don't worry sir, she looks like a wreck but that is just to fool the enemy. She flies over the water and she is sound. Trust me."

I didn't want to offend the old man's feelings and I didn't want to create a scene. We had been lucky with the E-Boat. This was just the other side of the coin. I nodded, "Of course. Right Sergeant get the lads aboard the schooner. We are going home in style!"

As they passed me I heard Lance Sergeant Lowe mumble, "More like a floating coffin if you ask me. I'd rather be in a submarine and I hate them."

"Lance Sergeant!"

"Sorry sir. Didn't mean for that to come out loud."

I shook my head, I could not blame him. I wondered if it would make it out of the harbour, let alone around the islands. Alan came over to me as my men began to board the ancient vessel. He took the cheroot from his mouth as he said, "Don't make the mistake of judging a book by the cover Tom." He pointed to the motor launches and motor torpedo boats in the harbour. "Hugo could have got any one of those for you. There will be a reason he has picked this one. Speak to Hugo before you say something you might regret."

"When have I ever done that?"

"Sorry. Listen I will get this repaired as soon as is humanly possible." He shook my hand, "Good luck eh?"

I stepped aboard and saw that my men were standing on the decks looking worried. I smiled at Lieutenant Magee, "Shall we stow our gear below decks?"

"Help yourself. There is plenty of room."

I saw an open hatch, "Right lads, down the rabbit hole eh? Let's see what our new home is like." I led the way feeling more worried than I looked. As I bumped my head on the way down I realised that this was not designed for tall men. The captain, however, had been right. There was plenty of room. We found ourselves in a large mess with a long table down the middle. "We will use this for home. It's only a little hop around the coast. There was none of the usual banter and humour. I shook my head. This was my fault, "Sergeant I am going on deck. When I come back down I want to see this section behaving like Commandos and not a bunch of prima donnas!"

When I reached the deck I saw that we were already at the harbour mouth. Lieutenant Magee had his pipe in his mouth and both hands on the huge wheel. I saw that he only had six ratings none of whom looked to be in regulation uniform. They looked more like pirates than Royal Navy. He nodded to the masts, "We'll get the sails down as soon as we clear the harbour, then she will fly!"

"Sorry about before. We have been in action for almost twelve hours."

"Don't worry, old boy. I know exactly what people think of my little beauty. I am not offended. Your Lieutenant Ferguson asked for a ship which the Eyeties and Jerry ignore. This is her. We have been bumbling around the Med for a year now. I speak Italian and German." He chuckled, "They think we are Irish. I make them believe we are gun runners for the IRA. Anyway we will have lots of time to get to know one another eh? I'll have you in Marsalaforn before you know it."

"Actually we are just north of Marsalaforn at a place called Qbajjar Bay."

He gave me a shrewd look, "I know it well. Clever too. No one would look there for an E-Boat sailing under false colours. I think we are going to get on, sir. You sound as sneaky as me."

"Forget the sir, it's Tom." I held out my hand.

He shook it, "Sandy. I am a relic from the Great War." He waved his pipe at the sea. "I stayed here after the war. That's why I am still a subbie! There was nothing back in Blighty for me. Most of the men I joined with were dead. I just stayed on. I ran fishing trips from Valetta. It was a nice little earner until the war. Hang on a minute." He shouted, "Lower the mainsail. Cut the engines."

"Aye aye sir!"

"Anyway when this lot started I volunteered again. Thank God someone saw the potential of a beat up old schooner which had always been here. I get to do my bit again and I don't have to worry about spit and polish."

I regretted my uncharitable thoughts. Here was someone like my dad. Dad had stayed in the RAF but other than that they both believed in the same things. The generation of the Great War were a different breed. I just hoped that we could match them.

"Well we shall need to be sneaky. Our orders are to get close to Sicily and scout out the beaches. We were just coming back from an operation when we were jumped."

"Invasion."

I nodded, "That is what we are thinking."

He nodded. "We can't do what your E-Boat did. We will have to drop you after dark and then stooge around during the day. You lads will have to lay up unless you want to risk a daylight voyage."

"We will have to play that by ear, Sandy. When we were ashore at Agrigento there was nowhere to hide. The place was crawling with troops."

"I see. This won't be as easy as I thought. You see, up until now, I have just dropped off agents and picked them up." He brightened, "Still it will stimulate the old brain cells, what?"

I suddenly remembered the piece of paper I had picked up at the machine guns in Agrigento. I took it out and began to read. It was a piece of German propaganda. It was in German and Italian.

Soldiers,

The gangsters from America and Churchill's dogs of war will soon make an attempt to take Italy from us. We will throw them back into the sea. Be ruthless. You are fighting for your loved ones. Your wives and your daughters will not be safe from these animals. You must fight to the last bullet.

I showed it to Sandy. He read it and nodded. "They used the same tactics in the Great War. You have to be a bit soft in the head to believe them."

"I know but this, added to the Hitler order about Commandos, makes our job even more difficult. Still, it's our job and we just have to get on with it."

The schooner lurched alarmingly as he put the wheel over and the wind caught us. We did begin to fly. He grinned, "Told you. Now you had better reassure your lads that we aren't sinking!"

When I re-entered the mess I saw that all of them looked terrified. "Are we all right sir? I mean I thought we were going over."

"We are fine Hewitt. This is a sailing ship. We will all have to get used to it."

Corporal Hay said, "I told them sir. This will be a lot quieter than an E-Boat."

Lance Sergeant Lowe said, "Aye but did you not notice? We have no guns on board! If Jerry comes then we are sitting ducks!"

I stayed below decks with my men just to reassure them although I dearly wanted to be on deck. There is no finer sight than a ship under full sail. I could see, from the mess, that the timbers on this ship were sound. Sandy Magee had deliberately let the paintwork look neglected but I guessed that the engines would be spotless. "Emerson, go and find the engine room. Have a look at it. Lance Sergeant Lowe, go with him."

"Are you certain sir? I mean it will be even deeper than this!"

"George just go eh?"

"Sir."

"Sergeant Poulson, this will be our home for a while, find the galley. It looks to have a smaller crew than the *'Lady'*. We might have to fend for ourselves a little more."

"Right sir, Scouse, go and find the radio room. Crowe come with me. The rest of you, stow the Bergens out of sight. It looks like a knocking shop in Pompey!"

With something to do my Commandos became more positive. "You heard the Sarge, come on, let's make this ship shape and Bristol fashion."

Now that they were all busy I left them and returned to the deck. It was dark but we were still flying. Sandy was still steering. "Half an hour and we will be tied up. I am guessing that if the E-Boat could anchor in the bay then it is deep enough for us."

"It is but we had a camouflage net rigged over her."

"We won't need one. If Jerry flies over he will assume we are stealing guns from the British Army." He pointed to the taff rail. There was no flag. "We rarely use the White Ensign. We have the Irish flag and a Liberian one. It makes us look more like smugglers."

I sat at the stern and wrote the first draft of my report. There was enough light from the binnacle for me to see and it was pleasant to sit with the breeze and the silence. The occasional flapping of the sail and the snap of the sheets was somehow reassuring.

We edged into our secluded bay under engine power. My men were happier about the prospect of sailing in the schooner once they had explored it and seen that it was not a death trap. They were less happy with the fact that the deeper keel meant we had to anchor in the centre of the bay and we had to paddle back to the shore.

Chapter 3

Hugo was waiting for us. He looked concerned, "It is true that the Chief Engineer is dead?"

"I am afraid so, Hugo. Jock didn't feel a thing. He couldn't have. We were shot up pretty badly."

He nodded, "I know you have just returned but his lordship is keen for a report."

I knew that Major Fleming would not be concerned about any losses we might have incurred. I flourished the report. "In a nut shell they can't use Agrigento to invade. It is a death trap with guns all over the place."

He nodded, "I think we knew that. We have lost too many aircraft who were trying to take photographs. You were just to confirm it."

"Well the family of the Chief Engineer will be happy to hear that, won't they?" I snapped at him. I knew it was not his fault. He didn't have to endure the dangers but it seemed a little cold for me.

"Don't be like that, Tom. You will feel differently in the morning."

"I doubt it. You will probably have more orders from him, won't you?" His silence was eloquent. "The next time you speak with him tell him that we need more Commandos. Nine of us are not enough."

He brightened, "Will do. And the ship; is it okay?"

I smiled. He was like a puppy eager to please, "Yes it will be fine. Where on earth did you find him?"

"I met him in Gibraltar. He used to pick up agents there. I heard that he was like a ghost. He appeared and disappeared. When we first came to Malta I saw him in the Grand Harbour. I kept him in mind." He looked worried, "We have only got him for a month you know. SOE are very precious about their resources. It was only the record of your unit which facilitated the loan."

"Alan will move heaven and earth to get his ship back in order. A month will be fine."

When I awoke, the next morning, Sergeant Poulson already had the men washing out the German uniforms. If we had to use them then the men would want them clean. Some were bloodstained. I looked out at the bay and saw Sandy and his motley crew working on the ship.   It was obvious now that it took as much work to keep it looking neglected as it would to keep it clean.

The smell of cooking bacon drifted over. Scouse shouted, "Ey up sir, tea and bacon butties!"

"Where on earth did you get the bacon Scouse?"

He tapped his nose. "Some dozy bugger wasn't watching when we docked last night in Valetta. I reckon there are some squaddies who will be less than happy!"

Later, replete with tea and hot, greasy bacon sandwiches liberally coated in HP sauce I felt ready to face the world. I wandered over to Hugo's shack. "Well?"

"New orders, I am afraid. You need to check out the coast south of Syracuse. It is about eighteen miles from there to Calabernardo." He shook his head, "I think you will have to overnight there. Behind enemy lines."

I nodded, "Lieutenant Magee and I had already worked that one out. Just between the two of us, Hugo, does he intend to have us examine every piece of Sicily?"

"Oh no, the north has already been ruled out. If this is not suitable for a landing then they will have to go with an airborne invasion."

"You seem well informed."

"I was studying military history at Oxford when all of this blew up. If they want Sicily and then Italy they have two ways to go, seaborne or airborne."

"Right. But there is no hurry is there?"

"What do you mean?"

"I want the men to have today off. I will see Sandy. We would be stupid not use the skills and knowledge he has eh?"

"Of course, Tom. But he will want a report in the next week, you know."

"I know."

I took Sergeant Poulson with me as we paddled over to the schooner. Sandy helped us aboard. He shook his head, "That was damned cruel you know, Tom."

"What was?"

"Cooking bacon and not sending any over to us!"

I felt guilty. We would have sent bacon butties over to Alan and his crew. Polly said, "Sorry sir, that was my fault." He hurried to the stern and, cupping his hands shouted, "Scouse! Bacon butties for the navy, chop, chop!"

Scouse raised his hand in acknowledgement.

"It is the one thing I miss from England. Bacon butties with HP sauce."

Polly grinned, "Then you are in luck sir, we have HP sauce too!"

The veteran beamed, "Ah nectar of the gods." Turning to me he said, "I am guessing our lords and masters have a task for us?"

"They have." I took out the map. "They want us to investigate the coast from here to here." I pointed.

"I can save us a journey. There are guns and wire all down the coast."

"The question is how much? They want boots on the ground. I thought we could leave tomorrow but we are in your hands."

He nodded, "We can leave mid morning. It will take most of the day to reach Syracuse. We will sail beyond the port and then turn after dark. There is a little spot here, about a mile north. It is a secluded bay, Scoglio Due Fratelli. It was popular before the war with holidaymakers but now..."

I looked at the map trying to see the place he meant, "Is that a village?"

"No, it is a little island a few hundred yards off the coast. It is a rocky coast and the nearest road is a good half a mile from the sea. After dark it should be quiet enough for you. We can hide behind the island and pretend we are repairing the ship. We can then sail south and wait for you..." his finger hovered over the map, "here. Calabernardo is a tiny place and the bay to the south is quiet. I can have the lads pretend that we are night fishing."

"Won't the Germans and Italians be suspicious?"

He reached into the locker which was next to his leg and pulled out a bottle of Spanish brandy. "They think we not only smuggle guns but brandy and American cigarettes too. It is quite profitable for us!"

I could see that the old sailor was resourceful. "Right, then we will get our gear sorted."

As we reached the stern Hewitt and Fletcher were approaching with the bacon sandwiches. Sub-lieutenant Magee cupped his hands and shouted, "Right you lubbers, bacon butties! Get them while they are hot!"

As we rowed back to shore I said, "We won't bother with the Bergens. They are too bulky. We will just take one. Hewitt can carry that with the first aid. So long as we have water we will be all right. And we will just take four Thompsons. The Colts with silencers are more use."

"Grenades, sir?"

"Four Mills bombs per man and half a dozen potato mashers. Scouse will need a signalling lamp."

We stepped ashore and Sergeant Poulson said, "The lads are a bit worried about being attacked when we are on the sea. We have no guns on that schooner."

"Lieutenant Magee seems to think that we will be left alone. We will have to trust him."

"Right sir, if you say so."

"Oh and another thing. They pretend to be an Irish boat. See if any of the lads can do an Irish accent."

"Scouse should find it easy sir. Liverpool is full of Micks."

That evening the three of us, Hugo, Sandy and myself, sat around the fire on the beach. Sandy had opened a bottle of brandy and we were drinking the fiery liquid as we went over the operation. "We will be away three of four days and we will be out of radio contact."

Sandy shook his head, "It could be four. The winds can be funny at this time of year and we just don't know what we might have to do to escape prying eyes. I would say six days. If we are away for a week then you can start the hue and cry."

"We will take the German caps with us. We now have enough for each of us. In the dark we might be taken for Jerry. Put in those five German Zeltbahn we found. They can cover the uniforms of five of us. "

Sandy nodded his approval, "Good idea."

Hugo asked, "What was that you said about the lack of harmony between Italians and Germans?"

"I got the impression that neither liked the other."

Sandy took his pipe from his mouth and pointed, "You are right there. We play one off against the other when we play the smuggler. The Germans think the Italians are lazy cowards and the Italians think the Germans are arrogant bores."

"If the invasion comes off soon then it might just push the Italians to break with Germany."

"Let's get on to the mainland first, Hugo. The last thing we want is the country being reinforced by Germans."

The only petty officer on '*Dragonfly*' was almost as old as Sandy. Chief Petty Officer Thomas had also served in the Great War and had been at Jutland. Like Sandy he had stayed on in the Med where he had worked on a variety of ships. He was a jack of all trades. He could fiddle on with engines, he could navigate, he could set a sail as well as Sandy. Against all King's Regulations he had a pipe jammed between his teeth when he was awake. I suspected that he had it there when asleep too. I am not certain it was always lit but he had this ability to speak with it while billowing clouds of smoke. The smoke was the same as that from Bill Leslie's pipe and I suspected they both soaked their tobacco in rum.

He knuckled his forehead as we clambered aboard, "Morning sir. A fine day for a trip across the bay eh?" He chuckled at himself. "Mr Magee is preparing the charts. He said to get you lads stowed away below decks and then we'll set sail." He leaned in, "Unless your lads have some civvies, sir, they'll have to be battened down all the way across. Its why we don't wear regulation rig, sir."

"We'll remember that for next time, Chief."

He shrugged, "Anything for an easy life. Having a smart uniform didn't help those lads we lost at Jutland did it sir?"

He left it at that and I followed my section through the hatch to the Stygian depths below. "I am afraid that we will have to stay below decks. Jerry might be suspicious of a bunch of khaki clad squaddies."

I could see they were disappointed but the resourceful Scouse said, "If we take off our battle dress, sir, we could stay on deck."

I was dubious. The white skinned Commandos would stand out against the gnarled mahogany sailors. I saw that they were keen and so I relented. "In ones and twos then and for no longer than an hour. The last thing we need is you lot with sunburn!"

I intended to spend as much time with the charts and the maps as possible. Although it was only seventeen miles between where we would be landed and then be picked up there were not a huge number of roads. We would have to find somewhere to lie up during the day and that would not be easy. As I scrutinized the maps I saw that the closer we came to Calabernardo the fewer were the number of roads. In one place there was just one for the mountains came very close to the coast. I had no idea what the terrain might be like. We would have to think on our feet. This time there would be little point in splitting up. We had to start and finish at the same place. I could not have my men swanning around by themselves.

I felt the motion from the hull as we set sail. Some of the section went on deck. I would not need to check up on them, the NCOs would sort them out. Sergeant Poulson joined me. "Problems, sir?"

"Yes Sergeant. I am trying to work out how to avoid the Germans and Italians who will be swarming all over the area we are searching."

Sometimes it helped having another pair of eyes and so it proved. "Well sir it strikes me that this Syracuse is a big place. We found out at Dieppe that you don't land at a port."

"Yes, that is right."

"So if we start here, at this little river a mile south then we can avoid the town. It looks quiet enough south of there."

I had not spotted that. The planners would avoid Syracuse itself and there was little point in us taking a risk getting through a heavily defended town. "Good idea. I will have a word with Mr Magee. If he could drop us there then it would save some miles anyway." As I studied the map I saw that there was a little isthmus south of Syracuse. If we went there we could cover a large area quite quickly. "If we head down here the first night and then lie up between Avola and Noto we can do the southern end while we are heading to be picked up."

Sergeant Poulson's finger jabbed out. "This looks rough ground. That would be perfect for us."

I rolled up the map. "Right, I had better see the lieutenant."

"Sir?"

"Yes, Sergeant?"

"Don't forget to take off the battledress eh sir?"

"Good thinking, Sergeant." I took off my battledress, shirt and vest and headed on deck. "Sandy, I have a request."

He grinned, "If we can oblige then we will."

"Instead of Scoglio Due Fratelli we want to be dropped off here." I pointed to the bay which was south of Syracuse. He frowned. "Problem?"

"For you, not me. I can still go back to Scoglio Due Fratelli but what about your dinghies? I don't have enough crew to row you in and back."

I had not thought of that. Once again our lack of numbers would hurt us.

"What is your plan? Scout out here and then what?"

"Head inland to lay up and then scout the southern end when we are picked up."

"Then there is your answer. Have your men row you in and back. I will take them down to land at Calabernardo. They can scout out the southern end and I will take you all off at the same time"

Already my plan to keep my men together was in tatters but Sandy was right. This made sense. "Sounds like a plan to me. I had better get my lads down and explain the change to them. Right lads, below decks."

I saw, from Fletcher's red back that he had not heeded my advice. He would suffer. "I have changed our plans. I will go ashore with Corporal Hay, Fletcher and Hewitt. The rest of you will row us in and drop us off. Lieutenant Magee will drop the rest of you off at Calabernardo and you will recce the southern beaches. We will meet up with you."

"Will you have enough men, sir?"

"You said it yourself, Sergeant, we have to lie up during the day. The fewer men the better eh? One of the drawbacks of the schooner is a smaller crew. We have to get ourselves ashore. Anyway it just means the rest of you have a day hiding behind an island eh?"

I spent an hour with my three men going over what we would need to do. We had found it paid to go over every detail in case we became separated. We were Commandos and they could survive without an officer peering over their shoulder. I was lucky in that Sergeant Poulson had good leadership qualities and he was intelligent. He would make a good officer. He would be able to scout out the southern section of the operation.

In the middle of the afternoon Lieutenant Magee stuck his head down the hatch, "Keep your heads down. We have company. A Jerry aeroplane is giving us the once over."

As we waited for the rattle of machine guns I reflected that if we were on board *'Lucky Lady'* then we would have been ready with our machine guns. We were now in Sandy Magee's hands. We would bluff the enemy and not fight them. We heard his engines as he came very low to investigate us. When his engines receded and Sandy whistled the all clear we breathed a collective sigh of relief.

With just four of us we needed less in the Bergen. "Fletcher you take your Thompson. Hay and I have our silenced Colts. That should be enough. We will just take six Mills bombs and two potato mashers. Make sure you all have a German cap. Put four Zeltbahn in the Bergen too."

"Right sir."

As dusk approached we blacked up. We had saved at least an hour by landing south of Syracuse and time was not such an issue. By the time it was dark the two dinghies which would row us ashore were ready and we headed in under silent sails. I had to admit that this was an advantage over the E-Boat. Even when we were barely moving the engines could be heard from a long way away. It took more skill to navigate with sails and I noticed that there was barely any canvas. Magee had been right, the schooner was well named, she could fly. We had covered the seas between Malta and Syracuse far faster than I had expected.

How Sandy knew when we were in the right place I had no idea but he spun the wheel and we came to a dead stop. There was no point in speaking. The boats were lowered and we quickly clambered down the ladder. The water was inky black and there were no lights to show the shore but we knew the direction and we paddled. We only had forty yards to paddle and we ground on the shingle and sand. Hewitt and I clambered ashore and ran up the beach.

The buildings were three quarters of a mile to the north of us. There was nothing save mud, sand and salt flats. We made our way as quickly as we could to the river. Hay and Fletcher soon caught up with us. I glanced over my shoulder and saw that I could barely see my men in the dinghies. We moved along the river bank. River was rather a grand word for an over grown stream but it was a marker. We made our way upstream. We walked along the edge of the shallow stream; that way we left no tracks.

We reached the railway line. I was surprised that, so far, we had seen none of the defences we had done further around the coast. We clambered up the railway line and walked along it. It was a safer way to travel. The rail would vibrate if a train came down the line. It was also a good place to observe the defences as it was raised up. It was a single rail. That meant that trains could only pass in stations. It was useful information to take back. Reinforcements could use the railway line but it could be easily sabotaged or even bombed from the air.

Bill Hay, who was on point, stopped and held up his hand. He pointed east. We could see, below us, gun emplacements. There was a battery of artillery there. Not as many as we had seen before but there were at least three of the seventy fives. We were above the emplacements and we could see the Italian sentries as they peered out to sea. We had been lucky. They might have seen us if we had walked along the road. I took out my map and marked them on it. I waved Bill forward and we continued south.

I heard traffic on the road ahead and we paused in the undergrowth at the bridge which crossed the road. It was civilian traffic which passed beneath us. However the coast was now a mile away and I wanted to make sure that we had investigated anywhere which might have defences. I decided to leave the railway line and risk the few roads. There were enough buildings for us to duck into doorways and hide behind walls. There looked to be no sign of enemy activity at all. This felt too good to be true. It was when we could smell the sea that we saw the first Italian soldiers. Forty yards away they had the road leading from the sea protected by two sandbagged emplacements and machine guns. There looked to be a moveable barbed wire barrier.

I pointed to the south and Bill led us down an alley way. We found another squad of Italians. It seemed they were using the buildings to make improvised strong points. I decided to keep on moving down the alley. It meant we could see each intersection as we darted to the cover of the next alley. They had a line of machine guns and were using the buildings to protect them. It was nowhere near the defence they had at Agrigento. And then we struck the sea again. They had the isthmus cut off by the machine guns.

Suddenly I heard Italian and we ducked behind a wall. A patrol of four men were on the other side of the wall. It was a cigarette break. I had no idea what they were saying. For once my French and German were of no use. After what seemed like an age they moved off. We headed for the shore. There was no beach; there were just rocks and stones and then a low wall. With few buildings it was a deserted part of the town. The narrowness of the shore also meant it could not be mined. Even in the dark I could see that the little bay was perfect for landing craft. This was no Dieppe with enfiladed machine guns and heavy weapons.

We made our way down the shore. I risked walking along the beach and over the rocks. This way we would see, close up, what the problems of an invasion might be. With just four of us we were able to move quietly and remain unseen. There were many tiny bays. We saw no more defences. I looked at my watch. It was three thirty and dawn was less than two hours away. We needed to be inland and hidden before then. When we found the small river, the Fiume Cassibile, I knew we were just a couple of miles from Avola. We headed up the river. It was shallow enough for us to walk up the middle if we chose. It was our safest route inland. We would leave no tracks and, hopefully, meet no one. Within half a mile we were in deep undergrowth. This was perfect cover. I gathered the three of them around me. "Let's find somewhere to lie up. I don't think we will find any better cover than this."

We found a small cave along the valley sides. It was really just four fallen rocks but it would hide us from above. Hay and Fletcher quickly set to making tripwires around the perimeter while Hewitt sorted out the rations. I took out the map and added all the features we had seen. The little General would be happy when we got back. When Hay and Fletcher returned I said, "We each have a two-hour stag. Use your watch to see what there is close by." I handed the glasses to Bill. "You can have first stag. I'll take second."

"Right sir."

Hewitt handed out the rations. We all had our own water. The rations were fairly tasteless but they would give us the energy we needed. I wrapped myself in my camouflage net and was asleep as soon as my head hit the ground.

Bill woke me up. He pointed to the high ground to the north east of us. "There are a couple of big guns up yonder sir. Eyeties again. They have machine gun nests in front of them."

"Thanks Bill."

I took the opportunity to look to the south and west. The high ground and my binoculars meant that I could see all the way to the coast. The Italians and the Germans appeared to have placed their anti aircraft guns facing the south. They were looking to Malta. This was crucial information. An attack to the east would be easier than an attack from the south. I returned to the camp and added notes to my map. I gave Scouse an extra half hour. My mind was filled with everything I had learned. I realised that we did not even need the others to land and investigate Noto and Avola. I had seen all that I needed to see. We had the time now to recce the defences on the hill.

"Have Hewitt wake me at three, Fletcher."

"Right sir."

We left the camp at four in the afternoon. It was a risk but we had the trees for cover. Making our way up the river we were able to skirt the Italian defences. The men there were very noisy. I could not understand their words but they suggested to me a relaxed regime. They contrasted with the Germans we had scouted at Dieppe. They had been silent and grim. They had been ready for war. These Italians were not. We crawled to within forty yards of their position. It was a well-chosen site for guns. The steep sided river valley would slow up an attacker and the guns were protected by, not only sandbags, but also the natural rock. Satisfied we had seen all that we needed to we made our way down the river to reach the road once more.

We reached the river mouth at six thirty and it was coming on to dusk. My map suggested we had a seven-mile hike to our rendezvous. The air was filled with the threat of rain and, even as I stared south the first drops of drizzle fell. As it would soon be dark I took a chance. Using the rain we washed the last of the black from our faces. We now looked more like locals. "Right lads put on the German field caps. Hewitt, take out the Zeltbahn." The Zeltbahn was the German equivalent of our oilskin. It covered the shoulders and the top half of the body. With the German caps it would complete the disguise. "We will just walk down the beach. That way we can check out the defences from the side our lads might be attacking. No English from now on. Scouse has a bit of German. If we meet anyone then I will chat to Scouse. Remember the Eyeties and Germans don't like each other. Don't smile at them. You are the master race, after all!"

I had noticed that the beaches were not as big as those in France. It was only ten yards deep in places. The sea deepened quite quickly too. There were few people around, in the damp evening air. The ones that we passed scowled at us and slammed the doors shut. We marched in step. It was what the Germans would have done. To the east the normally blue Ionian Sea looked grey. It could have been the sea off Scarborough.

The beach at Gallena was a little bigger and there we saw our first Italian soldiers. We saw that they had put barbed wire next to the road and the section had a machine gun behind sandbags. I heard the Italians shout something to us but we ignored them and marched on. When I heard laughter behind us I guessed that the comments had been unkind. The sand stopped altogether at

Caponegro. We had to make our way over rough stones but there were no prying eyes there.

It was almost midnight when we approached Avola. I knew that we would have to be more circumspect there for there would be a curfew. Any Italian patrol we met might wonder why four German soldiers were marching in the rain so far from their unit. There was a derelict hut close to the beach. I guessed it had been somewhere which had sold food to those using the beach in pre-war Sicily. The door hung off its hinges and the wind had blown some of the wooden panels off. I led the men inside. We had shelter and we could talk.

"We have three hours to get through Avola and then rendezvous the other side of Calabernardo. I think it is less than four miles away but we are going to have to avoid detection. Avola is the biggest place along the coast save Syracuse. It stands to reason it will be defended. We keep the disguises but have your weapons at the ready."

"Sir."

"Now have a quick bite and a drink. We need to be alert for this last section."

As we headed south I heard the unmistakeable sounds of a number of aero engines and the sound was coming from the south. It sounded like bombers. I had seen no military targets yet and I wondered what the target was. The sirens from the town told me that they had efficient air defences. We hurried down the beach. The flashes from the guns to our right identified the positions of the anti-aircraft emplacements. The bombers were heading inland. Searchlights played out along the hillside and we saw the large guns we had seen from the river as they added their firepower. We used the diversion to hurry past the town and clear the prying eyes of the Italians. Their eyes were to the skies and not on the ground.

Chapter 4

There were just a couple of hamlets between us and Calabernardo. They were silent as we passed through them. The guns had stopped by the time we saw the tiny harbour of Calabernardo. However, we saw the German flag flying and German sentries patrolling. Their coal scuttle helmets were unmistakeable. We could not pass the port. We would have to head through the town. As we headed towards the narrow streets of the fishing port I glimpsed the familiar sight of an E-Boat. I hoped that Sandy had seen the vessel. It would make mincemeat out of the schooner.

We turned south as soon as we could. We slipped through the streets like fleeting shadows. I could smell the sea. If all had gone well then, the schooner should have been just three hundred yards away over the other side of the headland. I led. Every sense was attuned to spotting the enemy. It was fortunate that I had my Colt out for as we emerged from the alley at the sea wall which overlooked the small bay I saw, twenty feet away, two German soldiers and they were pointing out to sea. I heard the one with the binoculars say, "There is a ship there and there are dinghies! Telephone the harbour!" As the other cranked the field telephone my Colt spat out four times and both men fell to the ground. The bullets killed them both.

"Over the wall with them!"

Even as my men took the guns and binoculars from them I was peering over the wall. I could see that Sergeant Poulson and his men were rowing back to the schooner. There was one crunch and one splash as one sentry hit the water and the other the rocks. When daylight came he would be discovered.

"Let's go!"

We ran down the path which led along the sea wall and then down the old stone steps which led to the small beach. It was a very narrow and dangerous path. If we had not been wearing rubber soled shoes then we might have slipped over the side. The recent rain had made it very slippery. When we reached the beach I said, "Scouse, signal!"

He took the lamp from the Bergen. The presence of the E-Boat was unexpected. I doubted that Sandy would have seen her. The harbour wall would have hidden the vessel from the sea and the *'Dragonfly'* would have stood well out to sea. The schooner would not reply to our signal. That would be seen from the land but Bill hissed, "Boats!" and I knew that they were coming for us.

There were two dinghies both crewed by my men. We said nothing and we all helped to paddle across to the schooner. I clambered up first and made my way to the stern. "Trouble, Sandy, there is an E-Boat in the harbour yonder."

"Bugger! That wasn't here last month. Chief, get the sails and the anchor up, we are leaving now!"

We barely managed to get the dinghies back on board before we heeled over and set sail south.

"You had better get below decks. I will head west, away from the harbour. The wind is from the north west. As soon as we turn we can make better speed."

We needed no urging and we went to the mess. With the blackout curtain in place we lit an oil lamp. "Maps!"

Before we did anything else we would collate our information and make copies. If the worst happened and we were attacked there was a chance that one set would get home. There was no point in taking such risks as we did and not being careful.

We were still adding to the maps when the curtain from the galley opened and the cook said, "Captain had some fish stew made for you lads and some stoker's cocoa. He reckoned you needed it."

I nodded. "You lads who have added your info get some grub. The sergeant and I will finish up." The smell of the food was inducement enough to hurry and finish the maps. "What do you think, Sergeant?"

"A better prospect than Agrigento sir. There were guns and troops but nothing to worry us. I reckon a couple of sections of Commandos landed before the invasion could knock them out. The stuff we saw was nothing like they had at Dieppe. There were no concrete tank traps and we saw no mines at all."

As I ate the stew I reflected that Dieppe was now the yardstick by which we measured degrees of danger. The poor Canadians who had been slaughtered in that abortive attempt to gain a port had, probably, saved thousands of lives. That plan would not be repeated.

I lay down on my bunk. There were just four bunks in the schooner's mess and the rest of the section insisted that we have them. I lay down and closed my eyes. I was too pumped up to sleep and I listened to the section as they spoke of the operation and smoked. I suppose I must have dozed off for I was suddenly shaken awake by Sergeant Poulson who whispered, "Trouble sir! It's that E-Boat."

"Weapons!" I grabbed my Luger and a grenade and went to the curtain. We had stopped. We bobbed up and down on the water.

I could hear the German captain's voice as he spoke to Sandy, "Next time you stop as soon as I order you to!"

Sandy was a fine actor and he managed to speak German with an Irish accent. "This is a sailing ship, Captain. You should know it takes time to lower our sails and come about."

"Do not presume to tell me what I should know. My men will come aboard and search you."

I dropped back down the stairs. "Sergeant take half the men and go out through the galley. Jerry is searching. If they get close we have to take out the E-Boat. Issue the grenades."

"Sir!"

I led the four men who were left to the stairs. All had their Thompsons and grenades festooned around their necks. We were armed and dangerous.

"There is no need for a search. Your colleagues never come aboard."

I heard the loud hailer again, "If by colleagues you mean those spaghetti eaters then do not insult me. I know you fly the Irish flag but I do not trust you. I will bring aboard twenty men and we will search your boat from top to bottom!"

There was a bump as the E-Boat nudged us. I heard the sound of ropes being thrown and I took the opportunity to slip out through the curtain and roll behind the mainmast. Hay and Fletcher followed. I held up my hand to hold the rest. Glancing around the mast I saw that the Germans just had one machine gun covering Sandy at the stern. I pointed to the gunner and then Bill. He nodded. The trick would be to wait until the Germans were all on board.

Sandy's crewmen were tying the ropes the Germans had thrown. The German captain was being careful. He would not attempt to board us until it was secure. I waved Lowe and Hewitt over and they joined us. The wooden dinghy was also next to the mast and it gave us cover. I caught Sandy's attention. I pointed to my gun and he nodded. He was lounging by the stern and I knew that he had a Webley concealed there.

The German captain snapped, "Board them and watch for tricks!"

I waited until half of the Germans had boarded before I hissed, "Now!"

I stood and, holding the Luger two handed shot the German captain three times in the head. Bill's Thompson scythed through the gun crew. While my men slaughtered the boarding crew with their Tommy guns I ran to the E-Boat's side. I knew exactly where the radio room was and I took the pin from a Mills bomb and lobbed it over the side of the bridge. "Grenade!"

I dropped to the deck and the grenade went off. As the air cleared I heard, "Grenades!" as my men threw their own grenades down the length of the E-Boat. It was carnage. Other crew men had heard the gunfire and were racing to help their colleagues. The chatter of Thompsons deafened me but I heard Sandy shout, "Cut those lines, lower the sail!"

Fletcher was next to me. I grabbed two of his grenades and said, "Bill, follow me!"

I jumped aboard the E-Boat. A German Petty Officer emerged from the engine room and I shot him at point blank range. I took my two grenades and threw them into the engine room before shutting the hatch and jamming a rifle through the handles.

"Down!" Bill and I took cover.

"Tom! Get back!" I heard Sandy's voice and then the deck below us moved as the two grenades took out the engine room and her crew.

I saw that the schooner had drifted a little way away from the E-Boat. We would have to swim back. "Bill, head forrard to the ammunition. Let's blow this bugger up!"

He grinned, "Right sir."

There was a sudden fusillade of shots as my men shot a group of German sailors who had emerged through the aft hatch. We knew from *'Lady Luck'* that the ammunition was stored below the waterline close to the bows. There were two ventilation pipes to take away dangerous fumes. Bill handed me a grenade and we stood over the two pipes, "One, two, three!" On three we pulled the pins and dropped them in and then turned to dive over the side. I dived deep and I kicked as hard as I could. The grenades had nine second fuses. How far could I swim in nine seconds? My legs kicked as fast as I could manage and I went as deep as I dared. The concussion from the explosion was more powerful than I had expected. It hurled me forward and I fought to keep my mouth shut. I thought my head would explode. The force threw me up to the surface and I popped up like a cork. I was forty yards from the schooner. I turned around and saw the E-Boat settling into the water. Flames leapt up and ammunition exploded as she slowly sank. Around her were the bodies of the crew. I desperately sought Bill. I caught sight of him ten yards away. He was face down in the water. I swam to him and turned him onto his back. Putting both arms around his stomach I pulled hard three time. He gave a cough and began to splutter. He was alive.

From behind me I heard Sergeant Poulson, "Just hang on sir, we are coming!"

Bill coughed for a few more minutes as I heard the dinghy approaching. "That's it sir, I am giving up the fags! I didn't have enough wind then!"

We were quickly hauled aboard, "Best get a move on sir, Mr Magee says that he is not certain if Jerry got a radio message off."

We all set to paddling and, even as we were dragged to the deck, the *'Dragonfly'* was flying. Sandy shouted, "Get below, you lads. They will have aeroplanes up soon. We need to be as far away from here as we can."

When we reached the mess deck I saw Hewitt tending to George Lowe and Alan Crowe. I looked at Sergeant Poulson, "Is it bad?"

He shook his head, "George didn't duck quick enough and he has shrapnel. Crowe was unlucky. Bullets hit the wooden rail and drove splinters in his arm. It looked a mess but Hewitt thinks they will be fine and won't need a hospital." He shook his head, "Sir, if you don't mind me saying so that was the maddest thing I have ever seen! You and Hay could have been killed."

"We both know that an E-Boat has a big crew. If they had stood off they would have made matchwood out of this little ship. Besides I know that Bill here is the best swimmer in the section."

Bill smiled, "Was, sir. You showed me a clean pair of heels. It was a good job you were there."

"I got you into bother, Bill, the least I could do was to get you out."

I thought we had escaped the scrutiny of the Germans but a shout from the deck dashed those hopes. "Ju 88 stooging around. Best grab a life jacket! We may be swimming."

I hated being below decks and not being able to see what was going on but I obeyed orders, "Right Sergeant, issue the life jackets. Corporal, put the maps in waterproof packets."

Bill handed one packet to me. He took one himself and handed the third to Sergeant Poulson. If we went down then the information would get back to Malta. Even if they found our bleached bodies the information would get through. "Better pack our Bergens too."

One of the ratings came below decks. "Captain says that the Jerry is circling. It looks like they have sent for another ship to investigate."

"Thanks."

That was a problem. We had already met an Italian Corvette and I knew that there were other naval vessels close to hand. The *'Lady Luck'* could easily escape any pursuer and even shoot down the Ju 88. We were a sitting duck. I took off my battle dress; it was soaking anyway and I went up on deck. I hated not knowing.

Sandy shook his head, "Sorry about this, Tom. They must have missed the E-Boat. I daren't even use the radio; they might be listening and if he decided to that bomber could blow us out of the water. We will just have to try bluffing it out."

"But you aren't hopeful."

"No. I think the German would have said he was investigating a schooner. When we blew it up it meant they would worry about it."

"How far from home are we?"

He pointed to a little blob on the horizon. "That is Ghawdex."

"That is so close we could almost swim."

He laughed, "You could, Tarzan! The rest of us would struggle!" He looked up at the billowing sails, "And the annoying thing is that we have never travelled as fast as this. Look at her! She is glorious!"

I nodded, "You are right, it is a beautiful sight. But I would trade it for an Oerlikon right now!"

One of the lookouts shouted, "Fast patrol boat approaching from astern, Captain!"

I turned and saw the dot in the distance. I could just make out the gun mounted in front of the bridge. "So close and yet so far."

"You had better tell your lads to get ready to bail. We'll try to fool them until the last minute but..."

"I know, we won't be able to pull the same trick twice, not with that big bird in the sky."

As I turned to look at Ghawdex I saw, high in the sky, three black crosses. I shaded my eyes against the sun. They were fighters. The question was; was it ours or theirs?

Sandy had seen them too, "I hope they are the Brylcreem boys!"

The three crosses began to descend. When the Junkers turned I knew what they were, "They are Hurricanes!"

The three fighters dived, in line astern. The Ju 88 had plenty of guns including two at the rear. The three Hurricane pilots knew their business and they came directly at the rudder of the Ju 88. The lower gun had no target and the upper rear could not fire for fear of hitting its own tail. The German dived towards the patrol boat in order to be protected by the ship's guns. The three Hurricanes were much faster than the Junkers and they peeled left and right as they zoomed alongside the Junkers. They divided the fire of the rear guns and I saw pieces of the rudder fly off and then smoke appeared. The three fighters banked and then closed in for the kill. The patrol boat used its limited machine guns to try to help the Junkers but when it plunged into the sea the Italian turned and headed back to Sicily, closely pursued by the Hurricanes.

The crew cheered and I shouted, "Sergeant, you can bring the men up on deck. We are almost home."

I went to the stern. Sandy and the Chief had their pipes going and were grinning. "That was lucky! Perhaps I ought to pray for the RAF more often."

The Chief said, "That was in the days when we just had Faith, Hope and Charity! Things are different now, sir."

Sandy nodded, "Take in a couple of reefs if you please. There is no rush now and I would like to finish this pipeful."

"Aye aye sir."

The sub-lieutenant nodded to me, "I can see that life with you will be interesting. The phrase mad as a fish springs to mind."

I laughed, "I think it runs in the family."

Sandy frowned and then said, "Harsker! Is your dad Squadron Leader Harsker, the British Ace from the Great War?"

"He is Air Commodore now but yes he is."

"Then I am not surprised that you do what you do. The papers were always full of his exploits. Won a V.C. and the Military Cross!"

Sergeant Poulson had joined us, "The Lieutenant has the Military Cross too, sir."

Sandy said, "Here you are Sergeant, keep her on a straight line." Much to Sergeant Poulson's consternation he let go of the wheel and came to shake me by the hand. "Chief Bosun, splice the main brace. This calls for a celebration."

The Chief hurried below decks.

"You have made my day, today, young man. After Jutland when the Navy was on its uppers and the lads on the Somme were being slaughtered it was the likes of your dad, duelling with the Red Baron and the others that kept our spirits up."

The Chief returned with four very large glasses of rum. He gave one to me, one to Sandy and one to Sergeant Poulson. Polly looked nervously at the wheel and the Chief said, "Give it here son! I can steer, drink a toast and still keep my pipe going."

Sandy said, "Here's to Bill Harsker and the Royal Flying Corps!"

I felt quite touched as I raised my glass to my dad. Sandy Magee and the Chief had both lived through the Great War and seen it all. For them to acknowledge my dad as their hero meant the world to me. The fact that the rum burned when it went down did not upset me in the least but we all laughed when Sergeant Poulson coughed and spluttered.

The Chief shook his head, "For Gawd's sake don't waste it! That is neaters! I didn't dilute it!"

I laughed at Sergeant Poulson as he fought the fiery liquor. I think it confirmed the old sea dogs' view that soldiers just couldn't handle their drink!

I turned to Sandy, "Thank you for that. Dad would have appreciated it."

Chapter 5

Hugo watched as the wounded were brought ashore. You could tell that he was a deskbound warrior. He paled at the sight of the scars and the blood. "Don't worry Lieutenant Ferguson, the lads will be right as rain in no time!" Sergeant Poulson had recovered from his close encounter with the rum.

"Quite. Did it go successfully this time?"

"Yes Hugo. All the way from Syracuse to Noto looks fine for an invasion."

He panicked a little, "Who said anything about an invasion?"

"Grant us a little intelligence, Hugo. We are not just killer dogs you let loose. We can think. Everyone of my men knew why we were sent to Sicily. A little more honesty would not go amiss." I handed him the packet with the maps.

He nodded, "You are right." He tapped the maps. "I will let his lordship know! He will be delighted."

"Any more news about replacements?"

He looked guilty, "Lieutenant Jorgenson's new crew members are on their way by convoy!"

"Which means you haven't asked him."

"Not true, old chap, I have but he is a little distracted with the planning for this new operation. I am sure that once he has this information he will move heaven and earth!"

"I somehow doubt it. We will have some mail ready to send soon. I hope that our own letters catch up with us."

"I check each day but you know how things are."

"Yes, Hugo, I am aware of the way of the world." I went to my quarters and took off my uniform. The salt from the sea water had dried, making it stiff. I would have to do some washing. I smiled, Dad had had a batman in the Great War. Uncle John would have done this for Dad. The world had changed in the last twenty-five years.

Bill Hay joined me as we washed our clothes the old-fashioned way using the rocks on the beach. The weather had improved somewhat although it was still far from warm. Any news about mail from home sir?"

"Sorry Corporal. Nothing yet. Are you waiting for something?"

"Just a letter from home, you know..." he tailed off lamely.

"One of the lads said you hadn't been married long, you know before you were sent to join us."

"Less than six months sir. I know most of the lads think you are daft if you get married while there is a war on but me and our lass had been courting a year or two and we thought, why wait?"

I nodded. My Auntie Alice was supposed to marry Charlie who had been one of Dad's pilots. They had delayed and he had been killed. Auntie Alice never married. "I think you are right to get married. God knows how long this war will last."

He looked relieved that I had said the right thing, "I am just glad that she isn't in one of the big cities. I know the bombers go everywhere but I just hope that Shrewsbury doesn't suffer like the rest. It is bad enough that her family live miles away."

"What about yours, Bill?"

"They got hit in the Blitz. There were up in town celebrating their wedding anniversary. There wasn't even enough to bury them. It's why we moved to the country. It is a bit lonely for her but it is safe and..."

He clammed up. "And you want your family to be safe."

"I don't know if she is, you know, sir in the family way but we were trying and... well I just want a letter to know she is alright.

I give my letter every week to Lieutenant Ferguson. I write one a week. Some are longer than others."

"I know." Hugo acted as adjutant and read all the letters before sending them on. My men were good about that. They didn't put in anything about our operation or even where we were. Hugo was quite touched by some of the things they said. "I'll tell you what, I will put a fizz bang up their arse, how about that!"

He brightened, "Yes sir. That would be great."

I laid my clothes on a rock to dry. In summer they would be dry within minutes and even at this time of year knew they would not take long. I went back to my hut and began to clean my weapons. I doubted that we would be away again anytime soon. It would take Major Fleming some time to come up with another operation. Being such a small unit we all mucked in with the food and I sought out Sergeant Poulson. "What is on the menu for tonight, Sergeant?"

"Lieutenant Magee sent over some of the fish they caught the other day. We are doing a fish stew. We still have some tatties left. We could do with a few things though, sir. We are running low on tea and sugar for a start."

"And that would never do." The British soldier was stoical about almost everything save his tea. If he had no tea he could become mutinous. "I will have a word with the Lieutenant when he returns."

Hugo was sympathetic to our request. "I think the *'Dragonfly'* needs a few things too. I'll send her tomorrow to Valetta."

"I think I will go with Sandy. I'd like to see Alan, and find out how things are going and I intend to have a rant about the lack of mail. Poor Bill Hay doesn't know if his wife is pregnant yet."

"I know, I feel sorry for them. You and I are fine, Tom, we have no entanglements but most of your lads either have wives or girlfriends."

That decided me. I was normally mild mannered but if some official was sitting on my men's letters I would show him the hard side of a Commando. I put on my one decent uniform. It would not do to turn up in a crumpled battle dress.

I enjoyed the cruise down to Valetta for we sailed under the White Ensign and I was able to stay on deck. Sandy needed tea, fuel and rum. Our celebration had meant he needed his requisition filling. Valetta harbour was filled with ships of every description but Sandy carefully and skillfully navigated every obstacle. When we came to the dock I saw our old ship. The *'Lady Luck'* did not look right sitting on a wooden framework while dockyard workers and her crew repaired her. We came in under engines.

Sandy nodded as the ship was tied up. "I'll need about four hours to refuel and get the supplies we need."

"Good. That will give me the chance to find whoever is sitting on our post!"

I stepped on to the jetty, grateful that I was not having to wade! Alan looked up from the stern. "How is it going, Tom?"

I was aware of the Maltese dockyard workers and so I shrugged, "The *'Dragonfly'* is different. When you return I will give you the lowdown. How about you? Have your new crew arrived?"

He shook his head, "The end of the week... or so they said. We have another six days, at least, of work here. Those cannon shells made a right mess of her. We are waiting for parts!"

"I am off to chase up the mail!"

"Good! I dare say my chaps are as annoyed as yours!"

There was a whole section devoted to mail in Valetta. It was sent on from Gibraltar and then sorted. The sentries at the military post office were smartly turned out. I wondered at the waste. I guessed there would have to be eight men guarding the building. I doubted that they needed that much security but what did I know? I was a fighting soldier. The sergeant who was reading the newspaper behind the desk had a neat little moustache and slicked back hair. I judged that he liked order. He stood to attention when I entered.

"Yes sir? What can I do for you?"

"We are the first special section, Number Four Commando based at Marsalaforn on Ghawdex. We have had no mail since we arrived. I wondered where it was."

The sergeant seemed to take in my Commando flash and my Combined Operations badge. He stood a little straighter and his eyes went to my medal ribbons. His eyes widened when he recognised the Military Cross.

"Right sir. There must be some kind of mistake. I will see Lieutenant Harper straight away!"

He was away for quite a while and then the sergeant said, "If you would like to follow me sir. Lieutenant Harper wishes a word."

Lieutenant Harper was another fan of order and neatness. His office was arranged perfectly and everything was in its place. Everything, that is, save for the huge sack of letters squatting untidily in the corner.

"Thank you, Sergeant." The lieutenant flashed me an irritated look, "Please take a seat, Lieutenant...?"

"Harsker, Tom Harsker."

"Now Sergeant Harris tells me that you are here about some missing letter." He smiled and it was like staring into the eyes of a dead fish. "We do not lose letters. Before we begin have you any papers of identification?"

I had anticipated this and I took out my own papers and the warrants I had been issued before we left England. He scrutinised them closely as though I was some sort of German spy. He reluctantly handed them back, "They appear to be in order but we can't be too careful about this sort of thing."

I wondered what he meant, *'this sort of thing'* but I let it pass. "So if you do not lose letters then I assume you know where they are."

His eyes involuntarily flicked to the sack. "Of course and we tried to deliver them. I sent a mail boat to Marsalaforn but neither you nor the Royal Naval chaps was there and my orders were quite specific. They were not to be handed over to anyone other than a ranking officer."

I sighed. I knew his type. We called them Jobsworths. In civilian life they were the ones who always shook their heads and said, 'More than my job is worth!' They could not think for themselves. "Lieutenant Harper, do you know what we do?"

This time he took in my flashes and medals. He shifted uncomfortably in his seat, "Well you are Commandos so I am guessing that you see a little action."

I laughed, "You could say that. Sometimes we are away for days at a time. We have an officer at our base, Lieutenant Ferguson, but when we are away he is glued to a radio. Unlike you we do not have the luxury of eight sentries to guard us. When we are gone there is no one to wait in for the postman!"

He coloured, "That is unfair! We do valuable work!"

I was becoming angry. My mother said that dad and I were the same we both got what she called 'mad eyes'. I knew that my eyes were becoming angry. "Listen to me, Lieutenant Harper, on our last mission one of those Royal Naval chaps, as you put it, died. He was waiting for a letter about his first grandchild. One of my corporals is also desperate to know if he is to be a father. Now if my men's minds are not on the job then they can make a mistake and that mistake will cost lives." I leaned forward, "I was at Dieppe and I know about costly mistakes so give me that sack of letters before I take them!"

"Are you threatening me?"

He was leaning as far back as he could get in his chair and was in danger of falling from it. I put my hands on his desk and leaned forward. My eyes still burned but I had a grin on my face. He was terrified, "Of course not. It is not a threat. I am leaving with those letters either with your permission or without it. Clear?"

I saw his eyes flickering from side to side as he sought a way out which gave him some dignity. There was none, "Then take the damned things. They are cluttering up the office anyway."

I walked over and hefted the sack on to my shoulder, "Good and now that I have explained the situation then I hope future letters will be delivered promptly whether we are there or not. I would hate to have to come back."

He nodded, "Of course. We are here to help."

I turned as I reached the door, "I did wonder."

Sergeant Harris snapped to attention, "Got what you wanted, sir?"

"Yes Sergeant and I shall be borrowing one of your sentries for half an hour or so. I have no intention of carrying this sack back to the harbour."

The ghost of a smile played upon the sergeant's mouth, "Of course not, sir."

When I left the building the two sentries stood to attention. I nodded to the bigger of the two, "You, Private, leave your rifle and grab this. You are coming with me." He had little choice in the matter for I thrust the sack at him.

"But sir..."

Sergeant Harris came to the door, "Just do it Smith. The exercise will do you good."

I gradually calmed down on the twenty-minute walk back to the harbour. It was not the fault of Smith and Harris. Lieutenant Harper had made them the way that they were. He wanted order and normality. I suppose we needed men like that. God knows it would be a disaster to have the likes of Harper with a gun defending anything save a sack of letters.

"Just drop them there, Smith, by that schooner."

"You sail in that sir? Are all Commandos as..."

"Watch it Private or I may take you with us on one of our little jaunts!" I was smiling when I said it.

He deposited the sack and said, "No thanks, sir. I'll stay in my cosy little billet. I'd like to see the end of this war."

"As would we all, son, as would we all."

Alan and Bill Leslie wandered over to me. "Petty Officer Leslie if you want to take out the letters and mail for your lads eh?"

He grinned, "Will do sir. I take it we will be getting regular mail from now on?"

"I think so, Bill!"

"Oy, Tosh, come and give me a hand eh?"

Alan lit a cheroot. "It is bad enough being over here and risking life and limb every day. A letter from home is all it takes to make these chaps feel happy."

I nodded, "Except for sad so and so's like us."

He laughed, "Well of course!"

That was not quite true, there would be letters from mum, my sister Mary, and, perhaps, even Auntie Alice but if they did not write I would not be as upset as the likes of Billy Hay and George Lowe who both had wives and families at home.

I nodded towards *'Lady Luck'*, "Is the work still progressing?"

"I said six days before. Make that eight. We need another part and E-Boats do not use standard parts. We will be ready eventually. Perhaps Fleming will let you rest on your laurels for a bit eh?"

I laughed, "There is no chance of that!"

It took longer for Sandy to get everything he needed and we left just before sunset. It felt almost like peacetime as we headed into the sun with the sails billowing above us. The Chief and Sandy leaned against the stern rail and let me steer. Their pipes puffed pleasantly as a gentle breeze made me think that the war was just a nightmare. The short voyage was an interlude which recharged my batteries.

There was a reception committee waiting for us. Hugo had told the men my mission and they were eager for their letters. I threw the sack to Hugo, "There you are Lieutenant Ferguson! Enjoy!"

I was walking to my hut when I heard Bill Hay give a whoop. "I am a dad! I have a son!"

Everyone crowded around to congratulate him. I turned to walk back. Suddenly he said, "Oh no!"

A deadly silence fell over the men. This sounded like bad news. "What's up Corp? Summat wrong with the bairn?"

"No Fred, well at least not yet." He looked up. "It's the name. She has named him after her uncle, Maurice!"

"What's wrong with that?"

"If it gets shortened it will be Mo Hay! You can't do that to the poor little bugger can you?" There was relief all around that the only problem he had was with a name.

We had two days without orders and then Hugo came one morning and shouted, "Lieutenant Magee, we have orders!" He waved his acknowledgment and clambered down to the dinghy.

"Where to this time, Hugo? Sicily again?"

"No, Tom, Italy!"

"Italy?"

He held up a hand, "Best I explain what Major Fleming wants when Sandy arrives. But he has promised us more men. There is some good news."

Sicily was one thing but a voyage to Italy on the schooner involved greater distances and more danger. Sandy was beaming as he strode over to us. "Don't tell me, the holiday is over? We have had our two days of relaxation and now it is back to the fray, eh?"

"You seem remarkably philosophical about the prospect, Sandy."

"When you went through the Great War then every day you are above ground seems like a gift from God."

Hugo had the maps out. "The Major was very pleased with the last operation. He wants the section to go to Italy to do a little sabotage." The surprise must have shown on my face for he said, "Let me explain. Your information confirmed that there is a lack of harmony between our enemies. The Major wants you to exploit that. There are Italian Communists who are opposed to Mussolini. Sadly they don't like us very much either. He wants you and your men to cut the railway line north of Reggio and make it look like the partisans did it."

"And how do we do that?"

"Use dynamite and an old-fashioned detonator. The partisans and resistance all use them!"

"That increases the risk for us."

"I know but you get to choose the place to do it. You could pick somewhere really quiet."

I sighed, "Give me the map then." The first glance did not appear to offer anything. "There are settlements all the way along the coast and look here, Messina! You can guarantee that there will be more patrol boats there than anywhere."

Sandy said, "Let me have a look."

I leaned back as Sandy examined the map, "We don't mind the difficult, Hugo, it is the impossible we don't like. I am not certain that this is worth the risk."

"It diverts Jerry from looking too closely at Sicily. The powers that be want the Germans looking further east for an invasion. I think, although no one has told me, that there will be similar attacks in Greece and the Balkans. Now that North Africa is sewn up we can strike anywhere in Europe."

Sandy said, "Here!"

"What?" I saw that his finger was almost on Reggio. "Are you mad? That is less than a mile from Reggio harbour!"

"And that is why it is perfect. Look, Tom, there is the railway line and nothing else nearby. The mountain almost comes down to the sea. It is like that bit of coast close to the Menaii straits in Anglesey. Why you could probably block the line for a long time if you set the charges to bring down part of the mountain."

"What about you and the schooner?"

"Oh, don't worry about us. We can play the wind trick."

"The wind trick?"

"Pretend we are poor sailors and get caught out. We have done it before. You lads paddle in and leave your dinghies, here." He pointed. "The nearest house is a good two hundred yards away. I have seen you operate. You are invisible when you want to be. Ten minutes to get to the railway and then however long it takes to set the charges."

"An hour, tops."

"Then there you have it. It will take that time for us to turn around and get back in position for you."

"The trouble is we only have seven men we can take. I am not risking the two wounded lads."

Hugo smiled, "Technically this just needs a couple of you."

"You two seem determined to make light of this."

"No, Tom, we are just doing what you normally do, seeing the positives. You have had two rough missions. This one might not be as bad."

"Right. I suppose I am resigned to it. We will need dynamite then."

"They have some in the stores at Marsalaforn. I'll nip over and get it."

As we walked back to the beach Sandy said, "We both do what we do, Tom, because we want to make a difference. There are risks in everything."

"I know." I whistled and my men looked over. "Front and centre! We have work to do!"

"I'll tell my lads. See you later and don't worry. You young lads can handle this."

I waved at him. My men squatted around on the sand. "We are off again. We leave tonight. We are going to Italy."

Unlike me they seemed enthusiastic. "Lance Sergeant Lowe and Private Crowe you will stay here. You have been wounded and I can't risk it."

They both looked devastated. "We'll be fine sir! Won't we, Doc?"

I shook my head, "There is no point in appealing to Hewitt. It is my decision. You can stay here and make this camp a bit more organised. It looks like we are getting more men."

I took out the map and laid it on the sand.

"We are going here. It is the railway line just north of Reggio." I looked at Ken Shepherd. "It will come down to you and you will be using dynamite not our usual explosive." George Lowe gave me a look of surprise. "I know Lance Sergeant but we have to look like Italian partisans. We want to be as primitive as we can be."

"It means he will have to use an electrical charge to set it off, sir."

"All sorted, George, and that is why we have chosen this place. We can run the fuse down to the shore. It is as safe as we can make it. Lieutenant Ferguson is getting the dynamite, fuse and everything else that we need. You need to work out how to blow up the line and bring some of the mountain down too."

George looked at his acolyte, "You and I will have to spend the next few hours going through this."

Bill Hay said, "I have used dynamite before. I'll give the lad a hand."

"Thanks Bill."

"Now it doesn't need us all so most of you will just be needed to row us in and guard us. Take the German guns and leave the Commando weapons here. We use German grenades rather than Mills bombs. You have the rest of the day to get ready. We will be at sea for a few days this time."

"How about wearing civilian gear, sir, like the crew of the *'Fly'*?

"Good idea, Scouse." I looked around the faces. They were good Commandos. I had given them a problem and they had come up with solutions. They were better Commandos than I was. "If there's nothing else, let's prepare."

I would take my Luger. It was a shame it had no silencer but if Sandy was right in his estimation then there would be no enemies nearby anyway. This seemed to me like it might be our easiest operation to date.

Just after two o'clock Hugo reappeared with dynamite, fuse and detonator. My three explosives experts scurried away to examine them. Sergeant Poulson came to see me, "Who will you take with you, sir?"

"Who would you take?"

He grinned, "Hay and Shepherd, sir. I just thought you might need me too!"

"I need you to watch our backs. The schooner is no E-Boat. Mr Magee will have to tack back and forth. We have to wait until he is on station before we set off the charges."

"What about trains using the railway line sir?"

"I know, that could be a problem. We will have to cross that bridge when we get to it."

Chapter 6

Hugo and Alan Crowe made the meal for us. We ate while the sun dropped in the west. We set sail at dusk when there was just a thin line of red on the horizon. George, Hugo and Alan Crowe waved us off. We looked just as piratical as Sandy and his crew. The comforter was the only piece of uniform, apart from my rubber soled shoes, that I wore. I had donned the bisht as it covered a multitude of sins. It kept you cool when it was hot and warm when it was cold. The rest of my men had been equally imaginative. We were able to lounge around the deck. To a casual observer the schooner might have appeared to be over crewed but as Sandy played the smuggler it might be expected.

"Have you been to Italy before then?"

Sandy nodded, "A couple of times. Once was not far from where we are going to land. It's why I am so confident about the site. I remember having the willies put up me by a train once. I know how close to the shore it is."

"How far is it then?"

"About a hundred and ninety miles." He pointed to the masthead pennant. "Light winds and from the wrong direction; it could take all night and most of the day to reach it. We are subject to the wind. Timetables are hard to keep to."

"We don't want to get there in daylight though."

"No. We will head around to the east if we are early. My worry is that those Jerries we ran into the other day will have reported us. The last thing we need is for inquisitive eyes on us." He pointed the stem of his pipe to the hatch. "You might as well get your head down for a bit."

"I am too wound up. I will stay here, if you don't mind, I find the sea soothing."

"I know what you mean. It is especially true when we are barely moving, like now." We headed through the dark and I sat with back to the stern rail. The Chief came on deck after an hour so that Sandy could go below decks for a call of nature. When the skipper returned he brought me a corned beef sandwich. They seemed to live on them in the navy. It was, simply, two huge wedges of bread filled with thickly cut corned beef and smothered in mustard. It was an acquired taste but I had had enough of them now to quite like the aggressively seasoned sandwich. He also gave me a huge mug of tea.

"Thanks Sandy."

"Don't thank me. Cookie made them for your lads too." He nodded north east. "I reckon four o'clock tomorrow afternoon should see us close so I will head further east. If any nosey aeroplanes see us they will think we are heading for the Balkans or Greece." I saw that we were flying the Irish Free State Flag once more. The rules out here were bent almost to the point of breaking.

At midnight I felt my eyelids drooping and I went below deck. Sandy had retired an hour earlier. They were working four on and four off. He had three watch keepers. Tosh Taylor was the youngest of the three of them and, as Leading Seaman, was the most junior. He nodded as I went below decks. "See you in the morning sir."

"And you, Tosh!"

The schooner was a little livelier when I awoke. I visited the side first and then joined the Chief whose turn it was to steer. "A little livelier than last night, Chief."

"Aye the wind got up an hour ago. The pressure is dropping. My teeth tell me there is a storm brewing. It doesn't change the plan though. We still head east and..."

"Italian aeroplane, nine o'clock!"

I shaded my eyes to see the reconnaissance aircraft which was heading for us. It was high up and posed no threat. That was as long as we behaved normally. We maintained our course and no one raced around the deck. Scouse was lying on the deck and he just said, "Just so long as he doesn't have any mates then we should be fine. This is the life, sir. It is like being a film star." I smiled. He said 'film' as 'filum'. It was a northern trait.

I nodded and watched the Italian aeroplane. He did not deviate from his flight but I had no doubt that he would report us. "Whereabouts are we, Chief?"

He jerked a thumb astern, "Sicily is forty miles that way." He pointed due north, "And Italy is forty miles that way. We stay on this course for another hour and then turn towards the north. It might fool our friend up there."

I went back below deck as the air was becoming a little colder. The rest of the team were gathered in the mess. Ken Shepherd said, "I'm off to make a brew."

"I'll give you a hand. I hate sitting around doing nothing." Doc stood to help him.

Hewitt and Shepherd disappeared. I saw Bill fiddling with the detonator. "Everything all right, Corporal?"

"It's a while since I have used one of these and young Ken here has never used one."

"They are simple enough and more reliable than a timer. Once you have connected the terminals up you just crank her up and push the plunger."

"True sir but we are bringing down a pretty big chunk of the mountain. We need to judge the charge just right. With a timer you can be to hell and gone. With this," he tapped it, "we will be close enough to see it! And, if we get it wrong, feel it too!"

I smiled. Bill was just being careful. He was a dad now and that changed things. There was someone else to live for. Some men changed too much. I hoped that he was not one of them. He was a good man. Soon I would consider promoting him to Lance Sergeant. George Lowe was ready to move on. I would hate to lose him but he deserved the chance to become a full sergeant.

By the time Hewitt and Shepherd came back with the tea the motion of the schooner was more violent. I heard the bosun's whistle, "All hands on deck!"

Fred Emerson started to rise. Sergeant Poulson said, "Just sit down Fred. We can do nowt! It is up to the sailors. They are all old sea dogs. They know what they are about."

We heard orders being shouted. I had done a little sailing myself and I guessed that they were taking in a reef or two. I heard Sandy's voice, "Lieutenant Harsker!"

I donned my bisht and clambered out of the hatch. A wave came over and soaked me. Sandy was laughing, "Sorry about that Tom! I was just going to tell your lads to hang on to something. We are going to come about and it might get a bit hairy!"

I glanced over the side. The normally benign Mediterranean was now like the Atlantic. There were troughs and peaks.

"Should we be worried?"

The Chief was hauling on a sheet, "Nah, just a bit of a blow. We'll be fine! Just warn your lads though, sir." He chuckled, "It's a good job they are all wearing brown trousers!"

I ducked back through the hatch. "Right lads hold on to something. We are going to come about. We might tip a little." I pulled the teapot closer to me. Thankfully, it was almost half empty.

I saw Scouse. He was cocky and he was lying on his bunk smoking a cigarette and blowing smoke rings as though he hadn't a care in the world. I shook my head. He would not have far to fall. I heard the call, "Prepare to come about! Come about!"

I was ready. I felt the hull as it began to lean. At first it appeared to be gentle but suddenly it pitched so hard that Scouse was thrown from his bunk and he landed on the wet deck, "Bloody hell fire! Are we sinking sir?"

"Not yet, Scouse. I told you, hang on to something!"

"If you don't mind sir, I'll stay here, I haven't so far to fall." He was wrong for, as we turned he was thrown against the bench. He cracked his head. Then we began to right ourselves as the boat came about. By the time we were upright Scouse's head was bleeding.

"Better see to him Doc. Don't get complacent, chaps. The storm is still raging. Expect a bucking bronco ride all the way to shore."

We tossed and pitched for another hour before the storm abated a little. I ventured up on deck. It was getting on to dark. Sandy and the Chief still had their pipes going. They had oil skins on and looked like old lifeboat men. Their beards were rimed with salt.

"That was handy that was, Tom. It meant we could turn about with no one noticing. There will be no one out there looking for us. We couldn't have planned it better." He pointed to the north. "We will make a turn in twenty minutes or so. We will be off Reggio in two hours."

I returned to the mess. "Right lads, we go ashore in a couple of hours."

"In this sir?"

"Suits us Fletcher. Who else would be daft enough to go out in weather like this eh?"

Scouse shook his head and Sergeant Poulson quipped, "You know what they say, Scouse, if you can't take a joke you shouldn't have joined up!"

Hay and Shepherd were the two who had Bergens. My job would be largely that of security. Thanks to our last foray in Sicily I had plenty of ammunition for the Luger. I also had four German grenades. In a perfect world we would have had Russian weapons for they supplied the Communist resistance but the Italian resistance would take weapons from the Germans as well as their fellow Italians.

When we drew close to the lee shore the wind became less violent and our motion easier. The waves were still so big that it would be hard for anyone to identify us. We clambered onto the slippery and slick deck with an hour to spare. We brought the rubber dinghies up, both of them, and inflated them. I made my way to the stern. "When we get there, Tom, we will have to be quick. We will drop you and then come about. If we hang around we will draw attention to you. This weather plays into our hands. It will look as though we are trying to escape the storm. We will sail west for thirty minutes and then beat back. Have your laddie signal three times in quick succession. We will answer with one flash when we have seen you."

"It is a bit rough, Sandy."

"Those dinghies are tough. Keep your weight low and you will be fine."

I was not so sure.

We passed the harbour mouth of Reggio but Sandy kept us well out to sea. We were a mile off shore. If anyone spotted us with binoculars it would have looked as though we were heading north for Messina. As soon as we passed the harbour light Sandy put the wheel over and we began to head towards, what looked to me, like a cliff although Sandy seemed confident that we could land.

Stopping a sailing ship was easier than one might think. The captain headed us for the shore and then turned into the wind so that we just stopped. The Chief and his deck party got the dinghies over and then pushed us unceremoniously into them. I was in the one with Bill, Hewitt and Crowe. It lurched alarmingly as Bill slumped into it. He had the Bergen with the detonator and dynamite. I grabbed a paddle and began to paddle towards the shore. It was just thirty yards away but it felt like a mile. The water surged back from the rocks. It was a case of two steps forward and one back. Our extra weight helped when we drew close to the rocky ledge I was aiming for. I jumped out just before we struck it but there was still a horrible grating noise from the bottom of the dinghy. I prayed we had not punctured it.

I was ankle deep in water but I managed to help Hewitt and Crowe to pull the boat out of the sea. I drew my Luger and ran up the slope. I saw, ahead, the cliff and, below it, the railway line. It was eighty feet away. I turned. Bill was struggling up the slope while the other two had their German rifles aimed up towards the railway line. Disaster struck when they tried to land Ken Shepherd.

They were lighter than we had been and a freak wave upended them. Ken was thrown into the sea and his Bergen threatened to pull him down. Poulson and Fletcher were struggling to hang on to the dinghy and I feared we might lose Shepherd. Doc dropped his rifle and dived in to pull Ken Shepherd coughing and spluttering on to the rocky ledge. Hay hovered half way between us, "Corporal, move yourself!" I scrambled up the slope and peered north and south down the line. It looked empty. I lay down and put my ear to the rail. I could hear nothing.

Bill Hay took off his Bergen. I helped him to untie the straps and remove the dynamite. "Railway line first. When Ken gets here we will look at the cliff." He nodded and I left him to it. I crossed the single-track line and went to the cliff. I found what I was looking for straight away. It was a large fissure which rose up the mountain and narrowed towards the top. It was a perfect fracture point.

Still coughing Shepherd joined me, "Sorry about that, sir."

"Later. Put your dynamite here in this hole. I will pack stones around it."

"Right sir." We emptied his Bergen and then I took it and went back to the track.

Hay had moved some ballast and I put it in the Bergen. "How long, Corporal?"

"Ten more minutes."

"Good then you run the fuse back to the ledge and attach it to the detonator."

"Shouldn't I wait until you are back?"

"Just do it!"

By the time I reached Shepherd he had most of the dynamite already in the hole. "You attach the cables and head down to Hay. I will finish up here."

"Are you sure sir?"

"I am sure." I continued to pack in the dynamite. There was no point in taking any of it home with us! Shepherd began to back towards the ledge, trailing the cables behind him. I was just finishing with the dynamite when he hurried back. I began to use the ballast I had placed in the Bergen to fill in the small holes.

"What is the problem?"

"I need to put the fuses under the rails sir, sorry!"

He had made a mistake; it was a small one but it could be the difference between success and failure. All this was wasting time. He took the fuses from the dynamite and half rolled down the slope to the line. I could not pack the rest of the ballast until he had attached the fuses again. He reached me and began to attack the fuses, "Sir, there is a train coming. I felt the vibration."

"Get these connected as quick as you can." I emptied the last of the ballast and packed it as quickly as I could. I could now hear the train. I slung the Bergen over my shoulder and half slipped and slid down the slope. I saw the dark shape of the train coming down the line. It was heading towards Reggio from the north. Hay and Shepherd were busy attaching the fuses. "Scouse! Signal the ship! Now!" All that I could see were four shapes but I knew that he would hear me.

"Ready sir!"

"Right, Corporal, whenever you are ready. Try and get the engine!"

He nodded, "Take cover!"

I lifted the plunger and Shepherd and I ducked down beneath the rock with our hands over our ears. The noise of the train was so loud that I thought he had missed it but he pushed the plunger down and buried his head next to ours. A wall of flame leapt out and there was a wave of concussion. Even though I was deafened I heard the second explosion a moment later. This time I felt the earth beneath me move.

Shepherd grabbed my arm and shouted, "Sir! The wagon!"

Above us one of the wagons had been derailed and was tumbling down the slope towards us. A freak of the explosion had severed its connection with the rest of the train and it was now a huge missile heading for us. We grabbed Bill and threw ourselves towards the two rubber dinghies. The wall of air had knocked the two boats a few feet from the ledge and we hurled ourselves into the sea. As I came up, spluttering I saw that our jump had saved our lives. The wagon teetered, alarmingly, on the ledge we had just vacated. I kicked hard, grabbing Shepherd's collar as I did so. We were pulled aboard the pitching, tossing dinghies. As I rolled on my back I saw that a huge chunk of the rock had slid down and had crushed the engine and the tender. The wagons lay spilled along the railway line. Stones still tumbled down the slope. Some of the smaller ones splashed into the sea just feet away from us.

"Paddle! Before we are seen!"

I was in the same boat as Hewitt and he said, "Sir, we can't see the *'Dragonfly'*. Scouse kept sending but there was no reply."

I shouted, "Keep paddling! We'll paddle back to Malta if we have to!"

Although the waves had abated the seas were still rough. As we paddled across the straits I think that the wild sea saved us. I saw the train and the wagons were on fire. I had no idea what was on board but whatever it was it burned well. The light from the fire illuminated the shelf where we had lain in wait.

I shouted, as I paddled, "Poulson! Come close to us. We'll tie the two dinghies together. "

He nodded. We dug in from our left and soon the two dinghies bumped up next to each other. I grabbed the painter and tied it tightly to the rope which ran around the edge of their dinghy. Sergeant Poulson did the same with his painter.

"Now we paddle on the two sides. I will be the rudder!" I put my paddle between the two hulls. It made paddling and steering much easier. We were bigger and had more stability. The easiest thing to have done would have been to panic. However, in my mind I had the map. The wind was behind us and, eventually, we would hit Sicily. We would make landfall. I still hoped that Sandy would find us but he would be tacking into the wind. Our problem was that we were such a small target for the crew to see. Behind us I heard more explosions. The train must have been carrying ammunition.

Sergeant Poulson's voice carried to me, "Right lads, we can make progress if we do this together. One, two, three, paddle! One, two, three, paddle! One, two, three, paddle! That's it. Now we are motoring!" Our motion was both smoother and faster. Poulson had them working as a team.

I reached under my bisht and took out the compass I had brought. There was just enough light from behind to see the needle. I made a slight correction. We had been heading west south west. When I was satisfied that we were back on course I replaced the compass. I would check it every ten minutes. It was too easy to get lost in the dark of night.

The *'Dragonfly'*, when we did see it, loomed up suddenly and silently out of the night directly ahead of us. "Bloody hellfire!"

Scouse's shout gave me just enough warning to steer to the port side of the schooner as I shouted, "Starboard side, back water!" The side of the schooner grated along the paddles. Luckily with the wind against her the schooner was barely making any way.

I looked up and saw white faces. I heard the Chief shout, "Get that scrambling net over the side, chop, chop!"

Hay and Hewitt grabbed hold of the bottom of the net and we bobbed to a halt. "Get aboard!" I took out my dagger and sliced through the ropes binding the dinghies together. I pulled on the scrambling net to pull us closer. Shepherd reached down to grab the front painter on the dinghy as Sergeant Poulson clambered up the net. I gratefully grabbed hold and then I reached down to help Shepherd with the dinghy. If the enemy found a floating rubber dinghy then they would know who had blown up the line. It was a struggle until hands reached down from above and pulled the two dinghies aboard. I flopped on to the deck with the rest of my men. We were exhausted.

The Chief said, "Best get below decks, Lieutenant Harsker. We are not out of the woods yet."

"Right lads. Mess deck!"

We tumbled through the hatch as the schooner caught the wind and began to heel over. No longer constrained by a headwind she would fly! It was pitch dark in the mess but it was warm and it felt safe. It would have been too easy to lie there and sleep but that would have been dangerous. "Get out of your wet clothes chaps. Sergeant, see if you can shed some light on us eh?"

"Sir!"

I had the easiest job for the bisht just slipped off me. Poulson lit the oil lamp and a golden glow filled the cabin. I found my Bergen and took out my dry clothes. I stripped off and dressed as quickly as I have ever done. I found myself shaking with the cold. It was still winter and the Mediterranean could be as cold as the North Sea!

The cook came through with a dixie, "Here y'are lads. A dixie of cocoa. I have some corned dog butties too." He shook his head, "Sorry about the delay. Lieutenant Magee saw a patrol boat and he took evasive action. It took us some time to get back on station."

"Don't worry, cookie, you got here and that is all that is important."

Bill Hay handed me a mug. I wrapped my hands around it to get some warmth from the enamel. When I sipped it the warm glow slipping down tasted like nectar. The shaking began to abate. I sat on my bunk. Sergeant Poulson shook his head, "That was close sir. I thought you and the other two were a goner when that wagon came towards you."

Bill hay said, "Too much dynamite and I didn't direct it the right way. Sorry sir. I could have got us all killed."

"We all survived but it is a lesson for the future." Ken Shepherd was still shaking with the cold and, I think, the shock. "Well done Shepherd. It will take them weeks to clear that mountain from the line."

"I know sir but I should have remembered to put the fuses under the line."

"No. Listen lads. All of this was my fault. We should have practised more before we left. Major Fleming barks and we jump. From now on we practise everything before a mission. It's what we did in England." I chuckled, "Sergeant Major Dean would have my guts for garters!"

They all laughed, "I bet old Reg is rattling around in that boarding house."

Scouse shook his head, "Nah, he'll be happy as a sand boy! Him and Mrs Bailey playing mums and dads! He'll be narked when we get back!" And that set them all talking about home. This time we had no maps to annotate and no reports to write. We had had one task and we had completed it. For a couple of hours they forgot the war and just talked of home.

When the conversation stopped I knew that most of them were asleep. I felt like sleep too but I had to speak with Sandy. I slipped on my oilskin and headed up on deck. The wind was still blowing strongly from the north east but the rain had ceased. Sandy was at the wheel with his pipe. He looked like a rock.

I made my way across the canting deck using the mast as a support. I grabbed the stern rail. He nodded at me, "A hell of an explosion!" I nodded. "Sorry we missed the pickup. Best laid plans and all of that..."

I shook my head, "It couldn't be helped. A train came along. The original plan to signal you and wait until you were close went out of the window. I think the train was carrying ammunition."

"You and your lads did well. If you hadn't tied the dinghies together I don't think you would all be on board." He nodded to the skies. "The winds are easing. I hope they don't ease too much. We don't want eyes in the sky, do we? I am not certain if that patrol boat saw us but the aeroplane yesterday did. All it needs is some smart arse to work out that we are the same boat which was seen in the vicinity of sabotage and they will be all over us. You and your lads get your heads down. It is a long way home!"

"I think I will take you up on that offer."

There was a warm fug when I entered the mess. The smell of stale tobacco, sweat and flatulent Commandos filled the air but I didn't care. I lay down in my bunk and was asleep before my head even touched the pillow.

Chapter 7

It took all day to reach our base. The winds did not cooperate with us at all. Added to that we had damage. The winds had proved too strong and we had lost one of the sails. Luckily the crew had a spare but it was a nerve-wracking couple of hours as we bobbed up and down feeling naked and exposed while they swarmed up the mast replacing it.

Sandy looked old and tired as Tosh brought us in to our anchorage. "Well I hope Major Fleming doesn't need us any time soon. We need some repairs."

"Valetta?"

He shook his head, "Nah, we can get what we need from Marsalaforn. It will just take a few days."

I pointed to my weary looking men, "And we need a rest too. I will tell Major Fleming where to stick his orders!" I shook my head, "We should be back with the rest of our lads in Falmouth. I don't trust this Major Fleming!"

"You should be grateful there is only one of him. In the Great War we had more Flemings than you could shake a stick at! That's why so many lads never made it home."

Lowe, Crowe and Hugo were like worried mothers as they stood waiting and watching on the beach. It was Lieutenant Ferguson who asked the inevitable question, "Well, how did it go?"

"Scratch one railway line, one train with ammunition and half a mountain!"

He nodded, "We know that. The RAF sent a bird to photograph it. I meant did it all go well. Did we lose anyone this time?"

"It was hairy but yes, it went well." I gestured at the schooner, "The *'Fly'* needs repairs and we need rest. If Major Fleming gets on to you let me speak with him."

"Don't be like that Tom. He is very pleased with the work and the replacements are on their way. They will be here at the start of next week."

"Good." I looked up and saw that Lance Sergeant Lowe and Private Crowe had built another four huts. "Well done lads!"

"We would rather have been with you. Did the lads do all right?"

"They did but I will let them tell you themselves." I headed for my hut. The men had no reports to write but I was the officer. Major Fleming would need to know chapter and verse. Over the next few days my men went through what had gone wrong with the demolitions. We were all very aware that things had gone wrong and we had been very lucky. No one had been hurt but it could have been so different. We also pitched in and helped the crew of *'Dragonfly'* with their repairs. We had no skills but we had strength and much of the work just needed that.

The weather was in our favour for it began to improve and we had blue skies and blue seas. This was more like the weather we expected from this part of the world. The men worked in shorts and soon the redness of their skin would become a golden brown. They would blend in a little more. In any spare moments we improved our camp. It was rough and ready but we had our privacy and we preferred that.

A week after our Italian adventure *'Lady Luck'* appeared around the headland. We gathered at the beach as she edged in. She was able to get closer to the shore and I saw the jumpers ready to leap off with the hawsers to secure her to the land. Even as they slowed I saw the camouflage nets being unrolled. I saw brown uniforms and white skin on the E-Boat and knew that our reinforcements had arrived. I turned to Hugo, "About time too. What do you know about them?"

He shrugged, "They are Commandos from Number Four Commando."

I turned to George Lowe, it was his squad's turn to cook the evening meal. "Better treble the quantities, Lance Sergeant."

"Righto, sir." I saw Hewitt and Fletcher scurry off to the stores.

When I turned back it was to see Sergeant Gordy Barker jumping into the water with his Bergen and kitbag. Polly laughed, "What the hell brings you here?"

"It was getting boring in Blighty. We had done nowt since St. Nazaire so when they asked for volunteers for Lieutenant Harsker's section I jumped at it. We all did!" He stood to attention in front of me with a big grin on his face.

I put my hand out, "Never mind that. It is good to see you, Gordy. How is Blighty?"

"Happier since we knocked the Afrika Korps out of Africa!" His men lined up behind him. "This is my section. All volunteers so there are none of the lads we served with, sir. Most are either promoted, in the bag or... well you know."

"I do indeed, Sergeant." It didn't do to speak of the deaths. There would be a time for that. It would be after this war was over.

He went down the line, "Corporal Jack Jackson, Private Jimmy Smith, Private Herbert, Private Grimsdale, Private Roger Beaumont and Private Peter Davis."

I nodded as each one saluted, "I dare say that I will get to know your names and your skills as we go along. We are a tight knit bunch here. I will say a few words; not that I like the sound of my own voice but you are volunteers and I owe it to you to let you know your prospects out here. What might have seemed fun in England might not be so much fun out here. If you decide, after a few days, that this isn't the life for you then I will happily give you a transfer out." I looked each of them in the eyes, searching for weakness. "Here we all pitch in. We are proper Commandos here! And it is dangerous. We have lost too many men and remember the Hitler order. If you are captured then it will probably be a firing squad." I smiled, "Sorry if I sound full of doom and gloom but I always worry about volunteers." I pointed behind me. "We made you huts. Feel free to make your own or improve those but at least you will have a roof over your head."

They saluted and, slinging their bags over their shoulders wandered to the huts. "A bit dour sir, if you don't mind me saying so."

"Sorry Gordy but there is little point in sugar coating the pill. There is an officer in Gibraltar, Major Fleming, who seems to really enjoy giving us difficult operations. We almost lost the E-Boat and our last mission almost resulted in half the section being wiped out by a railway wagon."

Gordy rubbed his hands, "Thank the Lord for that then. I was beginning to get bored!"

Sergeant Poulson picked up the kit bag. "Come on, we have special quarters for someone for your elevated status!"

"I would expect nothing less, my good man!" He suddenly stopped and turned, "Oh and I nearly forgot. Old Reg Dean married Mrs Bailey! It was a grand wedding! Daddy was best man."

That was the best news I had heard in a long time. Two people had found happiness long after they thought they had lost it. It gave me hope for the future and world without war. It put a spring in my step. When I reached the beach Alan was talking to Sandy and handing him something. I shook hands with Alan while Sandy opened the letter. "Good to see you. Fully crewed now?"

"We are and they even fitted a couple of depth charge throwers I am not certain why but they will come in handy."

Sandy looked up, "Well this looks like goodbye, at least for a while." He waved the paper in his hand, "Orders!" I knew enough not to ask where. Sandy worked for Major Fleming and SOE. That meant dangerous work behind enemy lines.

I held out my hand, "I hope we serve together again."

"Me too. You remind me of the young officers from the Great War, before they were either killed or had every bit of hope taken from them. Keep that spirit, Tom!" He shook hands with Alan and then shouted, "Right you lubbers! Its back to work for us!"

We watched '**Dragonfly**' as it raised its anchor and then sailed north. I would miss the old sea dogs on the schooner. They were the last remnants of a Navy which knew how to sail. In comparison Alan was a glorified taxi driver.

"How are your new crew?"

"Oh fine."

"Alan..."

"They are mainly like the old crew but the chief.... He isn't a chief! He is not even in his thirties. I have underwear older than him!"

"I think people say that about us. Is he any good at his job?"

"Well how do I know? We only sailed from Valetta! Your Fred Emerson could have run the engines for that little jaunt. The test will come when we are under fire!"

"And that is the way we all get tested, Alan. Come on. You know about my reservations about Bill Hay and I was wrong; totally wrong! Give your new chap a chance."

He nodded, "I suppose I owe him that." We started to walk towards the fire. The smell of cooking food was too much. "I hear you blew up half a mountain!"

"That we did and we were nearly killed by a runaway railway wagon!"

He laughed at the image. "What is it like on a schooner?"

"Different. It is quieter and slower. A sailing ship can just sit with idling engines. They were good sailors though. Two of them had been in the Great War."

"I admire them. I know my limitations. I could sail a sailing ship but not under fire."

"That's the other thing. They have no guns. They have steel running through their veins! Sandy's main weapons are bluff and bottle!"

Inevitably a couple of days were spent in catching up about Blighty. Then we began training. I had seen the cliffs in Sicily and Italy. The odds were that we would have to climb at some point and it was many months since we had had the opportunity to train. I left Gordy and Polly in charge. The two sections needed to work each other out. I went in the E-Boat with Alan and Hugo to Marsalaforn. Now that I had had my understanding with Lieutenant Harper we had regular delivery of letters. There was an anti aircraft unit and a naval patrol vessel in the port and they acted as our supply base, postman and, if we needed it, doctor. With more men to feed we needed rations.

"Well I don't know about your lads, Tom, but mine are raring to go. They have sat on their backsides long enough."

"Mine too. The old hands are keen to show the new ones what they do and the new ones are desperate for any sort of action. To be honest I am surprised that there hasn't been more movement towards Sicily."

"Rommel is still holding out in Tunisia. I can't see them lasting beyond April. Malta is now covered with aeroplanes. It is just a hop and a skip to Tunisia. They have to get rid of the North African problem first."

It did not take long to sail around the coast. We docked at the harbour and the three of us made our way to the Quarter Master Stores. We had developed a good relationship with the aged lieutenant, Bernard Devon, who was in charge. He was a regular but he had grown up in a peace time army and being in charge of stores suited him. That said, he enjoyed hearing of our suitably watered-down tales of action and excitement. He told us once that he would enjoy telling them to his grandchildren after the war. "I wouldn't want them to think their granddad sat on his backside for the whole war."

He beamed when we strode in, "Ah, real warriors! What can I do for you gentlemen?"

"We have more mouths to feed. "

"Not a problem."

"And my lads need new uniforms. Everything from socks and skivvies up!"

He tapped on the desk with his pipe, "Sergeant! Come and take the orders from our neighbours."

When he came in Sergeant Macpherson said, "Someone is with the adjutant asking about you chaps, sir. A major from Gib."

I had a sudden chill creep down my spine, "Not a little obnoxious chap who chain smokes?"

The Sergeant grinned, "The very chap! Are you clairvoyant then sir? If so I'll be in touch after the war. We can make a fortune with the football pools!"

Lieutenant Devon said, "Who on earth is it?"

"The bloke who sends us on half cocked missions. That is who! Do us a favour eh? Send that stuff to the boat. And any mail. I don't want to run into him unless I have to."

Hugo said, "I think if he came here, Tom, we ought to speak with him."

"He has to find us first!"

We hurried out, foregoing the opportunity to have a drink in the officer's mess. Of course it was all in vain. He was standing next to *'Lady Luck'* drumming his fingers on the harbour wall. He threw a stub away as he lit another. "Well gentlemen; you take some tracking down! I thought that this was your base?"

Alan smiled, "It was sir but we thought we might attract too much attention from Jerry aeroplanes. We have found a quiet, empty bay where we can't be seen. We thought you would approve."

"Don't try to flim flam me! You should, at the very least, have told me! Anyway that is by the by." He turned and shouted, "Harrington!"A harassed looking flag lieutenant hurried from the admin building, his arms filled with maps and papers. "Get aboard!" he turned to us, "I take it you have finished here?"

I looked up and saw a line of store men heading towards us. "We have now, sir."

It did not take us long to load the E-Boat and we sped around the headland to our little bay. Major Fleming wrinkled his nose when he saw the huts. "A little primitive isn't it?"

"We are Commandos sir and we are used to roughing it. The benefits of a comfortable bed are outweighed by the camaraderie and team spirit we engender."

"Hmn." It was not exactly a rejection of the idea neither was it a ringing endorsement.

As we edged into the beach I glanced at the charts under the Flag Lieutenant's arm. It was North Africa.

"Stop engines. Drop the anchor. Rig the camouflage netting."

I went forrard and whistled, "Right lads, get these store and letters taken ashore!"

For us this was everyday but I saw the look of horror on the faces of the Major and the Flag Lieutenant. Hugo and I leapt into the water and stood ready to receive the stores which were passed down. We formed a human chain.

"That's it Mr Harsker!"

"Thanks, Petty Officer Leslie."

I turned and began to wade towards the beach. Lieutenant Harrington said, "How do we get down?"

Alan had lit a cheroot and he smiled as he said, "Just jump in. It is only ankle deep. Take your shoes off if you are worried about getting them wet."

Neither officer was happy about the situation but they had no choice. They took off their shoes and socks. As he was about to leave Major Fleming said, "We will need you ashore, Lieutenant Jorgenson. We have an operation to plan!"

If he thought to upset Alan he was wrong. He just said, "Righto!" And jumped straight in. He grinned as he waded towards the beach.

Polly and Gordy came next to me and said, quietly, "We have company then, sir?"

"We do. Make sure the lads are on their best behaviour. I can't see them staying the night."

"It is just fish stew tonight sir."

I laughed, "It's always fish stew, Sergeant Poulson. Don't worry about it. Give the best chairs to the two officers."

That was a laugh in itself. Our best chairs were a couple of packing cases we had liberated and they had old cushions on them. The table was a door which rested on two other, smaller crates. It was functional furniture.

The Major caught up with me, "Do you want to eat first sir and then brief us or vice versa?"

He spied the cauldron which bubbled away, "Eat? Good God no! We shall brief you and then Lieutenant Jorgenson can take us back to Marsalaforn."

"The men will be disappointed, sir. We don't often get company."

"I can see why. I will need your sergeants at the briefing too."

"Right. Sergeant Barker and Sergeant Poulson would you join us. Lance Sergeant Lowe, take charge!"

Once we were around the table Major Fleming was more in his element. Lieutenant Harrington unrolled the map. Major Fleming jabbed a yellow finger at Bizerte. "You have been here before."

"Not the actual port but close by, yes sir."

"Same thing. We want you to go back and blow up the railway line which runs from Bizerte to Tunis. We nearly have the Axis beaten. Patton and Monty are banging on the door but the enemy are bringing supplies in by sea, at night. We need to stop them supplying Tunis. The air force is bombing during the day and the Royal Navy is stopping as much shipping as they can but the Germans are using U-Boats to bring in supplies. We want you to blow the line up as soon after dark as you can. That is when they are sending material down the lines. The USAAF and the RAF can then bomb the hell out of Bizerte and destroy the supplies once and for all." He lit another cigarette. "Lieutenant."

Lieutenant Harrington said, "There is a large lake and the railway line runs alongside it. We have identified somewhere here for the actual demolition." He pointed to an area a mile or so from the town and from the airfield. "It will be quiet and you should be able to blow up the railway line and escape."

It sounded simple but I knew that it wasn't. "How do we get in sir? And, more importantly, get out."

Major Fleming looked surprised, "I would have thought that was obvious. You sail in on the E-Boat."

I rolled my eyes at Alan who coughed, diplomatically, and said, "The harbour entrance is just a couple of hundred yards wide, sir. There will be guns on both sides. Assuming that we could get in, and I am not certain that we could, after we have blown up the railway every gun in the town will be aimed at the lake. Why not use the air force?"

"We have tried but they get repair crews out. We need a big section blowing up. This has to be a surgical strike. We want you to remove enough of the railway to require a week of work." He smiled, "It was your success in Italy which gave me the idea. When you hit the line at Reggio it took five days to repair it. A very impressive piece of work. Besides the two air forces will be helping you. The RAF will bomb the harbour just before dark and the USAF two hours later. That should give you the chance to get in and out."

I thought that Alan was going to choke. "You want us to get in and out while a bombing raid is going on?"

"Of course! It is the perfect window of opportunity." He pointed his cigarette at me, "Now I have given you more men so that you can use more than one team. The explosives will be delivered tomorrow and you sail the day after. You will have to sail most of the way in daylight. Still, Jerry appears a bit preoccupied with Tunisia so you should be all right. Any questions?"

As with all Major Fleming's plans there was no question of refusing. We would just have to make the best of a bad job. Alan and I shook our heads, "No sir."

"Well the explosives will be at Marsalaforn at nine a.m. Pick them up. And now Lieutenant Jorgenson, I am ready to return to civilisation. Good luck."

We sat and watched as Alan escorted them both to the E-Boat. Gordy shook his head, "Well he is a charming piece of work. Do we have much to do with him, sir?"

"I think, Gordy, that we are his little private army. The sooner we are back with Number Four Commando the better."

"Amen to that."

I shouted, "George, Bill, we need you."

The two of them joined us and took the seats vacated by the two officers. I briefly told them our mission. "Now the Major is right in one respect; we have more men. I intend to use four teams. Each of you will lead a team. I will have the E-Boat drop us four hundred yards apart. That should guarantee the maximum destruction. The last team to be dropped off will have the shortest time and the first will have the longest time to wait. Can't be helped. Now the airfield worries me so the first thing we will do will when we land will be to rig a line of booby traps half a mile from the railway line. Just simple grenade booby traps. I want to slow Jerry up."

The four of them looked at the map. George Lowe said, "I am not even certain we can get in undetected but, supposing we do, how the hell do we get out? I know the Yanks will be bombing the town but it will be night time. I would be happier if it was the RAF. The Americans are new to this."

"We will have to rely on the E-Boat. You have sailed in her, George. Is there anything faster?" He shook his head. "And having just spent a month on a sailing ship I reckon we might be able to pull it off. Anyway pick your own teams. I will be with Bill and we will be the last ones landed. It will be the biggest team. I will just need a crash course in explosives Bill."

He laughed, "You did fine at Reggio, sir. And this time we can use timers."

"Right, off you go and we will have a team briefing after we have eaten. I need to talk to Lieutenant Jorgenson."

When they had gone Hugo said, "I am no expert Tom but this looks impossible."

"Not quite. There will be panic when the bombers come over. It will not look unusual for an E-Boat to be flying through the water at such a time but George is right. Night time bombing over a dark target is not easy. Look at the Blitz. They bombed London by mistake! They thought it was an airfield. It could be that this time, our luck runs out."

When Alan returned he brought with him a bottle of whisky. "A present from Lieutenant Devon. There is little point in saving it. In three days time there might only be Hugo left to enjoy it."

"And I don't even like whisky!"

Alan beamed, "Don't worry, dear boy! Tom and I will enjoy your share. "What was it the old Roman gladiators said? *'We who are about to die salute you'*. Well we shall toast you dear boy and leave our letters for our loved ones with you. In my case that is a tailor in London and a rather sweet old aunt who still lives in Norway!"

Chapter 8

The *'Lady Luck'* was a little more crowded than we were used to. We had more men and more equipment. We had evolved a plan. Rather than heading directly for the North African coast we were heading north west to run parallel with the Sicilian coast. If we were to blend in with the German and Italian shipping we had to approach from the same direction they did. Once we were well away from the Maltese coast we ran up the German flag. I came on deck with half of my section. We wore the captured German uniforms. The distinctive coal scuttle helmets could be seen from some way away and would, we hoped, make us more realistic looking.

We had the radar array up but we disguised it with washing. I doubt that any senior officer on either side would have viewed it favourably but, until we found some enemy ships we needed it up. We could take it down in minutes. We sailed north west until Pantelleria, the enemy held island, which was forty miles south of us and then we began to head west. We were cruising rather than racing. The gun crews were closed up. It would be standard practice for German ships this close to combat and we had our arms too.

When we saw Sicily end to the north we were half way to our objective. Timing was key. Bill Leslie and Tosh came forrard with mugs of tea. "Thanks Bill! This is welcome."

Bill handed the tray to Tosh who went below. Bill took out his pipe and sat next to me. "It's quiet now sir but I reckon it will get a bit dicey when we spot Jerry. They will be a bit nervous."

I patted the deck of the E-Boat. "You aren't doubting your own vessel now, are you? We are faster than anything else we will meet."

"Nah. The *'Lady'* can fly. And she is lucky but last time when the old Chief copped it, well it brought things home. Those lads we lost were the first. Sailors are a superstitious lot. Some are wondering if we are no longer lucky."

The tea was hot and sweet. We would need the energy later on. I wiped my mouth with the back of my hand, "But not you."

"You know me sir, I don't believe in luck. Now Fate, that is a different thing. If your number is up then that is it. I just felt sorry for the old chief. He had just become a granddad and he was looking forward to getting home and seeing his grandson. It made me think about a family."

"You know Bill Hay has a son now."

"I know, he told me. He is chuffed to bits!"

"And how are your new lads?"

"Probably the same as yours sir; finding their feet." He glanced over his shoulder and began to speak quieter. "You are a mate of the captain, sir. Have a word with him. He has taken against the engineer. I don't know why but Tom McGee seems like a good lad. He might be young but he knows his engines. He is getting more out of them than the Chief did, God rest his soul. He just larks on a bit more than you might expect. He is newly promoted." He shook his head, "Sorry sir. I have spoken out of turn. Forget what I said."

"No Bill, we are old mates. You know rank doesn't mean much to me. I will have a word and thank you for confiding in me."

He grinned, as he stood, "It's the boat isn't it, sir? She deserves a happy crew."

I finished my tea and lay back on the deck. We were playing a part. We were what Auntie Alice would call window dressing. Any German aircraft would see an E-Boat carrying German soldiers to reinforce the garrison in North Africa. It would not look unusual. Eventually the tea kicked in and I had to take a leak. I went to the stern and, after I had finished stopped at the bridge.

"She is flying, Alan."

"She is and Symons says the seas are clear for the next twenty miles."

"Here you are, Tosh, take over until Petty Officer Leslie takes over. I'm going for a smoke."

"Aye aye, sir."

Alan took out a cheroot and lit it. We went to the leeward side of the bridge and the lookout vacated it. "I saw you chatting to Bill Leslie. Not talking mutiny are you?" He said it with a smile but I saw worry in his eyes.

"You know me better than that Alan. We were talking about the boat but the Chief's death came up. This new engineer, McGee, he seems to be doing a good job eh?"

"Well yes but..."

"But he isn't the Chief and he can never be the Chief. This is your first command and you wanted it to stay the same right through the war. We both know that can't happen. Look at my lads. We have lost some good blokes. Others have been promoted. How would you feel if they took Bill Leslie off you? Promoted him?"

He sucked on his cigar and stared at the distant coastline of Sicily. After a while he said, "You might be right. The engines do sound sweeter. Mind you they had a good overhaul." He grinned, "I'll give him a chance and..."

Symons voice broke in, "Sir, vessels ahead. They are on course for North Africa."

"How many?"

"Two bigger ones, they look like coasters and then some smaller ones, six of them. If I was a betting man then I would say E-Boats."

"We will keep the radar up until we sight them then get it down."

"Sir."

After glancing in the radar hut Alan grabbed the map and took out a ruler. He measured the distance to the convoy and then to the coast. He looked at his watch. "Tosh, slow down to twenty knots."

"Aye sir."

"We don't want to reach them too soon. Go around the lads, Tom, tell them that we will be going into action in the next couple of hours."

I went, first, to the mess deck where the two sergeants were doing a Bergen check. "We have just spotted a German convoy. One way or another it will get hot soon. Have the men all ready."

"Right sir."

Gordy shook his head, "I envy you, sir. It's like being in a bleedin' coffin down here!"

I went around all the gun positions and reached the bridge as Bill Leslie took over the helm. Bill Hay shouted, "Ships ahead sir, a convoy!"

"Right Symons, take the radar down. Wacker, listen for signals."

"Aye aye sir."

"From now on we speak German. If you don't speak German just grunt!"

Symons mumbled, "Same thing if you ask me! You talk to a Jerry and it's like talking to a Welshman. You get covered in spit and you still understand bugger all that they say!"

I smiled. The men were in good spirits. They could still joke. I went to the fore deck and took out the papers which came with the uniform. It was all part of our cover story. We were a detachment of Engineers from the three hundred and fifth infantry battalion and my name Feldwebel Kurt Planck from Innsbruck. The other four on deck with me had a smattering of German. They had been drilled to reply with their new names if questioned. We hoped it would not come to that for our story was extremely thin. Alan was wearing the uniform of a Korvettenkapitän. The equivalent rank in the Royal Navy was Lieutenant Commander.

With any luck anyone we met would be the rank of Kapitänleutnant or lower.

We edged closer to the convoy. I had no doubt that if we had seen them then they would have seen us. We had to appear as though we were relieved to see allies. Timing was all. The afternoon was passing. We needed to be entering the harbour towards dusk. We needed dark to perform our duties.

Wacker's voice came up from his radio shack, "Sir, we are being hailed by the commander of the convoy: Kapitan zur See Zeiss. He wants to know who we are."

"Bugger! He outranks me. Give me the mike." He slipped down to the shack and, after donning the headphones, began to speak in German. Wacker handed him the headphones." Korvettenkapitän Schloss in command of S-175 on detached duty from Reggio, sir." There was a pause. "Yes sir I realise I should have notified you when we first sited you but I did not want to break radio silence. We had to sneak by some destroyers just north of Malta." There was another pause while the convoy commander asked more questions. "Yes sir I am carrying German soldiers. They are railway engineers from Reggio. We have just repaired the damage caused by the partisans and we are ordered to help repair the line to Tunis. We are under the orders of Field Marshal Rommel himself." There was a shorter pause. "Thank you, sir. We will take station astern of the last boat."

He handed the mike and the headphones back to Wacker.

"Well?"

"They bought it. The mention of the Desert Fox was enough. That and the reference to the damage at Reggio. A clever plan, Tom!" he turned to the coxswain, "Let's catch up properly now. We have been formally introduced."

As we neared the ships I saw that none of them looked to be in good condition. The two merchant vessels showed fire damage while the E-Boats looked like they needed six months in a naval dockyard. We waved to the boat in front. It was about two boat lengths away from us.

One of the crew came to the stern for a cigarette. He cupped his hands and shouted, "Where are you from?"

"Reggio!"

He shook his head, "No, I mean where in the Fatherland?"

"Innsbruck!"

"I love Innsbruck. Do you ski?"

I shook my head, "Not since I broke my ankle as a child."

"I like the food there."

I nodded, "My favourite is the Goldenes Dachl."

"You must have money! Too rich for my taste." Just then a Petty Officer shouted something and the sailor waved. "We'll have a drink in Bizerte!"

Bill Hay said, quietly, "What was all that about sir? I caught a few words. Something about a golden roof?"

"My dad told me about it. There is a building in the town with a roof made of gold and below it is a fine restaurant. I was just making my story credible."

In the distance I could see the coast of Africa. We had made it. Just then I heard a shout from the ship ahead, "Aircraft! Tommies!"

I looked aft and saw three Beaufighters. They each had four cannons and carried bombs. We had discussed this already. The gunners had orders to fire but to miss! If the Germans ahead saw that we were not firing they might become suspicious. I took my rifle and knelt on the pitching deck close to the bridge.

Wacker shouted, "Orders from the Kapitan zur See. All E-Boats close up on the merchant men. He has ordered them to go full speed. We have to follow zig zag pattern F."

"What the hell is that?"

"I have no idea Tom. Petty Officer Leslie, just follow the last E-Boat and do whatever he does. Drop back half a length or two eh?"

"Sir!"

The Beaufighters began to dive. They were not the fastest fighter but, in a dive, could achieve over three hundred miles an hour. Dad had flown one once. I knew that they only had two hundred and forty rounds per gun. The cannon shells were deadly but they had few of them. The ship in front went to starboard and we followed suit. Alan shouted, "Shoot!" in German. I aimed well to the right of the leading Beaufighter. We did not have to fire fast. We just had to make sure that smoke came from our guns.

Then the leading Beaufighter opened fire. We had just turned and the shells struck the water where we had been. It would have been ironic to have been hit by our own side! The second Beaufighter, however, corrected his aim and his shells tore into the stern of the E-Boat in front of us. Smoke began to pour from the engine and Bill Leslie had to take evasive action. As we passed alongside there was a huge fireball and explosion as the ammunition exploded. A wave of fire and flames leapt towards us. It rocked the E-Boat to the side. When we righted ourselves all that remained was debris and bodies. My erstwhile friend would not buy me that drink after all.

Then the three fighters began to drop their bombs. Two struck the leading merchantman which began to list to port. The fighters made one last pass and raked the convoy with the last of their cannon shells. I had no doubt they would celebrate their victory in the mess that night. One other E-Boat had been damaged. The undamaged merchant man took the burning one in tow.

A few minutes later Wacker stuck his head out of the radio hut, "Sir, you are the senior officer now. The Kapitan zur See was killed in the attack. They are asking for orders."

"Tell them that we will cease zig zag pattern F and head at maximum speed to Bizerte. Tell them that we will look for survivors and guard the rear."

"That is a turn up eh, Alan?" This was an unforeseen stroke of luck.

"I shall have to ask for extra pay when I return to camp. I am a Commodore now!"

The attack meant that it was getting dark by the time we approached the narrow harbour entrance. The stricken merchantman would barely make it to the jetty.

"Wacker get on the radio and tell everyone well done. Let them know we are proceeding to Lake Bizerte to carry out our mission to repair the railway line. Tell them the Fuhrer will be proud of their achievements and add a Heil Hitler." He turned to me. "They will expect it."

The part we had thought would be the hardest was the easiest. As we overtook the other ships they all waved and cheered as though we were heroes. Then Wacker said, "Sir, I have the harbour master on the radio. He wants us to dock at the far end of the harbour close to his office. He wants to see our papers."

"Right Bill, let's head that way but keep it slow. When I give the order then full speed eh?" he looked up at the sky. "Where are those bombers?"

As we passed the eighty-eight-millimetre gun at the mole we heard the sound of sirens. I turned and saw the Martin Marauders. There were ten of them and they were high. They could carry a fair weight of bombs. Every gun in the port started blazing away and the other E-Boats began to speed up. "Right Bill, full power and head into the middle of the lake! It is what everyone else is doing!"

The harbour master had more important things on his mind now and we were, thankfully, ignored. Getting out might not be as easy. Alan's decision proved to be a wise one as the bombs began to fall on the docks and harbour. The stricken merchantman ended up on the bottom when a stick of bombs struck it. The buildings and warehouses adjacent to the docks were also engulfed in flames. Some bombs missed. I saw at least two sticks explode harmlessly in the lake. I guessed the RAF pilots knew nothing of us.

It was now dark and Alan said, "Right Bill, head for the first drop off point." Turning to me he said, "I believe this is your stop, sir!"

"Thanks. It is time to change uniforms." I went to the bow. "Right lads out of the grey and back in khaki."

Below deck the men were already blacking up. They looked at me expectantly as I entered, "Well lads we are in!"

Gordy nodded, "I heard all the German talk. I should have stuck in with the lessons."

"Remember, Sergeant Barker, you are the first one off. Your team will have to hold out the longest."

"Don't worry sir we will give any nosey Eyetie or Jerry the hot foot!"

The only team with just three men was Sergeant Poulson's. I hoped that I was not putting too much pressure on Private Shepherd. I knew that he still brooded about his mistake at the other railway line in Reggio. The explosives behind us lit up the harbour while to our right we saw the searchlights and heard the guns from the airfield. The fact that no fighters had taken off told us the lack of both aeroplanes and fuel. There was a large island which blocked our route all the way along the railway line. It was also the closest place to the airfield. Alan headed in to shore. We had four dinghies ready. Alan spun the wheel and Sergeant Barker and Lance Sergeant Lowe clambered aboard their boats and began paddling for the shore.

The island was less than a thousand yards long and, using the cover of the departing aeroplanes, he covered the distance in minutes. Sergeant Poulson and his men were ready the moment the E-Boat slowed and they were already ten yards from the E-Boat by the time Lieutenant Jorgenson had begun to move towards the last drop off. He would be waiting with us and all his guns would be manned. Even as he edged in the last of the British Marauders were heading east and their airfield in Libya.

We had a short distance to paddle and we all dug in as we travelled as quickly as we could. Time was of the essence. We drew the dinghy across the mud and hurried to the single-track line. I held my Tommy gun and led the four of us to the closest section. Hay and Hewitt had the explosives while Scouse and I watched the airfield. It seemed as though we had not been seen. The perimeter fence was a thousand yards away from us but it was much closer to Gordy and George. I did not need to nag them about speed. They understood the need as much as anyone.

Time seemed to drag and move slowly. I looked at my watch and the hands barely turned. The fires in the port were being fought and I heard the sirens of ambulances as they hurried to the wounded. Worryingly I heard the sound of engines at the airfield. Was it aeroplanes or vehicles which were moving?

"All done sir!"

I turned around and saw that Hay and Hewitt had finished. "Have you set the timers?"

"Twenty minutes sir."

We hoped that, by staggering the times of the explosions we could keep the enemy guessing. "Good, hurry, back to the dinghy."

The mud tried to suck us down and I waded a little in the lake to clean my shoes. Friendly hands dragged us up aboard the E-Boat and we were moving even before the dinghy was pulled up. The next air raid was fifteen minutes away. Sergeant Poulson and his men were waiting for us and we barely had to slow to pick them up.

"Well done, Sergeant Poulson."

"I was worried about the other lads, look."

He pointed and I could see that trucks were heading from the airfield. Even as I watched I heard the crack of small arms fire. I cocked my Thompson, "Better get a move on, Lieutenant Jorgensen!"

"Man the guns and begin firing as soon as the Germans are in range."

The Oerlikon was in range and it began pumping out shells. We were moving so quickly and bouncing around so much that any hit would have been a lucky one. I knew, however, that the men on the beach would appreciate it for it meant that the cavalry was coming. Lance Sergeant Lowe and his men were paddling as fast as they could to reach Sergeant Barker. I saw why. One of Gordy's men was down. We were turning around the island but we still had five hundred yards to go. The Oerlikon managed to hit one of the lorries but it was the half track with the machine gun which was doing the damage. Men spilled from the stricken lorry and they began to fire at Gordy and the dinghy they were trying to manhandle into the lake. Disaster struck when a second Commando, Private Grimsdale, was hit and the dinghy shredded.

Sergeant Lowe was left with no choice. He headed inshore to help Gordy. We were now in range and our Thompsons added to the Oerlikon, Pom-Poms and Lewis guns. Sergeant Poulson had brought up the LG 42 and its firepower was added. It was Sergeant Poulson who hit the gunner on the half track and the fire from the shore lessened, marginally.

We spun around the end of the island. My men and I raced to the bow firing as we went. The Tommy gun packed a powerful punch. We drew the fire from the shore and bullets struck the E-Boat. I heard Alan's urgent voice from the bridge. "Tom! We can't hang around here! We need to leave."

I turned, "I am not leaving those men to be captured and shot. Get in as close as you can."

"I'll do my best."

"Hay, Scouse, grab that dinghy and come with me."

I jumped into the water. It came up to my chest. Even as they were launching the dinghy I was striding towards my beleaguered men. I saw George Lowe pitch forward in his dinghy as he was hit by rifle fire. "Get back to the boat. I will take care of these lads!" I sprayed the half track. Most of the bullets clanged off the armour but a couple must have rattled inside for I heard screams as I reached the beach.

Gordy was firing like a madman. I saw that Grimsdale was dead and Jack Jackson wounded. I turned and saw Bill Hay drag the dinghy on to the beach. Scouse fire a burst from the hip. It was more in hope than expectation. I slung my Thompson over my shoulder and took out a couple of grenades. I pulled the pins and threw both as high and as far as I could. I dived at Gordy knocking him and Smith to the ground, "Grenades!" They both had five second fuses on them and they exploded in the air. The concussion and the shrapnel tore through the Germans. I stood and drew my

Luger, "Sergeant, get these bodies back to the dinghy! That is an order!"

"Sir!"

I began to aim at the officers and sergeants who were trying to give orders. The concussion had confused them and I hit two of them before the third shouted to his men to take cover. A shell from the Oerlikon hit the half track. It must have struck the ammunition for the whole vehicle lifted into the air. It was time to leave. I emptied my magazine and ran back to the dinghy. It was full! "Paddle back. I will catch you up. Go!"

Overhead I heard the sound of the American Mitchell bombers as they made their bombing run. I waded into the lake and, reaching the dinghy, pushed it. "Paddle!"

As they paddled I waded further out. Alan had brought the *'Lady Luck'* to within thirty yards. I saw George Lowe's section reach the E-Boat and haul my Lance Sergeant aboard. I caught up with the overloaded dinghy and I pushed it closer to the ship. My men on board were too busy firing to help but the remains of Lance Sergeant Lowe's section helped to pull the wounded and the dead from the dinghy. Bullets clattered into the side of the E-Boat as the first bombs dropped from the Americans.

As luck would have it the first bombs fell on the airfield at the end closest to the port. It made the Germans firing at us, hesitate. That hesitation saved us. The rubber dinghy was useless and we abandoned it. I was hauled aboard as the first of the demolition charges went off. It was the one my section had set. It was a bigger explosion that I had been expecting. It lit up the sky to the south and the confused Germans did not know which way to look. Alan took the opportunity to whip the bows around and head for the harbour entrance. As much as I wanted to see how my wounded men were doing I owed it to the living to help Alan extricate us from this hole. I had just reached him when Sergeant Poulson's charge went off.

Alan grinned, "That was definitely cutting it more than a little fine!"

I gestured with my thumb. "But we got the job done. At least two of the charges have gone off."

Alan pointed to the harbour entrance. A couple of fishing boats were being placed across the entrance. "We have to get past those two."

"Is there room?"

"There will be when we blow one out of the water. Go forrard and have every gun fire at the right-hand boat. Ignore everything else. If we can sink it we can escape."

The if was a mile wide and a grave deep!

I ran to the gunners. "Everyone, fire at the right-hand fishing ship. The Captain wants her sunk. Sergeant Poulson, it is made of wood, aim below the water line."

Bullets and shell were still hitting our port side but we ignored them as we fired at the sixty feet long fishing boat. They had a couple of guns on board but the Tommy guns of my men killed the gunners. The boat was crewless but it was in position. We could not go around it for fear of hitting the harbour wall or the other fishing boat. Suddenly I saw Alan Crowe with the grenade launcher. He fired high in the sky. Sometimes luck favours the brave for it arced on to the deck and exploded. We were less than thirty yards away and going so fast that I knew that a collision was imminent. The Oerlikon gunner chose that moment to pump four shells almost at the very spot which Bill had hit. Amazingly the boat began to split in two and we ground through the two broken halves. Our paintwork would be a mess but we were through.

"Fire at the harbour wall!"

As they cleared the walls of enemy soldiers, in the distance, I heard the last two demolition charges going off. It was hard to hear against the sound of the bombs which were falling on Bizerte but when I turned I saw the two glows which told me that we had succeeded. I waited until Bizerte was a dull glow in the distance before I relaxed. I smiled at the gunners, "Well done, chaps! Damned fine shooting."

I made my way back to Alan. "Do you have to take so many chances?"

"They are my men, Alan. You would do the same for yours."

"I am not so certain."

"Do we know the butcher's bill?"

"Three of my chaps are wounded. Johnson and your chap Hewitt are with your casualties."

"I'll go below. Call me if you need me."

He gave me a wry smile, "I think I can steer my own ship, Lieutenant Harsker!"

It was like a scene from the Crimean War. The mess was lit by emergency lights and there were bandages and pools of blood everywhere. I saw Gordy smoking a cigarette. His hands were shaking. "Are you hurt, Gordy?"

He had wild eyes and he stared at me as though he didn't recognise me.

"Gordy?"

"Sorry sir. I thought we had bought it. Grimsdale was killed outright and when Corporal Jackson got hit, well it was St. Nazaire all over again. Herbert was the first of the lads to be hit. He couldn't have known anything about it. My new men did not last long!" He ground his cigarette out in a puddle of blood. Petty Officer Leslie would not be impressed. "Thank you for coming back for us, sir."

"We never leave a man behind, you know that." I lowered my voice, "This is what I tried to say to you lads that first day. This is not glorious. Perhaps I should have just brought my section. This was too big a mission. I am sorry. I should have eased you in to it."

"Sir, with respect, that is rubbish! We are Commandos. We trained together! I should be able to handle it better. Next time I will!"

I decided to let it go. Gordy had his pride. He shook his head to clear it and asked, "What is the damage?"

"Lance Sergeant Lowe and Corporal Jackson are both dead. The SBA couldn't save them. Your chap Emerson and Peter Davis are both wounded. They should pull through."

He lit another cigarette. "Did all the charges go off?"

"They did."

"Then that is one positive thing to take home."

"I think we take home more than that, Gordy. We sailed into the heart of a German held port, and pulled off one of the biggest demolition jobs ever. I reckon we have something to shout about. Now you and the lads get some rest."

He nodded and slumped into a chair. I went over to Fred Emerson who was being tended to by John Hewitt. "How is it Fred?"

He tried to rise. Hewitt said, "Lie back you daft bugger! Do you want to pop these stitches?"

"Sorry Doc. I am fine, sir. I got a bullet in the arm. Doc here says it missed the bone. I'll be right as rain before you know it."

"I know you will. Well done Doc."

"You know about George?"

I nodded, "Where did he get it?"

"Machine gun in the spine. He knew nothing about it. It was just bad luck. He wouldn't want to be a cripple."

"You make sure you get some rest too."

"I will, sir."

I went back on deck to get some fresh air and to think about the letters that I would have to write. Major Fleming would be happy but George Lowe's wife and children would not. Another hero was not coming back. The others who had died would not have the chance to emulate my Lance Sergeant.

Chapter 9

We buried our dead on the headland overlooking the bay. For Jackson, Herbert and Grimsdale it was a short time they had served with us. They had been real Commandos, for however short a time and they had made a difference. We would remember them. We would raise a glass when all of this was over. Three days later we took *'Lucky Lady'* down to Valetta. Hugo, Alan and I had to report to Major Fleming. I guessed he was not enamoured of our idyll by the sea. Petty Officer Leslie and the crew made make shift repairs while Scouse and Shepherd appropriated a few items to make life a little more pleasant.

Major Fleming had a far grander office than Hugo had been allocated when he had been in Gib. The Major was going places. We were seated with the minimum of pleasantries.

"A good operation; no I will go further. It was an almost perfect operation. The railway line is still out of action." He smiled, "They can't get the rails. Already our chaps are pushing forward."

I gritted my teeth, "Good to know, sir."

He leaned back in his chair and blew smoke rings, "What you chaps don't know is that last week the Americans were knocked about a bit by Jerry at Kasserine Pass. Your attack has more than made up for it. And Rommel has been ordered out of Africa. Hitler must think we are about to win. We are almost ready to take Tunisia and we have played no small part in this."

I resented the '*we*', he had done nothing!

He rocked forward on his chair and pointed to Alan, "That was quick thinking with the convoy! We shall have to try to use you more like that in future."

"We were lucky and there were E-Boats which survived. They will remember us."

"Oh don't worry about that. We have Tunis and Bizerte surrounded. They can't get any more ships out and the Americans are bombing the hell out of their airfields. The Germans who know you will be in the bag soon enough." He stood and unrolled a map on the wall. "We can prepare for this."

The map was of Sicily. I read the name of the operation, 'Operation Husky.'

"Operation Husky, I take it that is the code name for the invasion of Sicily?"

"Yes, daft name I know, but it is an American led operation. It is all hush, hush. We are trying to make the Germans and the Italians think we are landing in Greece. They are already moving their most powerful units there." He pointed to a spot some fifty miles from the south coast, "Except for these. The Herman Goering Division. They are a top-notch outfit. You will see that the two attacks are to the east and the west of that division. I want you to stop the Herman Goering Division from reinforcing the forces to the east."

I looked at Alan who rolled his eyes, "Sir, I have less than a dozen men. How can we stop a Division?"

"You have shown great skill already. I am certain that you could come up with something. You are all bright chaps. Oh, by the way I have put you two in for promotion. With any luck you will soon be Captain Harsker and you will be Lieutenant Commander Jorgenson. Who knows; if you pull this off you may get another promotion or a gong out of it."

Neither Alan nor I were interested in his thirty pieces of silver. Hugo, however was interested in the planning of the operation. He liked chess and those sorts of games. He enjoyed puzzles. Hugo was no warrior but he was a thinker and he stood and went to the map to study it. "I think I see something here, sir."

Major Fleming said, "That's the spirit!"

I asked, "Sir, when is this invasion planned?"

"The beginning of July. You would have to be in Sicily by the end of June." He stood and went to a coffee pot. "Coffee? This is the real stuff."

Alan nodded, "Thank you, sir."

I joined Hugo at the map. I said quietly, "Hugo I do not want to write any more letters home. We have lost enough young men already."

He nodded and added, quietly, "I know, Tom. I am trying to come up with something which is less dangerous."

Major Fleming's waspish voice sounded, "What are you two whispering about?"

"Just coming up with the bones of a plan, sir. You know, eliminate the impossible and whatever is left, no matter how unlikely, is possible. The division looks to be in a mountainous part of the country. They have placed it so that it is equidistant between Syracuse and Licata. I take it that it was only moved there recently?"

"Yes, after Alamein."

"Then they are covering themselves in case we do invade. Now there are no convenient bridges for Tom to blow up. That is the easiest way to stop a division. It takes time to build a new one. But here, to the west of Ragusa, it looks like they have put hairpins in the road. Now if you could get some aerial photographs then Tom and his lads could do what they did in Reggio and bring down a mountain on to a road. Using nature is always best."

"I can get you photographs."

I looked at the place Hugo had identified. "Hugo, that is about fourteen miles from the coast! It would take a night to get there. We would have to lie up and then a night to blow it and get back down again. Alan couldn't wait for us for two days."

"No, of course not. You would have to go in by air. It is a remote area and you could blow the road and the mountain and get down to meet Lieutenant Jorgenson by dawn." Hugo had never dropped from the air and he knew nothing of the dangers. To him it was a logical solution to a problem.

Alan said, "Meaning we would have to get back during daylight?"

"I am afraid so."

"That is a risk worth taking, Lieutenant Jorgenson."

Alan shot a black look at the Major. "That is a matter of opinion."

"No, Lieutenant," he said coldly, "that is a matter of fact. If you do not feel that you can continue in this unit I have plenty other officers who would enjoy the freedom you have."

Alan stared briefly at the Major and then turned to me, "What do you think, Tom?"

Dad had always told me never to make decisions when you were angry. We needed to buy some time. "Let's study these aerial photographs and see what the ground is like. It might be possible. We have a couple of months don't we, sir?"

"Oh yes. The invasion date is already set. We are assuming that Tunisia will have fallen well before then." He put his hands on the table and stood. "Excellent! You will have to return here for the photographs, Lieutenant Ferguson. They will be top secret. Give me a fortnight to get them organised. That will give you time to refine your ideas eh?"

"Sir, we lost a couple of non-commissioned officers."

"Well I don't think it would be a good idea to draft in new ones before such an important operation. Promote a couple of your chaps eh? I am certain you have suitable candidates and I will see what I can to about expediting your own promotion. When you have the plan organised we will see if they have come through."

As we walked back to the boat Alan said, "The man is a snake! He is trying to buy us with a promotion."

Hugo said, "But you both deserve it! You deserve medals too!"

I shook my head, "This sounds like bribery. The title will stick in my throat. I want to be a Captain but not this way. Not paid for with the blood of my men."

Hugo said, sadly, "I am afraid that is the way it has always been. When you promote Hay to Lance Sergeant he will know that George Lowe had to die."

I stopped and stared at him, "How did you know that I would promote Bill Hay?"

"Easy, he is a corporal already and you have said to me, many times, that he is sergeant material." He smiled, "Besides he has just become a dad and you are thinking of the extra pay he will get. I am getting to know you, Tom."

Alan laughed, "He is right, Tom. That is how you think. What about the Corporal?"

"It is either John Hewitt or Scouse. I am inclined to Hewitt as he is slightly more dependable."

Alan said, "I would agree with that. I don't know if you have noticed but the others all defer to him. Scouse is your joker."

"Gordy Barker was a joker."

"I have only just met him but Sergeant Barker also strikes me as a leader. Is Scouse a leader?" Hugo was shrewd.

He was right, "Not yet but he will be."

"Then you need to develop those skills."

Fletcher and Shepherd were waiting guiltily next to the E-Boat when we returned, "Hurry up sir. We are ready to push off."

"Why the hurry Scouse?"

"No real hurry sir but some pongoes might be missing a couple of cases of peaches so a swift departure would help."

I shook my head, "Alan?"

"Everything ship shape, Petty Officer Leslie?"

Bill grinned, his pipe jutting from his mouth, "Oh aye sir! I think we need to move sharpish too!"

We were ready for sea in a matter of minutes. As we headed out of the crowded harbour I saw the distinctive red caps of the military police. I looked at my two men who shrugged. "They were just lying there on the harbour wall, sir. I mean any of the locals who work here could have had them. They would have been on the black market as sure as shooting."

I shook my head.

Petty Officer Leslie said, "They are right sir. The same goes for the tinned pears which are in the galley too!"

Alan turned to his petty officer and laughed, "Petty Officer Leslie!"

He kept staring ahead as he said, "Call it a reward for a job well done. We get bugger all else do we, sir?" He gestured with a thumb back to the harbour. "The blokes who would have had the tinned fruit were the store men and admin staff. They don't put their lives on the line like your lads do. No sir, I would never steal. This isn't stealing; it is redistributing the rewards!"

Alan nodded, "I can't argue with you there."

It was a pleasant spring morning on the Med and so the three of us sat by the rear gun emplacement and discussed this new operation. "I don't think it is a problem for us, Tom. It is only fifty miles from the base to the pickup point. At full speed we can be back in an hour. It is you lads who have the hard job. You would have to get through fourteen miles of enemy territory and, I am assuming, that you would have to blow the road up before you left."

"Yes. I know you meant well Hugo but it is a Herculean task you have set us."

"Sorry Tom but I know Major Fleming. If his chaps came up with the operation it would have been even riskier. It actually makes sense. The Germans wouldn't assume that blowing up the road was a prelude to an invasion. They might even put it down to partisans. It is like a chess game. The Major is thinking three moves ahead. I doubt that they will be in any hurry to repair the road. With North Africa falling there will be other priorities." Some of my men came on deck and headed to the bow to sun bathe. Hugo pointed at Fred. "Emerson is good with vehicles, isn't he?" I nodded. "Then steal a truck."

"Easier said than done."

Hugo smiled, "We use the aerial photographs; they show a lot more than you realise. They will show where cars are parked, garages, bus depots. Any of those vehicles would do. When I looked at the terrain it seemed to me that it was sparsely populated.

If you could steal a vehicle then you could be down the mountain in half an hour rather than three hours. You would need to land as soon after dusk as you can."

I nodded. Hugo was right. This was possible. It would be hard but we might just be able to pull it off. "And at least we get a couple of months to plan, prepare and ready ourselves."

When we reached our cove Gordy and Polly were already working with the men. We might have just had finished an operation but we were Commandos and training never stopped. Scouse whistled, "Ey up lads. Get this stuff ashore."

The ill-gotten gains had been shared and our allocation was ready to be carried ashore. Scouse had been a little free with the truth. They had more than a few tins of peaches. It was all foodstuffs and would last us for months; at least until our next operation. As the cases were carried ashore Hugo said, "Will you tell the two men tonight that they have been promoted?"

"No, I will see them tomorrow. I want to make sure I have made the right decision. I intend to sleep on it."

"Good idea. And when will you celebrate becoming a Captain... sir?"

I shook my head. "I never count chickens!"

"I think that is the right approach, Tom. I reckon our Major Fleming would have made a good used car salesman! I don't know about the Commandos but I am pretty certain that his word carries no word in the Navy. It takes a senior naval officer to make a promotion. I am not saying we won't get promoted but I am saying that Major Fleming will have little to do with it."

I nodded, "It might well be that he has heard, through the grapevine that Alan is to be promoted. He would use that to his own ends. I think I have the measure of Major Fleming. He sees a staff officer's cap and it will be us that wins it for him."

Poor Hugo looked so disappointed that I felt sorry for puncturing his balloon. Dad had told me the way some senior officers worked.

"Oh! Sorry I became excited for you."

I put my arm around Hugo, "It wouldn't change either of us anyway! Come on, let's get ashore. I think we will eat well tonight."

Alan came from the bridge flourishing three bottles of red wine. "And Petty Officer Leslie found these. I will give one for you gentlemen to share eh?"

We had a good night. It was more like a wake. We spoke of George Lowe, mainly, for we knew him the best but we spoke of others with whom we had served. It was just something we did to remember the dead and those who would no longer fight. I knew that Dad, Uncle Ted and the others from the Great War did so on their frequent reunions. They never forgot.

The next day there were thick heads for Scouse had also liberated some beer. However, the training did not stop. Despite the wine I had a clear head. I had only drunk four glasses. After an early morning swim and a bacon sandwich I sought out Corporal Hay and Private Hewitt. "Could you come to my hut in, say, half an hour?"

"Yes sir!" I saw the worry on their faces. Bill was still worrying about the Reggio demolition. He felt he had let the team down.

I waited until Sergeant Poulson and Sergeant Barker had organised the work teams. We had latrines to dig daily, fish lines to bait and huts to keep clean. After that the two of them would sit and work out the training for the day. "You two come along to my hut in twenty minutes. Bring some paper and pencils with you."

"Is it a test sir?"

"Sort of!"

I wanted to be ready for the four of them. I had no doubt that they would have questions and I wanted to anticipate them. I could not tell them the actual operation. Things might change but I wanted to give them an idea of what sort of problems we might face.

My sergeants arrived first and both looked worried. I smiled, "Nothing untoward here chaps. I just didn't want to repeat myself. Take an orange crate!"

They both relaxed and Gordy lit a cigarette. "I wondered what we had done wrong sir."

"Gordy, you know me well enough to know that I would tell you face to face if I was unhappy and I am not."

"Sir."

Before he could add any more Hay and Hewitt arrived. "Good. Pull up a crate. What I have to say concerns you all." They looked expectantly at me. "Our last operation was a success but we lost men. We lost soldiers who are hard to replace. Commandos are hard to come by. Good ones are as rare as rocking horse droppings! We need someone to replace Lance Sergeant Lowc; Corporal Hay, that is you. We need someone to replace Corporal Hay. Private Hewitt that is you. Congratulations." I did not believe in mincing words and dragging things out for effect.

My two sergeants had been through this themselves and knew how much it meant. They were effusive in their celebration.

"Your new pay starts today."

Gordy said, "Sir, what about Jack Jackson? I have no corporal now."

"Any of your lads ready for promotion?"

"No sir." The prompt answer was honest.

"I could promote Scouse Fletcher. He is ready too but he is from my section."

Gordy shook his head, "No sir. You are right. I will wait until one of the lads is ready." He smiled. "You always thought things through better than I did."

"There is another reason. We have another operation. It will be in July or perhaps the end of June. We have to parachute behind enemy lines, blow up a road and half a mountain and then escape through fourteen miles of enemy territory to be picked up by *'Lady Luck'*. That will be the sole purpose of our training for the next two months. I don't know any more details so that will have to do until we do discover them."

I had taken their breath away. Bill Hay was the first to respond, "Will we be able to use timers sir?"

"We can use whatever we want."

That simple question set the others off. "Will there be enemy soldiers nearby, sir?"

"A division of elite troops."

"Have all the new men had parachute training?"

Gordy answered that, "Aye, we had that not long before we left."

"I will tell you more when I know it. I want a training schedule from each of you. Identify those who will be responsible for the explosives. I want at least three teams. Corporal Hewitt you need to train a replacement for you. And lastly, we need to learn lessons from our last two operations. Neither went as smoothly as we would have liked. How do we eliminate the errors?"

They looked at each other.

"Don't tell me now. Think about it. Dismiss."

Hugo wandered over with his morning cup of tea. He was never an early riser. "How did they take it?"

"Well. They are Commandos. They don't expect reward for what they do. When they get it they feel they don't deserve it."

"I never understood that before I got to be your liaison officer. You are a unique force."

"That's what Dad said about the pilots in the Great War. I think every war has men who rise to the challenge. In this war that happens to be the Commandos."

The first two weeks flew by. My four non-coms filled the day with training. Men fell asleep, exhausted, each night.

The aerial photographs took ten days to arrive. Alan was convinced that Major Fleming had hung on to them to study them first. He wanted to come up with a better plan than Hugo's. It did not bother me. We would have to discover a way to complete the operation and survive. We studied them on the boat. The crew had been given a day off by Alan and they were sky larking in the sea. My men were still training and looked on enviously.

Alan took one look and said, "Here, north of Punta Braccetto is the best place to pick you up. It is an open beach with scrubland to the east and no houses within half a mile. I can be there from the middle of the night onwards; no problem."

"The problem is the road. The best place would be just south of Comiso but I can't see any vehicles to steal."

Hugo took out a magnifying glass. "What about here, in Comiso itself. There looks to be a couple of garages here. These were taken in daylight but I am guessing that they would have to park up local buses somewhere and trucks too."

Alan said, "Look you have twelve men. Surely you could spare two or three to capture a vehicle."

"You are right. In which case it is here, a mile south of Comiso. If we hit the mountain here and the road at these two hairpins we could destroy half a mile of road."

Hugo nodded excitedly "And you could use the road south to escape. Comiso has the nearest garrison and the road would be blocked. It sounds like a plan."

It took another three hours and two bottles of wine to work out the timings. However, I was pleased that we had something on paper. More than that we had something which stood a chance of success. Things could still go wrong but if everyone did their job then we might come through it unscathed.

"Right Hugo. Tell Major Fleming we have a plan. We will need the aircraft to leave here an hour before dark. I want to get there as soon after the sun has set as possible."

"Righto. You know he will want to come here and discuss it with us."

"Of course, but he won't stay long. He is no Commando and he does not like roughing it."

I enjoyed standing back and watching the two sections joining into one. Gordy and Polly had served together before and that helped. The attack on the railway at Bizerte had done much to fuse them into a single force. I think, however, that the defining element was the loss of the three comrades.

Bill relished his new promotion. He had come to me, privately, afterwards to thank me. He had told me that the new responsibility of fatherhood made him even more determined than ever to look after the younger soldiers. His smile when he said that the extra pay would come in handy made me feel good. I had never had to worry about money. Mum and Dad had never spoiled us and Mary and I had had to work for the money we were given but I knew that we were well off. The likes of Bill and the others had to scrimp and save for everything. Even a few shillings extra each week would make all the difference.

We had refined the plan. Gordy and Fred would head into Comiso and steal a vehicle. One night Alan took Gordy and Fred over to Malta. They spent the night breaking into the types of vehicles we might find in Sicily. We discovered that we could make a master key which would fit most vehicles and Fred was confident that he could use the wires beneath the dashboard to start one if they did not have a starting handle. The two of them also went to Marsalaforn each night. They sat in the bar, nursing a beer and learning Italian. The Maltese spoke a similar language to those on Sicily. They learned a few valuable phrases which, we hoped, might get them out of trouble.

The Major sent for us and approved the plan. "You will be leaving Valetta on the sixth of June. We have the new American Douglas C-47 transport aircraft. They are what will be used to drop the paratroopers on Sicily in July."

I was relieved. The Hampdens we had previously used were not called the flying coffin for nothing.

"Has anything changed around the target sir? Do we know what the garrison in Comiso will be?"

"No, nothing has changed. We send photographic fighters over once a week and we have chaps who compare the photographs. As far as the garrison is concerned we believe it is an Italian Brigade. Since the surrender in Africa the morale amongst the Italians is very low. A quarter of a million Italians and Germans were captured at the surrender. Sadly, most of their best units fled before the end and they have been moved to mainland Italy. Still we cross that bridge when we come to it."

I nodded as I made a note of that information. There was no such thing as useless knowledge. It was just that you hadn't found a use for it yet! "So we come to Valetta on June the fifth, sir?"

"Yes. I daresay as this is the first time you have used this aeroplane you will want to familiarise yourself with it."

The way he said that implied he didn't understand why but I nodded, "Yes sir. None of us liked the Hampden but we were familiar with it."

May came and went quickly. We had found a place close to our new cove where we could practise with charges. We had only one experience of blowing up a mountain. Hay and Shepherd had Hugo get as many books as he could on the physics of explosives. The problem we had was that we would be in the dark and have a short time to achieve what we wanted to achieve.

"Don't worry, sir. That attack on the railway line at Reggio gave Shepherd and me some ideas." He pointed to Private Roger Beaumont who was working with Shepherd. "He is a star with explosives, sir. He is posh, like you." I had long ago ceased taking offence at that judgement; it was my voice and I couldn't help it. The men meant it as a compliment. "He was at University studying chemistry. He actually enjoys playing with explosives. Sergeant Poulson will baby sit him as it is his first operation but I am confident he will handle it."

"Who will be with Shepherd?"

"Davis, sir, and I will have Smith. It seemed right to mix up the two sections." He said it with a worried look on his face.

"That's fine. I just needed to know who I had for security."

"Most of our section, sir, Corporal Hewitt, Fletcher and Crowe."

That was good. I could rely on the three of them and they had been under fire enough times not to panic. I gathered the three of them. "Right chaps. We don't need to worry about blowing up the mountain but we do need to worry about protecting the lads while they do their stuff. Scouse you will have the radio so forget your Thompson you will have enough weight to carry. Make sure you each have a silencer for your Colt."

"Sir."

"All of you will need at least eight grenades. Scouse, you won't have your Bergen as you will have the radio so get extra webbing from the Quarter Master. Alan, I want you with a grenade launcher rather than a Thompson. How are you with one?"

"I haven't used one much. I will practice with one. We still have a week before we go."

"Corporal Hewitt you and I will have the Thompsons." He nodded. "Pack as much cord in our Bergens as we can carry. We will take the German grenades and make booby traps. When the mountain and the road goes up then the Eyeties from Comiso will be all over us. We may have a vehicle but we may not. However, we escape I want our pursuers delaying."

"Right sir. If you give me your Bergen I will see how much I can pack into it."

"Don't forget you are still the Doc. Don't forget the medical kit."

"Right sir." He grinned. "We will look like pack mules sir!"

Chapter 10

Alan and I went over the arrangements for our rendezvous. Scouse and Wacker sat in with us for they would be talking to each other. "We will be on station from three a.m. I am not expecting you much before six but we would struggle to wait much beyond seven. It is a quiet bay but someone would come along and ask us our business."

"If we aren't there by seven it means it has all gone pear shaped! Even if we have to march down the mountain we can make it in three hours and we intend to leave long before three a.m."

"We have the code words, sir. The boat is 'Pier Head' and we are the 'Toffees'."

I nodded, "Both Liverpool references." I looked at Alan, "How are we for using the radio?"

"A heads up to say you are on the way and then a second blast when you reach the shore but we have the back up of a signal lamp anyway."

"We will keep messages short. I doubt that they have time to use radio location devices. It is a fairly remote area."

"That is my worry, Tom. I have seen the road. You have to go damned close to Ragusa on your way down."

"I know. That is why we are setting the timers for a good hour after we leave the demolitions. We will be beyond Ragusa by then."

"And if the explosives don't go off?"

"Then Lance Sergeant Hay will have a rapid demotion!"

Scouse sprang to support his comrade, "Don't you worry, sir, Bill Hay is a good lad. Won't be no cock ups with him, sir!"

There was something about his accent which made Alan and me smile. Wacker and Scouse did not understand it and they both shook their heads.

A lorry whisked us to the airfield. We arrived at six. I saw that there were dozens of the new Dakotas. It meant that we had to camp in the same hanger as our aircraft. The crew were waiting for us. Flight Lieutenant Cross was young but he sounded enthusiastic. "I say, sir, this is exciting." He patted the rudder of his aeroplane. "I am dying to use these properly!" He leaned towards me and spoke conspiratorially. "The big one is not far away you know."

"I know Flight Lieutenant but I would keep that to yourself. It is supposed to be a secret." I pointed to the non service workers. "Loose lips and all that."

"Quite sir. Sorry sir." He hesitated and said, "Er sir, there is a rumour that you are related to Group Captain Harsker."

"It is more than a rumour. He is my father."

"Gosh sir. A real ace!"

"Yes Flight." I did not want to go into the inevitable questions about what was he really like and so I became business like. "We have never flown in these. We trained and used Hampdens and Whitleys before."

"Totally different beastie, sir. These are purpose built for dropping parachutes and carrying heavy loads."

"Hang on a moment." I turned, "Right lads, gather round, Flight Lieutenant Cross is going to tell us about our new bus!"

The Flight Lieutenant began, "We have a crew of four. Flight Sergeant Williams is the radio operator and he will let you know when to jump. Notice that we have a door. None of that jumping through a hole in the floor here and we have racks for your parachutes. They are oiled and there will be no delays when you jump. The door is aft of the wings but make sure you jump when you exit. You don't want to smack into the tail plane."

They all looked at the huge tail plane. I doubted that would be a problem but it was a consideration. Dropping through a hole in the floor was not good but at least there was nothing to hit you there. It was too late to practise now.

"It will only be a short flight but you are being dropped down to a one thousand feet high mountain and so we will have to drop you at three thousand feet. Mount Etna is much higher than that and we don't want to hit it. It is likely that the wind will be from the west and so we will make our run from the east. That way you should hit your target. Any questions?"

"Could we look inside the fuselage, Flight Lieutenant. It will be dark when we exit. It is always good to get your bearings."

"Of course, sir. Be my guest."

I could see the hand of a good designer all over the interior. It could hold twenty-eight men and there were steel benches along both sides. There was a rack running the length of the aeroplane. I saw that it would be impossible to foul your lines. We would be able to stand close together and exit very quickly. The door was wide enough and high enough for the biggest paratrooper. I was happy and I left.

Some of the more nervous jumpers stayed inside longer but when they all emerged I could see that they were all as happy as I was. The Flight Lieutenant said, "Well that is it until tomorrow." He strode off.

Flight Sergeant Williams shook his head and wandered over, "Sorry about that, sir. The young gentleman was supposed to say that there is hot food for your men in the mess. You are expected in the officer's mess."

"Thanks Flight. He seems excited."

He shook his head, "Like a bloody puppy with a new toy sir but he is a good pilot. You'll be all right."

"I never doubted it for a moment." I turned to the men. "You take charge, Sergeant Barker. We will be sleeping here. I will see you after dinner."

It was some time since I had eaten in a mess. I felt a little strange as I headed to the main buildings. A helpful sentry pointed me in the right direction. I was the only soldier in the mess. The rest all wore the Air Force blue. It meant I was a curiosity and I spent the meal answering questions about the Commandos. Since the raid in the Lofoten Islands, St. Nazaire and Dieppe we were seen as mad men. I had to smile as I saw young pilots looking for a nervous tic or something similar.

When Flight Lieutenant Cross entered he couldn't wait to tell everyone about my father. I had merely delayed the inquisition. One slightly older pilot said, "Didn't I hear that you dropped behind enemy lines to rescue him a year or two back?"

"We went in for a General actually, but yes we did."

"Had to fight your way through enemy lines, I heard."

I nodded, "Yes, I lost some good men that day."

The older officer nodded. "We heard that the Germans execute your lot if they capture them."

I smiled, "The operative word is '*if*'. We make damned sure that they don't."

He shook his head, "Rather you than me. If we get shot down it is just a prison camp."

"We don't take chances, you know. Everything is planned."

He laughed and the others joined in as he said, "Like jumping out of an aeroplane over a mountain behind enemy lines in the middle of the night." He suddenly stopped. "That's a thought. How do you get out?"

It was my turn to laugh, "I told you, we are Commandos. We have a plan!"

The mess president insisted on buying me a drink. I had but the one. They had far more. As I listened to them I realised that they fought a different war. It was remote. Even Dad had been closer to the action and to danger in the Great War. He had been less than a hundred miles from the enemy. They faced a perilous existence. These men could be shot down and suffer a fiery death but generally they slept soundly and safely in their beds. When they dropped their paratroopers in Sicily it would be totally different from the airborne troops who would be subject to the wind, the elements and the terrain not to mention Germans and Italians trying to kill them. We all fought our own wars but we fought for the same cause.

I slipped quietly out of the mess and headed for the hangar. I needed my sleep. I was the first back. My men were taking advantage of the beer in the mess. I knew them well enough to know that they would all be ready the next day. The double whisky I had consumed sent me directly to sleep.

I rose early and breakfasted in the mess before heading for the operations room to find out about the weather. I was pleased to see that Flight Lieutenant Cross was there too and he was bright eyed. He had not drunk too much. "Morning sir. The weather looks to be about the same. Little chance of rain and the wind isn't too strong."

"Cloud cover?"

"That could be tricky, sir. We might have to come in under three thousand feet. Is that okay with your chaps?"

"They can manage. Better a lower drop than a blind one. Is your navigator good?"

"Oh yes sir, Bob is the best. We will get you there, don't you worry about that." He looked concerned. "I just hope you can get out."

"We will manage but thank you for your concern."

I spent some time talking to the meteorological officer. It was not that I didn't trust Flight Lieutenant Cross but I had done this before and there were questions I might ask which he would not. Satisfied I went to the hangar where tables were already being laid out by WAAFs and Ercs. They would be for the parachutes. In ones and twos my men wandered over from the mess. By the time we had all returned the parachutes and their packs were laid out already. The Ercs disappeared leaving the WAAFS under the command of a stern face female Warrant Officer.

I wandered over to her and she saluted, "Warrant Officer First Class Lindsey. My ladies are ready to pack your parachutes, Lieutenant Harsker."

"Thank you but some of my men may well wish to do it themselves."

She looked offended, "My girls are very good at this, sir!"

"They may well be but I for one will pack my own. I have seen too many Roman Candles to worry about offending a Warrant Officer." I turned and shouted, "The parachutes are ready. The WAAFs are happy to pack them for you."

As I had expected my men all chose to pack their own. The WAAFS, with the exception of their officer were not offended and they chatted and flirted with my men as they packed their chutes. It meant less work for them. I took my time folding and packing my chutes; main and reserve. I made sure that they were secure before writing my name with a chinograph pencil on the pack. We all wanted the parachute we had packed. By the time it was finished and the chutes laid neatly in order I went to see about the weather conditions.

The met officer said, "Sorry sir but the cloud cover will be two thousand eight hundred feet. The C-47 will have to drop you at two and a half thousand feet. If the cloud gets any lower than this then the mission will be scrubbed. We can't have them flying too low."

"Quite. I will return to my men. Keep me informed."

I let the men have lunch before I gave them the final briefing. I wanted to leave it as late as possible. "Right chaps, we have a lower drop than normal. We drop at two and half thousand feet and the deck is a thousand feet. On the positive side it should be easier to keep together but we will have to be aware of the ground coming to meet us a little more quickly than is normal. Sergeant Barker you will be tail end Charlie. Sergeant Poulson and Lance Sergeant Hay, you will be number six and number four respectively. I want no hanging around in the door. The stick is twelve men. Remember that." I looked around and they all nodded. "Get some rest. We eat at five and I want us in the bus by seven booted and chuted!" They all laughed. "Now get some rest. Sergeant Poulson, equipment check at six."

"Sir."

Flight Lieutenant Cross and myself waited anxiously in the operations room watching the weather. A chain smoking met officer finally came over at four in the afternoon and said, "You are good to go but cloud cover is two seven."

I nodded, "That is fine for my lads. How about you, Flight Lieutenant Cross, are you happy with the tolerances?"

"Pongo Race is the best navigator in the air force. We will get you there, sir!"

As I went back to my men I remembered a confident Hampden crew who had dropped us at St. Nazaire and then plummeted to a fiery end. I hoped the affable young officer and his crew would not suffer the same grisly fate.

It was almost pleasant seated in the back of the Dakota. There was no overwhelming smell of fuel and it did not feel claustrophobic. We sat in order in the aircraft. I had Davis opposite and Beaumont next to me. They were the least experienced jumpers and Bill Hay was ready to give them a shove if they needed it. We sat with knees apart cradling our hooks. This would be a short flight. Flight Lieutenant Cross had told me that it took nine and a half minutes to reach ten thousand feet. We would not need half of that. The plan was to head north east and come from the east. There would be anti aircraft, we knew that but, hopefully, the low cloud would prevent fighters from being scrambled.

The take off was almost silent compared with the Hampden and the huge Pratt and Whitney engines sounded reassuringly powerful. I smiled as I saw those who were not happy fliers as they unclenched their fists or replaced their good luck charms. I had been brought up in aeroplanes and I never feared them; I respected them and would not take risks with them but they were a tool. They were like the Thompson I carried.

The Bergen was heavy. We wore them on our fronts as we had chutes on our backs. Fortunately, we would not have far to travel once we landed; if the winds did not carry us too far off our course. There were no power lines to worry us and the trees were few and far between. The danger lay in the rocks. You could not predict where a rock might lie; especially in the dark. We were all silent in the aircraft. I was running through the plan and imagining what might go wrong. Those who had done this before would be going through their part in the operation and the new ones would be just wondering what it was like.

The shelling, when we crossed the coast, was sporadic. I doubted that they would bother wasting ammunition on a single aircraft. They probably thought that we were lost.

Flight Sergeant Williams came from the flight deck, "We are ten minutes out. If you would care to hook up."

"Right, Flight. Stand!" As one we stood. "Hook up, One!"

"Two."

"Three."

"Four."

"Five."

"Six."

"Seven."

"Eight."

"Ten."

There was a smack, "Smith you are a half wit! Did you never learn to count?"

"Sorry Sergeant Barker."

"Corporal Hewitt."

"Nine."

"Ten."

"Eleven."

"Twelve. All hooked up, sir!"

"Check chutes."

Private Davis checked mine and then the others were all checked. Scouse Fletcher, number eleven would check Gordy's. It was his voice which carried down the fuselage. "All chutes checked, sir. We are good to go!"

Flight Sergeant Williams came down, gave me the thumbs up and I said, "Bunch up!" He reached the door and plugged his headset into a socket next to the door.

He waited and then said, "Roger."

He opened the door and we heard no more. There was just a rushing and roaring from the wind. It was incredibly noisy. He placed the door to one side and gestured for me to get closer. I stood in the doorway. Davis was doing the right thing. He was as close to me as my parachute. I stared down at the black ground racing below me. I did not look at the Flight Sergeant he would tap me on the shoulder and then push me off if I hesitated. There was no rank in a stick of paratroopers! I caught occasional glimpses of lights below and then there was a tap on my shoulder. I leapt.

The slipstream and the speed of the Dakota took me well below the tail plane. There was a jerk as the release mechanism opened the chute. My hands went up automatically to feel for the cords. Then there was a second jerk and I looked up to see the billowing parachute I had packed less than twelve hours earlier. I took a quick glance astern and saw line of parachutes. I then shifted my attention to the ground. We did not have long before we hit the ground and the others would all follow me. I was looking for a grey snake that was the road. I twisted around until I saw it. It was behind me. I pulled on one set of cords and I began to spiral and to turn. Then I grabbed the cord with my other hand and began to aim to land sideways on a slight upslope. If I landed downhill I might not be able to stop. The ground was coming towards me rapidly. I braced myself and pulled up my feet ready to use my knees to take the impact. At the last minute I saw a rock and turned to the right. My feet touched the ground and I began to run. As my chute came over my head I stopped and began to collect the parachute.

I heard a cry from behind me. Davis had not managed to miss the rock I had spotted and his chute was dragging his body across the ground. I took out my dagger and slashed the cords on my chute. I would have to gather it later for Davis was in danger of being swept off the side of the mountain. I ran after him and managed to grab his chute. I pulled it towards me. He looked up at me. His face showed his pain. "Sorry sir. It's me ankle. I think it is broken."

I cut his cords and said, "You stay there. Here, roll your chute up while I find Doc."

I wanted him occupied. Rolling up his chute would keep his mind from the pain. I hurried towards the others. The second man down and he was hurt. The operation was not going well. Beaumont had rolled up my chute for me.

"Good man. Go and stand guard over Davis. He has broken a leg or an ankle."

I saw that the rest, although spread out, had all landed intact. I hurried towards Hewitt. "Corporal, Davis has broken something."

"Sir." He hurried past me.

Sergeant Poulson and Lance Sergeant Hay joined me. "Davis has broken a leg or an ankle. Unless we find a vehicle we are in trouble."

"Are we in the right area, sir?"

"I think so. The road is ahead and the mountain is there. I have left Hewitt with Davis. He will have to stay with Davis and that will leave Fletcher and Crowe with me. I'll find the best site for the demolitions." I looked at my watch. It was nine thirty. Time was wasting.

Fletcher and Crowe appeared at my side. I waved them left and right and headed to the west where I had glimpsed the road as we were landing. The ground was rough and I could see why Davis had hurt himself. He hadn't had enough practice at landing, especially in the dark. That was my fault. I would make sure that they were all checked out next time.

Scouse was the best scout I had. He could move silently and he did not seem to need to look where he put his feet. As we crested a rise we saw the road. The hair pin was just fifty yards from where we were. "Crowe, go back and tell the others we have found the road. Bring Davis!"

"Sir."

Scouse and I clambered down the side of the hill. It was almost a cliff. I saw that, in places, they had reinforced it with steel gabions packed with ballast. We could use that to our advantage. If we put charges in the gabions and then cut the steel we could direct the charge. Once on the road I took out the map. Scouse placed his body next to mine to shield the light and we turned on the torch. I knew exactly where we were. I looked to the north west and saw the outline of Comiso a mile away. We were far enough away from the enemy to talk. "Scouse, follow the road around. There should be another hairpin about three quarters of a mile down the road. Scout it out."

"Sir."

The others arrived above us. Leaving Hewitt and Davis at the top they scrambled down. "Gordy, take Fred and get to Comiso. It is over there."

He nodded, "Sorry about Davis, sir." He was his man and felt responsible.

"It was an accident. These things happen."

"Sir. "Right Emerson, let's go."

I pointed to the gabions. "I reckon charges up there should bring down half the mountain but you lads are the experts. I thought we could cut some of the steel and use that to direct the avalanche."

Hay and Shepherd nodded. "Perfect."

I took out the map and said to Crowe. "The road twists and turns. Climb back up and help Hewitt take Davis here." I pointed to a bend in the road. If we get a vehicle we will join you there. If not then we will all be walking."

"Sir."

"Sergeant Poulson, come with me. Your team can have a go at the next hairpin."

Already I saw the two teams snipping the steel hawsers and wires. We hurried down the road. Scouse whistled as we approached. "Here sir. I have seen nowt. The Sarge and Freddie Boy headed up the road."

"Take point up there." I turned and looked at the slope above us. This was too sheer to climb and there were no gabions. I turned to Beaumont. "Right Roger. It is time for you to earn your pay."

He looked up at the wall of stone. "There are natural fissures up there, sir. They are natural lines of weakness. We place bigger charges in the bottom and smaller ones higher up."

Sergeant Poulson said, "Smith, according to your sergeant you are like a monkey! You take the fissures up there."

"Right Sarge."

Beaumont said, "Here are two charges and two timers. Make sure that they are secure. I have set the timers already. Get as high as you can and then put the second in a third of the way down." He handed him the two bundles. Smith took off his Bergen and laid his Tommy gun down. He jammed the two devices in his battledress. I watched him climb. He was careful but he moved up the wall like a spider.

While Sergeant Poulson and Beaumont unpacked the rest of the demolitions I ran around to Scouse. "How is it?"

"Quiet as the grave, sir." He pointed to Comiso, a mile away. "I have seen a couple of lights come on and then go off but I haven't heard anything."

"That is good news. Hopefully you will hear the Sergeant and the vehicle soon."

I checked my watch again. It was gone ten thirty. My two car thieves would have reached Comiso. I went back to check on the progress of the others. Smith was half way down the cliff helping Sergeant Poulson place more charges.

Private Beaumont was ferreting away at the bottom. He had found a tiny cave. It would have been big enough for a large Alsatian. He had just finishing packing the explosives in the hole and was now making a wall of stones at the entrance. "This will force the explosion upwards." He pointed to a fissure just twenty feet up the cliff. "I am hoping it triggers that one."

"How much time do you need?"

"Five minutes, no more."

I went back to wait with Scouse. As I walked I couldn't help thinking that we could have set the charges and double timed it back to the boat. It was only eleven fifteen and we had finished. But and it was a big but, we now had a wounded man and that meant we had to have a vehicle. Our plans were now in jeopardy. Scouse was well hidden. His head popped up from behind the parapet at the corner of the hairpin.

"Anything?"

He shook his head, "I thought I heard an engine but it was my imagination."

We watched the minutes tick by. It was frustrating. I knew that the Sergeant and Emerson would not be wasting time but it was irritating to have to wait when the charges were all set. It was eleven forty-five when we heard the sound of the truck as it left Comiso. It was noisy. If there was a curfew then we were in trouble. I assumed it was Gordy and Fred. "I will go and warn the others. Jump on board when they reach you."

I ran to the next bend and Sergeant Poulson and his team were waiting. "I think they are on their way. Smith, pop up the road and tell the others. Best be ready."

As he ran off Sergeant Poulson said, "If Davis hadn't hurt his leg this would have been a perfect operation."

"Don't say that, Sergeant, we aren't on the *'Lady'* yet!" We had about three hours before the charges went off. By then I hoped we would be at the coast. The truck chugged slowly up the hairpin. We waited on a flat part. Emerson would have a hard enough job driving it without trying to go up a steep gradient. When I saw the truck, my heart sank. It was an Italian army truck. Firstly they were unreliable and secondly it would attract attention.

I cocked a head at Gordy in the cab. "An army truck?"

"It was all we could get. We have two dead Eyeties to get rid of too."

"Will they be missed?"

"Hard to say. They were driving out of Comiso and we jumped them when they stopped at a quiet intersection. It depends if they were meeting someone."

"When we put Davis in the back we will get rid of the bodies and lay a few booby traps."

I climbed in the back. It could not be helped and, at least, we had a vehicle but soldiers and an army truck were more likely to be missed than civilians. We stopped at Lance Sergeant Hay's party and they climbed in. "Everything set?"

"Has been for some time sir. I almost wish we could watch it go up. This will be spectacular." He suddenly noticed the two bodies. "Do we have company?"

"We will get rid of them when we pick up Doc and Davis."

We drove further than I had anticipated and I jumped down when we did so. "Get the bodies out. Sergeant Poulson, rig some booby traps. You three come and help us get Davis on board." I walked over to where my three men waited. "How is he Doc?"

"Broken ankle. A leg or an arm I can set but an ankle?" He shook his head. "There are too many bones. Stevie Johnson on the *'Lady'* might be able to do something. I gave him some pills to knock him out. "

We carefully lifted him in the back of the vehicle and laid Bergens around him to cushion his legs. I looked at my watch and it was one o'clock. We had plenty of time but I wanted us down the mountain sooner rather than later. We laid the Italian bodies at the side of the road and booby trapped them with German grenades.

Chapter 11

We had to head east before the road turned south to the coast. We would be within a mile of Ragusa. The truck was not the fastest in the world. The Italians were not noted for their engineering. We only had half a mile to go before the turn. Suddenly there was a squeal of brakes and I heard Gordy shout, "Shit!"

I took my Colt and moved to the back of the truck. I dropped to the side. I saw that there was an improvised road block and there were three Italians. They had two logs across the road and they had a motor cycle and side car combination. They spat Italian out at Gordy. He was not the best linguist in the world. Had it been me I would have shouted back at him in German. Gordy just reacted. He fired his silenced Colt at the speaker. I ran down the side of the truck and sent five bullets at the other two. They both fell.

"Out of the back, four men. We need a road block moving."

"Sorry sir!"

"My fault Gordy. You best get in the back with Davis."

"Sir?"

"What if we meet more soldiers?"

He nodded, "You are right sir!"

He jumped from the cab and Sergeant Poulson and Bill Hay brought Crowe and Smith to move the barrier. As they passed me I said, "Tell Scouse to send the signal. This may get a bit dicey!"

"Sir."

The bang on the side told me that they were aboard. "Right Fred, drive!"

"Should I use headlights, sir?"

"I don't think it makes any difference. They will soon find those bodies. Go on!"

The dimmed headlights did make a slight difference. The road we were now on was very narrow and very rough. The lights showed us the direction and the worst of the pot holes. Every jolt would be agony for Davis even with the pills Doc had given him. The condition of the road gave me hope for it meant it was little used. I took out the map and used the torch to work out where we were. I saw that there were no towns or settlements until we reached Donnafugata. It was an old place. It had an old, derelict castle but I guessed that there would not be many people in the place. We had not lost much time disposing of the bodies but it was now one thirty. We had eight miles of empty road and I hoped that we would make better time. The road, however, was like an English cart track. We were doing barely ten miles an hour. By two thirty we passed the eerie castle and then the truck decided to play up. We had just passed the castle when the lights went out and the engine stopped.

I looked at Emerson, "Can you fix it or shall we take to our legs?" I saw the panic on his face and I smiled. "Come on Fred, give me the truth. If you can't fix it we can walk. By my reckoning we have five miles to go. That is just two hours. It is not a disaster."

His face set into a determined grimace. "I'll get it going, sir!"

He went to the front and I went to the back. "Well Scouse?"

"The *'Lady'* is on station sir."

"Fred is trying to get her going but if he can't then we will have to walk. Doc, rig up a stretcher. It is only five miles to the sea from here!"

I hurried back to Emerson. He had the torch in the engine. Being seen now did not matter. I looked at my watch. It was ten to three. Soon the hillside would light up when the demolition charges went off and the ants would be disturbed. I knew there was no point in hurrying Emerson. He was working as fast as he could.

After what seemed an age he said, "Sir, grab the starting handle from under the seat and turn her over."

He ran to the cab as I took the handle and began to turn the engine. The first two turns yielded nothing. Then, on the third there was a cough. Fred shouted, "One more time sir!"

I gave it all and the engine fired. It struggled and then caught.

"Get aboard sir."

I jumped in the cab and he set off slowly. "It is the alternator sir. We can't use the lights. They are draining the battery. I will have to drive at walking pace."

I used the torch to look at my watch. It was three o'clock. We would make the beach in an hour. Suddenly I heard the loud crack of an explosion from behind us. I looked in the mirror and saw a flash high above us. Then there was a second. I heard a rumble and felt the ground move. The demolition charges had worked but the enemy would know where we were! A heartbeat later the other two explosions sounded and I really felt the earth move as rocks, stones and earth slid down the mountain.

I turned to Emerson, "I know you are doing your best but every second counts."

"I know, sir and it is getting marginally lighter but you don't want me to turn this over, do you?"

"No Fred. Just keep on."

I took my silenced Colt out and wound down the window. I made sure I had a spare magazine in my top pocket.

Suddenly we saw buildings and homes. We saw people. There were Arabs in bisht as well as Italians. This was a cosmopolitan island. The day's work was beginning. We were an Italian lorry and they were not surprised to see us. Then I heard a sharp crack from the north followed by another three or four. They had tripped our booby traps. They were less than fourteen miles behind us. I had to map read now. There were more roads and some of them were dead ends.

"Fred! Take a right!"

The wheels squealed, despite our slow speed as we left the main road at the quiet farmhouse. We were on a narrow track. It was not even a road but I could see that it led to the sea. I shouted, "Scouse, get on the radio. We are heading for the sea. Tell them to watch out for us!"

Perhaps it was the noise of our engine or maybe our luck running out but when we could almost smell the sea we passed a guard house. Three Italian soldiers stepped out when they heard the engine and saw us. One of them walked in front of the truck and held up his hand. Fred was tired and he did not brake in time. He hit the Italian who fell to the ground. One of the other two raised his gun, aimed it at Fred and cocked it. I fired. He fell and then I fired at the second and he, too, fell.

"Go! Go!"

The two shouts and the dying shout from the man Fred had run over had roused the others in the guard room. A fusillade of shots rattled behind us. Then I heard the scything sound of three Tommy guns and all shooting stopped.

"Sorry sir, he just stepped out and the brakes are rubbish on this truck!"

"Don't worry Emerson we are almost there now."

Ahead I could see that the houses ended and that meant the coast was close. I was getting ready to tell the others when the road took us left, north and away from the sea.

"Stop!"

I jumped out and looked at my map. There was five hundred yards of rough ground between us and the sea. We would have to walk. "Right Emerson. Leave the truck we are done with it." I ran down the side banging on it. "Right lads. We have to walk."

As I reached the back I saw, in the distance, the lights of vehicles. Someone in the guard house had sent for help. Sergeant Poulson saw them as he jumped down, "That's buggered it, sir!"

"Corporal Hewitt, take three men and carry Davis to the shore. Scouse, run on ahead and signal *'Lady Luck'*. If you can't see her then use the radio. They know we are here now."

I was left with five men. "Gordy, Shepherd, booby trap this truck." I handed them a half dozen grenades and cords. "You others come with me." We ran across the rough ground to the only cover I could see. Sixty feet from the road it was a large piece of rock covered with lichen and grass. It was only three feet high but it was six feet long. We could use it for shelter. I turned to Private Crowe. "Right Alan, you have lugged that grenade launcher all over this island. Now you get a chance to use it."

"Sir!"

I saw that the trucks were closer now. "Gordy! Move it!"

He raised his hand and a moment later he and Ken Shepherd ran to join us. They threw themselves behind the rock. "We have to buy those lads ten minutes at least. It won't be easy carrying a wounded man over this stuff and Scouse has to get the ship close in." They nodded. "Crowe, when I give the word I want you to lob all the grenades you can at the enemy. They won't know where they are coming from. Then I will give the order for the rest of you. Empty your magazines and then run when I give the order. Clear?"

"Yes sir!"

The vehicles all stopped when they saw the stationary truck. There were two trucks, one German and one Italian. I saw two Italians, with guns drawn, approach the abandoned truck. As one pulled on the handle of the cab the grenade went off and the two of them were thrown into the air. The German officer shouted orders and they machine gunned the truck. It triggered another booby trap.

The officer took out his binoculars and scanned the land behind us. It was getting light. It was the thin light of early dawn. He must have see something for he pointed and shouted orders. The two groups began to move towards us. "Now Crowe!" He was ready and the first grenade sailed high. He loaded a second and traversed it to the right. It popped up into the air. He loaded a third as the first grenade exploded. He had sent the fourth one when the mechanism on the grenade launcher broke. They were prone to that. The four grenades sent shrapnel and smoke across our front. They made the enemy take to the ground.

"Right chaps. Time for some fire power." As we raised our heads we saw that some of the enemy were still advancing but there were many writhing on the ground. "Fire!" Three of the men had Tommy guns while the rest of us had Colts. It took four of the enemy to fall before they fired back. It was a withering wall of fire which we threw up. After the Thompsons were empty I deemed we had bought enough time.

"Back to the boat." I holstered my empty Colt and took out two Mills bombs. I threw them in quick succession as far as I could and then followed my men. I drew my Luger as I ran. The two sharp cracks behind me were accompanied by flying shrapnel. Something smacked me in the back. I had been hit by my own grenade. I ran as fast as I could; weaving from side to side.

It was much lighter now and I saw the others were close to the shore but there was no sign of the *'Lady Luck'*. Scouse had said she was on station. "Spread out and weave! We are a tight target for them!"

I stopped and turned. I knelt to make a small target and aimed the Luger. The nearest Germans were just fifty yards away. They were firing as they ran. That was a mistake! Their bullets flew over us. With my arm resting on my knee I squeezed off four shots at the leading Germans. I hit two and the other two threw themselves to the ground. I squeezed off another four rounds and hit one of them as he raised his rifle to fire. I turned and ran. The others were two hundred yards ahead of me now and had almost caught up with the Corporal and his patient. Further ahead I saw Scouse with the radio. Like Crowe with the grenade launcher he had carried the radio since we had landed. Now it might be our lifesaver.

I glanced over my shoulder. The enemy had learned their lesson and were approaching in a solid line. They were running but whoever commanded them had stopped the heroes from running too fast. When I looked back I saw that the others had reached the sea and were forming a defensive circle around the injured Davis. I ran directly to Scouse, "Well?"

"They are just north of us, sir. They had a bit of engine trouble and drifted. They are coming…"

"I know Scouse but so are the Germans!" I turned. "There is nowhere left to run. Use the sand and lie down. Make small targets of yourselves." I lay down and pushed a wall of sand before me. Sand could slow down a bullet. Enough sand could stop one. I put a fresh clip in my Luger. I squeezed off four shots at the advancing Germans. They were sixty yards from us. I saw one clutch his arm as I winged him. Gordy's Tommy gun tore into one of them and they went to ground. I saw three Germans bringing a heavy machine gun. "Get those machine gunners!"

Everyone fired at the three of them. Although two were hit another two ran to help them to set it up. The rifle bullets were kicking up sand close to our position. If they used the heavy machine gun then we were dead men. I cursed the damaged grenade launcher. It would have eliminated the machine gun with just two grenades.

The Germans had gathered their forces and were protecting the machine gun. I heard a cry from my left as Smith was hit. As Doc ran to him, he, too, was hit. I emptied the Luger at the machine gun. I managed to wing the gunner and delay the start of the slaughter. I saw a replacement gunner cock the gun and then the whole crew disappeared as the Oerlikon from the E-Boat began to fire. I turned and saw the *'Lady Luck'* just twenty yards out.

"Get on board, The wounded first!" Every gun on the E-Boat was dealing out death. The Germans and the Italians who had finally caught up with their Teutonic allies were taking whatever cover they could find. I waited until the three wounded men were hauled aboard and then I led back the rest of my men. I was the last to clamber back on board and Lieutenant Jorgenson helped to pull me up. Alan said, "Sorry, Tom! Damned engines and damned engineer!"

As I rolled on to the deck I looked up and saw three black crosses in the distance. "Alan! Fighters!"

He turned and ran to the bridge. "Hold on! Coxswain, full power!"

I barely managed to hold on as we turned and headed south like a greyhound released from its trap. When an E-Boat moved at full speed it was a frightening sight. I managed to stand and I made my way to the bridge. I braced myself against the metal side and reloaded my Colt.

I saw that the three aeroplanes were the old 109. They just had machine guns. The FW190 had cannon! We had had some luck at the very least. The gunners on the *'Lady Luck'* now had their eye in. As the first of the fighters roared in they were met by a furious fusillade. It takes a brave man to fly into such a storm and an even braver one to be able to return accurate fire. The bullets from the first aeroplane went over our heads. Petty Officer Leslie was throwing the E-Boat from side to side. There appeared to be no pattern to it but his gunners knew his rhythm. They had practised this in the sea north of our cove. The second and third Messerschmitts actually struck the boat but they struck nothing vital and, as they banked to come around a second time I saw that one of them was trailing smoke.

The German fighters climbed to attack us beam on where Petty Officer Leslie's manoeuvres would not have the same effect. Alan shouted, "When they attack we are going to turn and face them. I want every gun to open fire at the same time."

I was aware that every second took us closer to Malta and safety. We just had to buy a little more time. The three fighters were coming in wing tip to wing tip. They would have a wide platform which they thought would blow us out of the water. Their attack negated our speed.

Alan shouted, "Now Bill!" As Bill spun the wheel and we heeled over the three Germans fired. Alan shouted, "Fire!"

The bullets from two of the German fighters blasted the empty sea while the bullets from the third tore through the Oerlikon crew and into the steel of the bridge. I emptied my Luger blindly by holding it over the bridge guard. As the fighter zoomed overhead I saw that it was hit. It did not rise, like the other two, but plunged into the sea some hundred yards astern of us. The sheer weight of bullets had done for the aeroplane and pilot.

"Resume course, Coxswain!"

As we turned a look out shouted, "Hurricanes!"

Someone had seen the Germans on radar and scrambled the fighters. The last two Messerschmitts turned tail with the three Hurricanes in hot pursuit.

"Doc!" We heard the shouts from the forward area. I peered over the bridge and saw that three men had been hit. Two were torn in two but the third might live. With Hewitt wounded that left SBA Johnson. I holstered my Luger and ran to the Oerlikon. It was Taff Jones who was lying wounded. He had been hit in the leg and he was unconscious. I took a piece of parachute cord from my battledress and tied it above the wound to staunch the bleeding. I checked him over to see if he had any other wounds. He had a gash to his head. I took off my Bergen and found my medical kit. As I did so I saw that one of the gunners had no head. His torso lay before me. I shook my head and found the medical kit. I had just applied a piece of gauze to the Welshman's head when the SBA joined me.

"Thanks sir. I was busy with your lads. They are a mess."

I had almost forgotten them. "They will be alright, won't they?"

"Smith and Doc will be out of action for a few weeks but Davis has an infection in his broken ankle. He might die or lose his leg. We need to get him back as soon as we can."

I stood and went to Alan. "Better set a course for Valetta. We need a hospital."

"Righto. Full speed Petty Officer. Wacker, get on the radio. Tell Valetta we need ambulances at the harbour. We have casualties."

I saw our island home ahead. We would be in Valetta in less than twenty minutes. Would Davis have twenty minutes?

Alan lit a cheroot. "I am sorry that we were delayed. I told you it was that engineer. We have had nothing to do for weeks and he didn't keep on top of the engines. Despite the recent overhaul they need cosseting. The Chief spent every waking minute down in his little hole. The new boy likes the sun too much. I am having him transferred."

"Are you sure? Sleep on it. You are angry and people don't make good decisions when they are angry."

He pointed to the Oerlikon crew. "Damned right I am angry. If he had done his job we would have been on station and been home before they could have scrambled those fighters. Your lads wouldn't have been shot at on the beach. It is down to him! You did your job and every other man did theirs. God knows those poor sods on the Oerlikon did their duty, right to the end. That's what we do. You can't have a weak link. He goes!"

I caught Bill Leslie's eye and he shook his head.

Wacker's voice came up from below, "Ambulances are waiting at the harbour sir. Head for berth ten, sir."

Anticipating the order, the Coxswain said, "Got it sir."

I went below decks. Doc was awake but pale. "Johnson says it will be weeks before you are fit again, Hewitt."

"We'll see sir. I still haven't trained my replacement."

The SBA said, "Mr Harsker did a fair job, He saved Taff's leg."

"There you are Doc." I looked over at Smith. He was out for the count. "How is Jimmy?"

"He copped one in the leg, sir. I have cleaned it up and he will live but I am not certain what damage was done inside."

I looked at the holes in the mess walls. The fighter's machine guns had not hurt the boat as much as cannon shells would have but she was damaged. "I don't think we will be going anywhere in a hurry. You both have the chance to recover."

I felt the boat slowing as we approached the harbour entrance. I went on deck and saw that the four ambulances had their back doors open and were waiting for us. Davis and Jones were taken off first as they had the most serious injuries. By the time the others had been carried to the ambulances we were tied fast to the harbour and my men and the crew began to relax. I could see that Alan was still angry. That anger was about to be inflamed as Petty Officer McGee came on deck. He was smoking and laughing with his stokers. It was the last straw and it set the Lieutenant off.

"Petty Officer McGee come here! Now!"

None of us had ever heard the captain speak like that to his crew and even Bill Leslie looked shocked. The Petty Officer threw his cigarette into the harbour and, scowling, strode to the bridge.

"Yes sir?"

"I want you off my ship now. I am transferring you."

"You can't do that Mr Jorgenson!"

Alan's voice became cold and he said, "I think you will find that I can. Get your gear and go ashore. I will tell the Port Admiral that there is an engineer available to him."

I saw Magee's hands bunch into fists at his side. "Is this because the bloody engines failed? They are rubbish! You can't blame me."

"So we add insubordination to incompetence. Get off my boat or I shall throw you off!"

Bill Leslie stepped forward and he put himself between the two men. "Tom, get your gear. Don't get yourself into more trouble." Bill was all muscle and he used his strength to move the Petty Officer towards the stern.

Magee thought about continuing and then he shook himself free and strode astern, "Good riddance. I hate this ship. This is a bloody death trap!"

He had said the wrong thing. He had insulted their ship. Any sympathy his crew mates might have had evaporated in that instant. There was an uncomfortable silence on the whole ship until the Petty Officer emerged with his sea bag and cap. He did not look at anyone, nor did he salute. That in itself was a mistake for there were destroyers and frigates in the harbour and all saw his actions. Few captains would take him on. Insubordination could not be tolerated.

Alan put his own hat on and jacket, "Take over Middy. I had better get this sorted out. Be ready to leave at noon. Get some fuel in her." He saw me and gave an apologetic smile, "Sorry about this Tom. You should be back at camp resting not listening to two sailors squabbling like a pair of cockerels!"

Midshipman Higgins was as shocked as the rest of us. However, he didn't deserve the attention of my men too, "Sergeant Poulson and Sergeant Barker, we have a couple of hours." I took out the bundle of money I always took when we were abroad. "Go and buy the lads a pint. They have earned it."

Their eyes lit up. Gordy said, "What about you sir? Aren't you joining us?"

"I don't want to cramp your style. Besides I have a report to write for Major Fleming. If I write it now it will save me a job later on."

They went below to get the others. Midshipman Higgins said, "Use the Captain's cabin, sir, he won't be needing it for a while."

"Thanks Middy."

It was quiet and peaceful in the cabin and the act of writing and thinking helped to calm me. It had all been going so well and now we had problems which we could not have foreseen. I finished it by eleven and went on deck. As I emerged I heard the bosun's pipe and the shout, "Up Spirits!"

There were smiles on all the faces as every man lined up for his ration. When they had it in their mugs and the barrel put away they raised their mugs and said, "The King!" None of them downed the fiery liquor. They sipped and savoured it. I walked to the stern to look out to sea. Bill Leslie joined me. He had a second mug. "Here y'are sir. Taff won't need his ration today and he owes you a leg. He wouldn't mind."

"Thanks Bill. Cheers. Here's to the boat."

"Aye sir, here's to her ladyship!" We both sipped it. Rum was an acquired taste. From the way Bill smacked his lips he had the taste. I suppose I was getting it. "I was wrong, sir."

"Wrong Bill?"

"About Tom Magee. I thought the captain had misjudged him but he was dead right and I was wrong. The Engineer knew his business but he didn't take the job seriously. He did just enough and no more. The old Chief, now, he spent every waking hour with the engines. He knew them inside out. Before we went anywhere he stripped them down and put them back together. You lads nearly died because of him." He shook his head and took out his tobacco pouch. "And what he said about the ship!" He had a drop of rum left in his mug and he carefully dripped it on to the bar of tobacco.

I handed him mine. "Here you are Bill. Every little helps."

He grinned, "You ought to try a pipe sir. It would suit you."

"Dad has one. I enjoy the smell of pipe tobacco but once you start you can't stop. I have enough vices already."

He laughed, "If you ask me, sir, your worst vice is putting yourself at risk too often. This war will last a bit longer than the last one. Don't burn yourself out."

It was a sobering thought. We had been at war for four years now and barely set foot in Europe. When would we reclaim what the Germans had taken?

Part 2

Sicily

Chapter 12

SBA Johnson had accompanied the ambulance to the hospital and it was him we had to wait for before we heard anything. It was good news. They had caught Davis' leg in time and he had been given a new wonder drug called penicillin. The bullet had gone straight through Smith's leg and he would be back sooner than we thought.

Alan was the opposite of his SBA and he came back with a face like thunder. He said nothing save the orders necessary to get us to sea. We all gave him a wide berth. My men, in contrast with the ship's crew, were happy. The three hours in Valetta's bars drinking with Commando money had been an unexpected bonus. They had had neither the time nor the money to become legless but they were full of bonhomie. I was happier when we saw the secluded cove hove into view. Things always looked rosier when we were back in our cove. There we were cocooned from senior officers and protocol. Alan was silent on the journey back. I did not know if he had been reprimanded or not. I decided to let things calm down before I broached the subject. Hugo had been kept informed through the radio. He knew why we were delayed but nothing of the dramatic scenes in Valetta harbour.

The two sergeants had also been shopping in Valetta's market and we had some fresh goat. I have no idea how they got hold of it but they were resourceful. Two years earlier and it would have been impossible to get hold of any meat but now things were easier on the small island fortress. "We'll get this sorted." Gordy nodded to Bill Leslie. "Tell your lads they are invited! There is more than enough for us all." He glanced at the stern-faced Lieutenant Jorgenson. "If it is alright with the skipper."

Alan smiled, "Of course, Sergeant and I may join you too!"

I nodded, "I will see you later then."

Once ashore I filled Hugo in on the events aboard the ship. The last thing we needed was an inadvertent comment to set off the fiery lieutenant. "Thanks for telling me. I would probably have put my big foot in it otherwise! First reports are that the raid was a total success. Those three Hurricanes pursued the 109s all the way back to Sicily and they passed over the road. They reckon it is totally blocked. The Herman Goering Division can't get to the British beaches without a hundred-mile detour."

"And I have travelled those roads. There is no chance of that. Good, I didn't relish having to go back." Hugo threw me a funny look. "What?"

"Sorry about this Tom but Major Fleming is so pleased with you that he wants the section to go in the night before the invasion and cause trouble behind the enemy lines."

"You are joking?" He shook his head. "But it will warn them that something is up!"

He spoke conspiratorially, "Major Fleming does not like the Yanks. He is trying to score points. Your recent raid means that the Herman Goering Division will attack Patton's Americans and not the British. By having your section fighting behind the lines he hopes he will guarantee success. The British objectives will be achieved quickly."

"At the cost of my men's lives."

"I think he relies on your skill, Tom. You have fewer losses than any other troop."

"Are you saying that if I lost more men he might not send us on so many operations?"

"Listen to yourself, Tom. You couldn't do that even if you wanted to, could you?"

"He has me over a barrel."

"It looks like it."

"And when is the invasion?"

"The 10th of July. You will go in on the 9th."

"And that means we will be short of three men and Alan will be short of a Chief Engineer."

Hugo had no more words of solace and he just shrugged. "You just keep, keeping on."

"And that is cold comfort." I was aware that I had snapped at him. "Sorry, Hugo. It isn't your fault. You are just the messenger."

He laughed, "Listen, if a tongue lashing from you is the only wound I suffer in this war, I will live with that."

I decided not to mention our next operation to Alan. He had enough on his mind as it was. He brought over some red wine he had bought in Valetta. As we washed down the goat stew he raised his mug. "Here's to the promotion I won't be getting!"

"How do you know?"

"That snake, Magee, put in a complaint about me. Lucky for me enough others saw his insubordination but the Admiral was not happy that dirty naval linen was washed in public. He left me in no doubt that I have dropped down to the bottom of the pecking order."

"We will soon be back in Blighty. I can't see them keeping us here too much longer."

"Why not?"

"Well the whole point of using a captured E-Boat is that it deceives the enemy but they have seen too much of us for that to be effective."

He gave me a knowing look, "And you want to be back in Blighty, I take it?" I nodded, "A girl?"

"Don't be daft! When would I have time to meet a girl? No it is just that the skills we have are more suited to France and the Low Countries than Sicily." What he would make of the new operation I did not know.

We made it a good party. The next day, when heads had cleared I summoned my sergeants. "Come on. Let's go to the *'Lady'* We need to talk to the liuetenant."

"What about sir?"

"You will find out." I turned to Hugo. "Lieutenant Ferguson. I think we will need you too." My three sergeants were bursting to know the reason for our visit. I did not enlighten them.

Alan was in a better frame of mind. I suspected that it would not last long. "Ah welcome." He frowned. "This looks ominous. I didn't drop my trousers last night did I?"

Polly smiled, "Not that we saw sir!"

"I asked them to come, Alan. When we got back yesterday Hugo here gave me the news that Major Fleming has another operation for us. We are going to land on the beachhead the day before the invasion. We have to cause mayhem behind the enemy lines."

"What? Is there no rest for us? My boat is shot to hell and back."

Hugo smiled, "You have a few holes Lieutenant Jorgenson. I know that there is nothing mechanically wrong with your boat."

"And that is where you are wrong. Didn't Tom tell you that we broke down and that is why he has two wounded men? Until I get a chief engineer and a repair to my engines then we are going nowhere!"

He sounded like a petulant child and Hugo burst his balloon quickly. "There is always '*Dragonfly*'. Major Fleming would happily use her. He doesn't care that she is unarmed. She is back from Greece and in Valetta."

"Alan, resign yourself to this. We are going in."

"You won't be alone, you know. The 1st Airborne Brigade are dropping too." I know Hugo was being positive but Alan was not in the mood.

"Well I hope someone has told them about the terrain or they could be in for some serious casualties." I shook my head. There was little point in feeling sorry for ourselves. "The 9th of July is not far off. We need a detailed plan and maps not to mention photographs."

Hugo nodded, "I will get on to our lord and master immediately. I think I can guarantee that he will expedite everything."

"Oh good! That fills me with joy!"

My sergeants laughed. Gordy stubbed out his cigarette, "You know what they say, *'if you can't take a joke...'*"

"*Then you shouldn't have joined*! I know, Gordy. Right Hugo, go and find out what we need. You three get the men reorganised into three sections. Find someone who can take over from Doc. I am afraid we will all be chiefs and no Indians!"

"Right sir. Leave it to us."

When they had gone I said, "Alan, snap out of this. We are fighting a war here. We are not prima donnas. We have a job to do and we have to get on with it. We don't get to pick and choose. We are a good team and we are leading the finest soldiers and sailors. I don't want the next generation to say that we let them down because we were too wrapped up in ourselves." I wondered if I had gone too far for his eyes narrowed and he began to breathe heavily. Then he relaxed.

"God, you are right. The trouble is I served with the Chief so long..." he waved a hand. "Right, back to work. I will have this boat ship shape in four days. I will get on the blower to the Admiral and demand a decent Chief Engineer!" He smiled and spread his hands, "What is the worst he can do to me?"

"He could always court martial you but I don't think he will."

I hurried ashore. Although we were in the dark until our targets came through there were still many things we could do. The best way to cause mayhem was to blow things up. Although we had no new maps and photographs we had the old ones and I hurried to my hut to get them. I took them out on to the beach. It was a lovely day and I could spread them out and weigh them down with rocks. We knew where the British were going to land: between Syracuse and Noto. There was a single railway line and a pair of roads. They would be good targets. I went to Hugo's hut, he was speaking with Valetta, and I borrowed his magnifying glass.

The fact that airborne troops were going in was a good thing but they were subject to the winds and the weather. We, landing from the sea, were not. I could guarantee that we would make it ashore but I was not certain that the Airborne Brigade would. Whatever target Major Fleming came up with I would pick either the railway line or the two roads. As I recalled the roads and the railway passed over a gorge. That would be a tempting target. I spent three hours analysing every inch of the material we had. I realised that this could be done. We knew the coast, or at least, part of it and we knew that our ship could get us in. Our lack of numbers was the only problem which I could see.

Hugo hurried from his hut to see me. "The generals and the planners have allocated the bridge at Ponte Grande to the Airborne Brigade. We are to attack the railway line and the road bridge which is a mile inland from Arenella. It looks like they need the roads and bridges running inland holding. That is why they are using paratroopers but the coast road and railway needs cutting"

I grabbed one of the maps I had been looking at, "I have just spotted this. It is a good target!"

"Except that there are houses and people between the sea and the bridge."

I grinned, "And when we escaped last time I saw Arabs in the towns. We go disguised in bisht. If we have to move in daylight we go in disguise. There are only nine of us. Besides it is a rocky island and there are places to hide. We can pull this off."

It did not take as much planning as some of our other operations. We had landed close by already. We knew that they would have machine gun posts and barbed wire at the strong points but we also knew that small groups of men could just slip through the back alleys and streets. If we dressed as Arabs then it might make us blend into the scenery. Hugo went to Marsalaforn to get the extra bisht. My own had been damaged and repaired in the past. It had a patina of age which cannot be manufactured. It looked like it had been well used because it had been.

My sergeants acted like quartermasters. They gathered all the timers and explosives which we would need. We would need Thompsons this time. We had to defend ourselves until the infantry and the tanks arrived. Once the road and railway bridge had been blown we could move through the hinterland making a nuisance of ourselves. Consequently we would take as many grenades as we could carry.

Alan had a much better attitude. He set to repairing his ship with a great energy. When the Admiral finally sent over an engineer the whole crew were relieved. The engines needed a complete overhaul before the *'Lady'* went to war. Albert Hanley was, like Sandy, an old sea dog who had been brought out of retirement. He had worked on the old Great War destroyers. He knew small ships but, more importantly, he knew engines.

When Alan took him below decks to show him the huge German engines he was not put out in the least. "An engine is an engine, Lieutenant Jorgenson." He had added, "Leave me and these lads alone with them for a couple of days and they will sing!"

Alan came over to see me when the Yorkshire man fiddled with the engines. "He is a proper engineer, Tom. There is grease and oil beneath his fingernails. He reminds me of the old Chief."

I knew that a great deal of this was in Alan's mind but it was important that he liked the Engineer. Perhaps if he had liked Magee then things might have turned out different.

The Oerlikon was given a new guard and we had three new gunners. Taff was still in hospital. He would return to his beloved gun but we had three new ratings. They were keen to be in the war and excited to be with a unit that had the reputation we did. The days flew by. By July the 8th we were ready and Major Fleming made a personal visit to ostensibly wish us well but, in reality, to make sure we understood what we were going to do.

"Your last operation was a huge success. The General was more than delighted with what you achieved. The Germans and

Italians have had to devote valuable resources to repairing a road. They have neglected the beaches. Our subterfuge has worked. They have shifted many soldiers to Greece. They think we will invade there!"

He had come by motor launch from Valetta and as he stood to leave he said, "Lieutenant Harsker, if you would care to walk me back to my launch." He leaned in to me and I was almost overpowered by the smell of smoke which permeated his uniform. "I wanted a word alone. I am well aware of your part in the success of these operations. As I said I am still working towards a promotion for you but be careful of your association with Lieutenant Jorgenson. He has incurred the wrath of the Admiral. You might be as well to distance yourself from him. We always have *'Dragonfly'* that we can use."

"I am quite happy to be working with Lieutenant Jorgenson and as for the Admiral well we all know that senior officers often don't know their arse from their elbow don't we sir?"

He was such an arrogant man that he failed to hear the insult. He shrugged, "I was just giving a word to the wise but I believe there are great deeds within you, Lieutenant Harsker and under my guidance you shall achieve them."

After he had gone I felt like having a shower to cleanse myself. He thought himself a puppet master controlling me. I did what I did for Britain and not the little Major.

Alan asked, "What was all that about?"

"He warned me that you were trouble." I shook my head and laughed, "As if I didn't know that already! Come on everything is ready for tomorrow let's enjoy a bottle of wine eh. I suddenly feel like drinking."

The plan was to leave on the afternoon of the 9th and arrive off the coast just before ten. That gave us the night to get through the defences to the railway line. We would lay up during the day and then blow the bridge at three a.m. That was supposed to be about the time the Airborne Division would be landing. We would then have two hours before the landing craft began to land their men. On paper it sounded easy but none of us were under any illusions. If something could go wrong it would do. We were Commandos and we would adapt.

Once Alan had dropped us off he would return to Malta. We would only get off the island if the invasion was successful. We had no radio with us and no means of asking for help. I had no doubt that the invasion would succeed but I had contingency plans if not. We had seen enough fishing boats to know we could steal one and Malta was less than fifty miles away.

We left well after dark and both the skies and the sea were stormy. There was a strong wind blowing from the north west. As we blacked up in the mess Sergeant Poulson said, "I wouldn't like to be parachuting in weather like this."

"Lieutenant Ferguson said that they have some gliders this time. Perhaps that will make life easier." Even as I said it I was not convinced. Gliders were subject to the wind. Dad and I always preferred to have an engine in front of us! The motion of the E-Boat was more violent than we were used to. It was a wild and stormy night. For once I would be glad to get ashore.

"Well this might keep the Eyeties heads down! They don't like the wet do they sir?"

Scouse shared the view of most British soldiers that the Italians weren't good soldiers. I knew that was true in Abyssinia and North Africa but the men we would be fighting would be defending their own country. That might make all the difference. We would be landing at a rocky and deserted headland which overlooked the beach at Arenella. We had found a narrow valley which followed a stream. It would add a mile to our journey but we would be hidden and we would be able to lie up just half a mile from the bridge with open fields before us. The tricky part would be the landing.

Tosh came down to the mess. "Captain says we are ten minutes out sir."

"Right, Tosh, we'll be up directly." I slung the Bergen on my back and grabbed my Thompson. We would don the bisht during the day; if they were needed. We would wear oilskins and they would help disguise us in the rain. The storm meant that there would be no one around. Even the sentries would take shelter. We would rely on the weather to help us slip through their lines. The deck was pitching and slicking with seawater. The three dinghies were already inflated and the two crew who would paddle each of them were waiting looking like drowned rats already. My men all went to their allocated boat and I slipped up to the bridge.

"How is it Alan?"

"Rough as. I am afraid it might be a wet landing."

"I don't mind a soaking so long as we land unseen."

"I think that the weather will be our ally." He nodded to the skies. "I don't think the glider pilots will think so." He shrugged. "The weather might have eased by tomorrow night. Best get to your dinghy. I can see the shore. Good luck and I shall see you back in the cove. I will get some wine in to celebrate."

We shook hands and I went back to the stern. The coast looked dark and foreboding. The headland rose to our left and Alan took us as close to the shore as he could. He held the engines against the swell and began to turn us. The *'Lady'* would give the dinghies some protection from the sea. The sailors threw the dinghies into the sea and slipped over. The two held them against the side while we climbed down. There were spare paddles and once we were aboard we paddled like mad the forty yards to the beach. We avoided the rocks to our left but once we landed they would become our friend. As soon as we felt the sand under the bow we jumped out. There was no time for goodbyes.

I crouched in the wet sand as I scanned the land to our right. I saw, on the beach, barbed wire. It blocked the easy route to the river valley. The land to the north looked quiet. I raised my hand and led my line of men to the headland which lay to our left. We could get around the wire. The stones were slick with rainwater and we moved carefully. We had plenty of time and a careless step was unnecessary. We only had to go a hundred yards and I saw the gurgle of water which marked the stream. It was swollen by rainwater. I headed towards it. Now that we were off the rocks it became much easier going although the ground was not as firm as it might have been twenty-four hours earlier.

There were trees running along the tiny valley and they gave us some protection from the rain and the wind. I led knowing that I need not turn around. We had plenty of time and we moved slowly. Sergeant Poulson was bringing up the rear. After a mile I saw the road ahead. We would pass under the bridge. We had identified this as a secondary target. We paused to take shelter beneath it and to examine the structure. I pointed to Lance Sergeant Hay. He nodded. This was his bridge. We moved on. Soon we would need to find somewhere to lie up for the other bridge, the main target, was three quarters of a mile ahead.

I smelled lemons on the wind and I stopped. The aerial photographs had shown a lemon orchard to the south of the valley. It also marked the place where we could cut across fields to the railway bridge. I looked around. This was as good a place as any to camp. I waved my hand in a circle. The sign for make camp. We all had a job to do. I took off my Bergen and dropped it to the ground. I tapped Scouse on the shoulder and I waded across the shallow stream with Fletcher in close attendance. We clambered up the other side and emerged into an open field. I had no idea what the crops were but I knew where we were.

I dared not risk a light to read the compass. I estimated the angle from the valley and set off. We would follow our own footsteps back. If the rain continued through the night then they would be washed away, eventually. The arable field led to another lemon grove and we moved through the aromatic fruit trees. The wild wind wafted the smell and then dissipated it. I suddenly stopped. There was a tiny road which lay ahead. I had seen it in the photographs but could not tell if it was metalled or not. It was. Once we crossed it I knew we were close to our main target.

The olive trees were closer together than the lemon trees had been. I took that as a good thing. We would have more shelter. I heard in the distance the sound of an engine. I hurried forward to the edge of the olive grove and I lay down. A car with dimmed headlights showed me where the road bridge was and I heard the train as it approached. It must have left Syracuse station and was building up speed. It was going quite quickly when it passed us.

The soot and smoke were somewhat dispersed by the rain. I saw that it was a goods train but I could not see what it carried. When it had passed we ran to the railway line. It was single track and we would be safe for some time.

Scouse knew what to do as well as I did. He went to one side while I went to the other. It was a stone bridge and there were gaps in the mortar. The bridge would come down and would block the line. A charge on the line itself would guarantee that no one would use it. Once we were satisfied we crossed the line and explored the area on the other side of the bridge. A hundred and fifty yards from the bridge was a farm. It was not big but it was a consideration.

I tapped Scouse on the shoulder and we retraced our steps. The rain had abated a little by the time we reached the camp. My men had rigged camouflage nets and made crude shelters from branches and undergrowth. We had brought flasks and Sergeant Poulson handed me a mug of hot sweet tea. It tasted like nectar.

"Gather round." They huddled close to me. "The bridge is just a couple of hundred yards away. We have to cross a road but it is very small. The bridge can be blown by two teams. Bill you and your team can go back to the road we just passed."

"Sir!"

"When you have set your charges then you join us at the railway bridge. We will head down the side road and make our way to Syracuse. That is a major target. A Commando Brigade will be going in there. Happy?"

"Sir!"

"Right, it is now four a.m. Team one on sentry duty. Two hours on, four hours off."

We had one scare in the middle of the afternoon. It was the sound of the truck on the road to the south. We had heard vehicles using the road for it was a busy one but this one stopped. I was on duty with my team. I left Sergeant Poulson and Private Fletcher on watch and I walked down the middle of the stream. The rain had stopped but the small rivulet was still swollen by the rains. The wind still howled. I hoped that I could make a silent approach.

After a hundred yards I moved across to the bank. It was slippery. Forty yards from the bridge I stopped sheltered by a couple of large trees. I saw an Italian truck and soldiers were swarming all over the bridge. They began to walk up the stream towards me. I knew that the rain would have washed away tracks that we had made but I worried that they might investigate the whole length of the valley. I remained frozen knowing that with my blackened face I would be hard to see, unless I moved.

The two Italians stopped just twenty feet from my position. They took out their cigarettes and lit them up. I had no idea what they were saying but from their laughter I assumed it was nothing to do with us. They had barely had two puffs when a stentorian voice from the bridge made them discard their butts and hurry back to the bridge. After ten more minutes of searching they left. Perhaps this was a weekly routine, I did not know. However a nagging thought that ran around my brain was that they were on to us. There were Italian sympathisers on Malta. Perhaps someone had wind of our raid.

I made my way back to the camp. I waved away the questioning looks. I did not want my men to be jumpy. I kept the information to myself; at least for a while.

We were all up and ready to go before dusk. The rain and the wind had returned with a vengeance. The glider pilots would have an almost impossible job. I shook that from my mind. We had our job to do. We ate and prepared ourselves. Bill Hay and his team would be the first to leave. They would begin to mine the bridge at ten. The timers we had used recently had proved to be very efficient but Bill would use four timers on four charges. The odds on all four timers failing were long ones. I took Bill to one side. "I saw the Italians checking the bridge. I didn't see any sentries there last night but just be ready in case they have some tonight."

"Right sir. We'll join you as soon as they are set."

Bill left at nine to allow plenty of time to check out the bridge. We left at nine thirty. It was less than half an hour to our target but, like Lance Sergeant Hay I wanted as much time as possible to scout out the target. As I packed my Bergen I realised that we had not needed our Arab clothes. It was better to be prepared than to need something you didn't have. I led the way with Scouse behind. We knew the route. We were much earlier than we had been the previous day and we heard a train as it thundered towards Syracuse. That would be a consideration. We would need to be aware of trains heading down the line. The small road was empty and we crossed it quickly. Once close to the bridge we waited in the olive grove.

My patience was rewarded when I saw the tell-tale glow of a cigarette end. They had put sentries on the bridge. I guessed now that there was an informant in Valctta. I took off my Bergen and fitted the silencer to my Colt. I pointed to my team and made the sign for kill. They dropped their bags and took out their weapons. Scouse had no silencer but he was deadly with a knife. The Sergeant had his silenced Colt. I pointed to Gordy and tapped my shoulder. He nodded, he was in command should anything go wrong.

The three of us moved along the woods using them as cover. I tapped Scouse on the shoulder and made the sign for follow. I got Poulson's attention and I pointed across the railway line. We would make a two-pronged attack. I watched the bridge. I could see the white face of a sentry and the glow from his cigarette. I could see that he was cupping the end from the wind. It was almost as though he was signalling. I waited. He finished and threw it on to the line. When he turned I hurried from the cover of the trees towards the railway line. I scrambled down the bank, grateful that my rubber soled shoes would make no noise on the rails. We walked on the sleepers and the rails. The ballast could move and make a noise.

We hid under the bridge and listened. I knew that Sergeant Poulson would make his way to the far side of the bridge and watch from the shelter of the trees. The range was only forty feet and he was an excellent shot. I heard two voices above me and they were speaking Italian. I heard their boots as they walked to the far side of the bridge. That was our chance to move and we clambered up the bank. It was slippery from the rain. We reached the top and I peered over. There was a small truck parked on the side of the road leading to the farm. It had not been there the night before.

I drew my Colt and slowly peered around the edge of the bridge. I saw that there were three Italian sentries. Two were in the middle, huddled together under their oilskins while the third was looking north, to Syracuse. I pointed to the one by himself and Scouse nodded. He silently scurried across the road. I crouched and began to move down the side of the bridge. I could have risked a shot for the two of them were just thirty yards away but we had to get all three. I did not glance to my left. Scouse would get there when he got there. He had fast feet and fast hands. I was just twenty yards away when one of them turned. He had seen Scouse. I used the two-handed position and fired two shots. I swivelled to my left but Scouse was already there. He was kneeling on the Italian sentry and he ripped his dagger across the sentry's throat. I turned back to shoot the other one but he was already dead. Sergeant Poulson had shot him.

"Carry them back to their truck and then booby trap the doors."

"Sir!"

"Well done Fletcher. That was fast."

It took two trips to put the bodies in the truck and ten more minutes to rig booby traps on the doors. While the Sergeant and I finished the booby traps Scouse ran to fetch the others. We had lost almost forty-five minutes.

By the time we reached the bridge Gordy and Beaumont were already working on the side walls. "Scouse, keep an ear to the rail and listen to the trains. Sergeant Poulson, get the spare charges out."

I went to the ballast and started dragging it from under the rail. I chose a spot some twenty feet from the bridge. The debris from the bridge would cover most of the track. This would add to the damage. Polly came down with the charges. We had learned to bury them and that provided the energy to seriously bend the rails.

We did both rails and then put a smaller charge on the other side of the joint. We had almost finished when Scouse shouted, "Train sir!"

"Hide!"

It was still pitch black and the rain and wind were blowing, I doubted that anyone would be scanning the embankments for saboteurs. We lay face down in the earth and the train thundered past us belching smoke and soot. As soon as it had passed we were on our feet. We had to move quickly as I wanted to be well away from the bridge when it blew. I put the timer in the explosive and began to cover it. I had set it for an hour. I hoped that, perhaps, we might even hit a train. Polly and I had the easier job and we had finished before Gordy and his team.

I ran back to the road and peered down it. There was no traffic but that was to be expected. It was the middle of the night. Then I heard the sound of anti-aircraft guns. It was the airborne brigade. It meant that we could blow the bridge any time we chose. In the distance I heard the sound of air raid sirens. I guessed it was from Syracuse. The wind kept taking the noise away and then bringing it closer. I feared for the Airborne Division. This was neither the night nor the terrain to be landing in a glider. I saw a movement in the woods. I dropped to one knee and levelled my gun. To my relief it was Bill Hay.

"Everything go according to plan?"

"They were three sentries there but we disposed of them."

I would have to report this to Major Fleming when we returned. Our two targets had been identified. If ours had been then what of the paratroopers?

"Get ready to move out when the others return. We will have to be on our toes. Word of this got out. They may be expecting us." He nodded. "You set the bombs for forty-five minutes from now?"

"Thereabouts."

I pointed to the skies. "Now that the Airborne are here it doesn't really matter." The rest of the section ran up. "I just said to Bill that I think the Italians know that we are here so let's be careful. They don't know that I decided to go down this road and hit them there. It might give us back the edge."

Scouse nodded, "I'm game, sir."

Gordy shook his head, "Gawd help us!"

I smiled. I liked Scouse's enthusiasm. "Scouse, you take point. Polly, tail end Charlie!"

He laughed, "So what is new?"

Chapter 13

It was getting close to the time of the first explosions. We ran. If anyone was out at this time in such a deserted area it would be bad luck. We reached the road just before three. There was no one in sight. We could hear, in the distance, sporadic gunfire. That would be the Airborne Brigade. What worried me was that there was not more firing. I could picture the landing craft, out there in the dark. They would land just before dawn to catch the defenders unawares. Our bombs should discomfit and disrupt them even more.

"Gordy, take your section on the other side of the road; to the east. Bill you go to the other side of the road, to the west. We will cover this section. Have grenades ready,"

"Sir!"

Suddenly there was an explosion to the west of us. I saw Bill's face light up. That was his bomb. The road to the west was now, probably, cut. "Bill you better stay on this side, go to the east."

He cheerfully shouted, "Yes sir!"

The explosions from the north were louder. There were six of them. We must have set the timers close to each other for there was a ripple effect. The sky lit up."Find some cover and wait!"

I had my Thompson ready. We needed no subtlety now. We would need maximum firepower. Eerily there was silence for five minutes or so and then I heard, in the distance, the sound of trucks and, I detected, tanks. The enemy were mobilising. I settled down in the drainage ditch and took out two hand grenades. I knew the manuals said to take on liquid and to eat but I was too much on edge for that. We were alone, behind enemy lines and, any moment now, all hell could break loose. The coast was but a mile away; however, thanks to the nature of the ground we could not see the sea. I just had to hope that the landing craft were on their way in.

At three thirty we heard a couple of dull cracks to the north. Polly chuckled, "I am guessing that they found the booby traps!"

"And now they will start to look for us. You and Scouse go back up the lane and set an ambush."

"Sir. Right, Fletcher; on me!"

I was now alone. That suited me. If we had to retreat then I wanted it to be towards the twentieth division who would be coming ashore. I heard vehicles from the east. They had sent someone to investigate the sudden explosion. I cocked the Thompson. Within an hour it would be light but now it was that half light murk which suited us and not the enemy. The engine noises drew closer and I saw the two faint pinpricks of dipped headlights. I took a bead on the middle of the road and then placed a grenade within my eye line.

It was Lance Sergeant Hay and his section who opened fire first. They waited until the Italian truck was less than thirty yards away and then they let rip. Someone must have thrown a grenade for I heard a shout of, "Grenade!" I buried my face. Then there was a dull crump and I saw the truck lurch towards the drainage ditch. It was covered in flames. Bullets hurtled in our direction but we were in the ditch and we were camouflaged. They were firing blind.

A second vehicle, a half track tried to get around the burning truck on the seaward side. Gordy and his men were prepared and I heard the three of them shout, "Grenade!"

I buried my head in the ditch and the three Mills bombs went off almost together. The concussion washed over me and shrapnel filled the air. I heard screams and shouts from the east. I could hear nothing but I peered over the top and saw the half track was on its side. Gordy half stood and sprayed the survivors with his Tommy gun before ducking back down. The moans stopped and it went quiet. Then I heard the sound of a naval bombardment as the invasion fleet pounded the beaches. Hugo had assured me that it would not last long but I felt vulnerable as we were just a mile from where their shells were landing. I hoped they were accurate.

"Take shelter until they stop!"

"Too bloody right I will!"

The shelling lasted twenty minutes and then all went quiet. The silence did not last long for, behind us, to the north, I heard the distinctive sound of Thompsons. Sergeant Poulson and Private Fletcher were under fire. "Bill! I am going to see how Polly is!"

"Right sir."

I left the safety of my ditch and ran, couching up the lane. I saw the muzzle flashes from a fire fight. My two men did not return fire. They would not give away their position. I guessed they had gone to ground. I lay in the middle of the road, a hundred yards from Bill and the others. I watched for muzzle flashes. I saw four and rifles barked. I raised my Thompson and gave a burst. I was rewarded with a few cries. As I had expected fire was returned but they aimed at the muzzle flash and the bullets pinged off the road ten yards ahead of me. The sky was lighter now, despite the clouds, the wind and the rain. I discerned shadows. I knew that Poulson and Fletcher would be off to the side. I rolled on to my back, took a pin from a grenade and then threw it down the lane. I heard it land and rattle towards the Italians. I turned back on to my stomach and covered my head with my hands. The shrapnel tore through the Italians and then over my head. I grabbed my Thomson and fired the rest of the magazine before rolling to the ditch at the side of me.

I heard moaning up the lane and saw two soldiers writhing. Then Scouse stood up and fired his Colt at the two of them. My two men returned to me. "That's it sir. The last grenade and burst took them all out."

I looked at my watch. It was five a.m. and the soldiers would be coming ashore. "Let's get back to the road. It could get interesting now. Our lads will be jumpy when they land and could shoot at us!"

The intersection was quiet but I could hear, from the south, and east, the sound of gunfire and explosions. I took the opportunity to reorganize. "I want a perimeter around this intersection. We will have more men trying to reinforce those at the beach. They have two ways of doing that, from Syracuse or from the north. Gordy, reposition your men to face Syracuse and the beach. Hay, you take your men to the left of this road and face north. Sergeant Poulson we will link the two." As my men took up their new positions and used their Bergens to make a protective wall I said, "Scouse, come with me."

I led him to the burnt out half track. The Italian crew were spread around in various poses of death. "Find any grenades we can." It was a grisly task but we eventually managed to find six. "Take them up the lane and make some booby traps.

He sprinted off and I dropped down behind my Bergen. Sergeant Poulson had made a parapet of our three bags. The colour would help to camouflage our position whilst the contents would give us protection from shrapnel. Behind us I heard the sound of tanks. That was a good sign. The tanks sounded like Shermans. We had seen no anti tank defences. I began to become hopeful.

Scouse ran back and threw himself behind the barricade of Bergens. "Done sir. I trip wired the sides of the woods too. I used my last Mills bombs."

I handed him two of my last four and put the last pair close to hand. I had barely done so when I heard the sound of men running down the lane. Their boots rang off the surface. "Heads down! I hissed. Suddenly there were four or five explosions and screams. Then another couple of explosions. Some shouted a command in Italian and there was a rattle of rapid rifle fire. The branches at the top of the trees were shredded. "Don't return fire yet! Wait until you see them." Dawn had finally broken. It would be a grey day but we had visibility.

I risked a peek over the top of the Bergens. I had a clear view for about fifty yards and I saw a huddle of bodies in the road. I heard more orders shouted and then shadows began to move through the trees, avoiding the road. It was a pity we had not found more grenades. We could have made them even warier of the woods. I saw a pair of grenades rise up and drop thirty yards from us. We dropped our heads. The Bergens protected us from the concussion. The air above our head was filled with deadly pieces of flying metal. Then I heard an Italian order. This time I worked out that it must have been, '*Charge!*' for I heard a cheer. I lifted my head and placed my Thompson on the top of my bag. The Italians were forty yards away. A line of them advanced quickly.

"Fire!"

I dropped the officer and sergeant with the first burst. Six Thompsons sent out a hundred and twenty bullets in less than ten seconds. We reloaded and fired blind. The smoke from the weapons made our view hazy. When I had emptied my second magazine I took my grenade and hurled it high in the air. As I did so a survivor from the attack appeared above me with his rifle raised. He had a bayonet poised to plunge into me. I grabbed my Bergen and rolled back. Two things happened at once. The grenade I had thrown exploded and he lunged at me with the bayonet. The grenade tore into him and the bayonet struck my Bergen. His body tumbled over my head. I replaced my Bergen, drew my Luger and began firing. When the magazine was empty I suddenly realised that there were no more Italian bullets.

"Cease fire!"

I raised my head sand saw that the only Italians ahead of us were dead or dying. Then I heard Gordy. "Sir, they are coming from the beach! Eyeties!"

"Quick lads turn around and support Gordy!"

We jumped up and dived on the other side of the bags. The dead Italian who had tried to kill me now lay before us as an extra barrier. Sergeant Poulson nodded at him, "That bugger almost had you sir."

"I know. Thank God for the Bergen." The holes in the Bergen told me that its life as a bag was finished but it had saved my life.

Italians, in ones and twos appeared from the direction of the beach. Gordy's section opened fire. Others began to spread in our direction. We fired. Then they tried to go around us but Bill Hay's team fired. An officer shouted to his men to take cover. They hid in the drainage ditch Gordy had recently occupied. They began to fire blindly at us.

"Hold your fire lads. Let me try something." The rifle fire diminished and I shouted, "Italians, surrender! We have you surrounded. We have machine guns!"

I had no idea if they understood me but I had to take the chance. There was silence and then a hurried conversation in Italian. A voice said in broken English, "My Capitano says for you to surrender!"

"The whole British Army is about to catch up with you. They are tanks you can hear. You have lost. There is no point in throwing your lives away is there?"

There were heated voices as my words were translated. Polly said, "Do you think they will surrender sir?"

The sound of the tanks was much louder now. "I think they will."

Sure enough the Italian voice said, "We will surrender. Do not shoot."

"Stand with your hands in the air. Lads, cover them." I risked standing. I held the Thompson in my hand. The Italians stood. There were thirty odd of them. "Gordy, take your men and disarm them. Bill cover the right flank."

I saw a young Italian whose mouth opened. "There are nine of you? You said you had us surrounded!"

Sergeant Poulson held up the Thompson. "Son, these would have slaughtered you! The Lieutenant did you a favour. He saved your lives!"

Some of the Italians began to lower their arms. "Tell your men to keep their hands up. Our lads from the beach might be a little trigger happy!"

The young soldier nodded and rattled out some Italian. The hands were all raised. I walked through the Italians. I saw that the Captain glowered at me as I passed him. I found myself beyond the prisoners. I could see a Sherman. It was fifty yards away and its gun traversed towards me. I raised my hand. A huddle of men ran towards me. I saw that they had the Commando flash on their shoulders. A captain strode towards me with a grin on his face. "You chaps did well to get ahead of us!"

I smiled, "That's because we have been here for two days. "I held out my hand, "Lieutenant Bill Harsker, Number Four Commando!"

Captain Jack Durrant, Number Two Commando. I heard we had men on the island but I thought they were all paratroopers."

"We were sent to blow up a few bridges." I pointed to the west. "The bridge over the culvert yonder is blown and the one over the railway to the north is too. There is a road into Syracuse here and if you follow that lane you will find another road next to the railway."

The Captain shook his head, "You fight a different war to us, Lieutenant."

"No, sir. It's the same war we just fight it differently. With your permission we will try and get a ride back to Malta." I turned, "Right chaps. Let's leave the war to these blokes eh?"

Scouse handed me my Bergen. The Captain shook his head when he saw the damage. "It looks like you have a tale to tell. Look me up when you get the chance."

"I will do, sir."

We began to trudge towards the beach head. There were other units advancing now. I saw us getting strange looks. We were dirty, bedraggled and we all still wore the remnants of the boot polish on our faces. When we reached the beach I saw that it was being organised. There were medics and doctors treating the wounded. There looked to be mercifully few of the latter. The landing craft were still unloading men. They marched ashore looking for an enemy who had retreated. All up and down the coast we could hear the sound of gunfire but in this section it was quiet.

We sat on the sand. "Well sir, how do we get home?"

I pointed to the wounded, "They will transfer them to landing craft. Malta is the closest place. We will hitch a ride with them."

Just then Fred Emerson said, "Sir, is that an E-Boat? It looks like *'Lady Luck'* to me."

Four hundred yards offshore, sailing amongst the destroyers and cruisers was our ship. "Scouse, get on the signal lamp and ask them for a lift eh? We might as well go home in comfort."

Scouse took out the lamp he always carried. It had survived. I am not certain how. As he unwrapped it from the bisht he shook his head, "Good job we didn't have to wear these sir. It looks like the mice have been at it."

The voluminous garment had indeed done its job. It had protected the lamp and taken much of the shrapnel from the grenades. I peered out to sea and when I saw the flash from the E-Boat, I knew they had seen us. "Right lads, to the waterline. I guess we are going to get a little wet!"

Gordy chuckled, "We are alive sir and, with respect, we haven't been dry since we landed on this island. I thought Sicily was supposed to be a hot place."

"So did I."

Fred Emerson snorted, "Scarborough in winter is drier than this." We began to wade into the sea. "Mind the water is a damn sight warmer here. You freeze your bits off in the North Sea, even in summer!"

The E-Boat negotiated its way through the landing craft. Bill Leslie turned it and Tosh threw down the net, "All aboard the Sky Lark. Trips around the bay, sixpence a head!"

As we climbed up Polly said, "Just so long as there is some Stoker's Cocoa then I am happy."

Lieutenant Alan Jorgenson shouted, "That is the least we could. Well done lads!"

Polly led them down to the mess deck and I joined Alan on the bridge. "What brings you here?"

"We couldn't sit at home. I thought you might need a lift and the chaps were all keen. Weren't you Petty Officer Leslie?"

Bill grinned, "All part of the service sir. Good to have you back and intact." He skilfully navigated the smaller boats and, as we passed the last destroyer he opened her up.

I looked astern, "It went better than Dieppe."

Alan pointed to starboard and shook his head, "Not for some." I saw the half sunken fuselage of a glider and bodies floating in the sea. "The Airborne part didn't go according to plan. We heard that half of the aeroplanes never even reached Sicily. The weather conditions were too bad."

The sweet taste of success which had been in my mouth now turned sour. I had assumed that it had all gone well. The handful of casualties on the beach had suggested that but, as we headed back to Malta the drifting bodies told a different story.

Chapter 14

Over the next few days, as the advance across Sicily gathered momentum, the full story of the invasion began to emerge. Our success had been offset by the appalling losses experienced by the Airborne Brigade. It was a disaster for that newest of arms. Many of their aircraft and men had crashed into the sea. The terrain had taken their toll so that objectives which were planned to be held by five hundred men had had to make do with twenty or thirty. If we thought that we would gain any respite we were wrong. Hugo gave us the news just four days after our return.

"Our little holiday camp is about to move. Major Fleming wants us on Sicily. It seems they want to use the momentum of Sicily to springboard into Italy and Major Fleming thinks that we are needed again." He shook his head, "Sorry."

"Not your fault and besides when I think of all those paratroopers who didn't even get to see action but died on the way there it puts our job into perspective. Any news on our wounded?"

"Davis has been invalided back to Britain. He will need months to recover. The other two will be back before we leave."

"And when will that be?"

"The end of the week. We are going to be based in Augusta, north of Syracuse. It has just been taken by the Marine Commandos." He tapped the map. "It looks like your attack on the road paid dividends. The Americans have been attacked by the Herman Goering Division. They couldn't reach the British lines. It explains why Monty had such great initial success.

"It is a pity they couldn't have blocked the other road too. We are on the same side you know."

"I know, Tom, but we can only fight our own war. We can't do it all. No matter how much you want to."

He was right. That evening as Alan and I enjoyed a glass of whisky after dinner I said, "At least nothing went wrong this time. All the obstacles we met were predictable and the men dealt with them well."

"You have a good team. It has balance." He waved an airy hand towards the E-Boat. "We have it now too. As soon as Taff returns we will be complete." I gathered from that he was happy with his new engineering officer.

Hugo hurried over. I guessed he had been speaking with the galloping Major. He had that look in his eye. "The Americans have made huge advances. They have cut off the German fifteenth Panzer Division."

I shook my head. Major Fleming was so predictable. "And he wants us to go to Augusta early."

Hugo looked amazed, "How did you know?"

"Major Fleming has two wars: one against the Axis and the other against the Americans. The little man wants to score points over our allies. You can tell him that I am not leaving until my men are returned."

"But..."

"What is the worst he can do, Hugo? Have a hissy fit? There is nothing we can do yet anyway. We have nine men. There are two Commando Brigades on the island already. I suspect our Major is looking ahead to Italy. We have time."

Major Fleming was not happy but I knew that he was now operating outside the remit of his role. He asked to speak to me on the radio. His voice was reasonable and he tried to be persuasive. "Look, Tom, you have done very well up to now. Why spoil your record? All I want you to do is to set up your base on Sicily."

"And I am happy to do so, sir but I want all of my men with me. With Davis back in England we are short handed as it is.

I have no medic and no corporal. When they return then we will go. Setting up a new base is easy, sir... if you have the right men."

"Leave it with me. I shall get them for you."

He was as good as his word. The two of them arrived back on the sixteenth of July. Neither looked to be fully healed but both were glad to be back with us. "We heard about the Sicily invasion and knew you would be involved. How did it go sir?"

"It went well Corporal and we had no casualties. Unless, of course, you count a Bergen and a bisht!"

It was a shame to have to dismantle our former home. I would miss the cove. Outside of Mrs Bailey's it was the best digs we had ever had. We loaded the E-Boat and headed north. The waters between Malta and Sicily were now safe. As we headed across I asked Hugo about the new role for the Commandos. Number Two Commando had come ashore like regular infantry. I had seen them with Bren guns and Lee Enfields. "Has there been a change in directive?"

"I think so. There are still a dozen or so units like ours but most, like your old Brigade, are now seen as elite infantry who spearhead invasions." He pointed to the Colt on my hip. "They use regular infantry weapons. They retain the dagger but almost everything else, except for the flash, is the same as ordinary infantry. They even wear tin lids."

We had been away from England since the end of 1942 and so much had changed. My letters from home were about the war in general and neither Daddy nor Reg Dean were writers. I had no idea what changes had been made. No wonder Gordy and the others had jumped at this chance for independent action.

Although there had been fighting in Augusta it had escaped serious damage. The harbour was filled with vessels of all shapes and sizes. Alan shook his head, "This won't do! I want our privacy! We will find out what is happening and then scuttle off and find somewhere secluded again."

The three of us left the Petty Officers and Sergeants in charge while we went to find Major Fleming and report to him. As I left I said, "If you find anything we may use..."

Sergeant Poulson tapped the side of his nose, "No problem sir!"

Hugo had a piece of paper with the address of the headquarters. It was on the Piazza Duomo. Thankfully it was easy to find. The Union flags were a giveaway. The red caps looked at us dubiously as we approached. I did not blame them. It was months since I had had a haircut and my beard needed a trim. My uniform was due for replacement. I think if it had just been Alan and I then they would have refused us entry. Hugo looked a little tidier and when we gave the name of Major Fleming we were admitted.

In Gibraltar and Valetta he had had a tiny cubbyhole for his headquarters. Here he had a large office with a fine view of the Piazza. The rewards of his success. The sentry at the door said, "If you could just wait sir, Major General Laycock is with the Colonel. He won't be long."

I looked at Hugo who shrugged.

The door opened and an aide came out. He looked shocked at our appearance. He was followed by the Major General who commanded Number Two Commando. He frowned when he saw me. We stood to attention. Then he glanced at my ribbons and he smiled. "I am guessing that you must be Bill Harsker's son."

"Yes sir."

"My chaps who landed at Syracuse were impressed by you. Captain Durrant could not speak highly enough about your action. They say you saved a brigade from being badly mauled by your quick thinking. In the best spirit of the service; well done, Captain."

I shook my head, "I am just a lieutenant, sir."

The General turned around, "Didn't you tell him that he had been promoted after the Reggio raid?"

Colonel Fleming said, "We have been busy, sir. I was going to tell him the next time I saw him."

"Make sure you do." He leaned forward, "Get your hair cut eh? Trim the beard. You look like one of those Long-Range Desert chaps!"

He and his aide strode off. The chain smoking Colonel waved us through. "See, I told you that you would be promoted if you stuck with me."

As I recalled he had said that after the Reggio raid which meant he had already known I had had been promoted and was keeping it from me. I smiled, "The back pay will come in handy, sir. It will be backdated to the date it was awarded won't it?"

"Of course," He waved an irritated hand, "that's just paperwork. Now sit down the three of you. We have much to plan."

He turned to the map which was pinned on the wall. "The General and I were just discussing you and how we can use your section and unit effectively. You are the scalpel where the rest of the Commandos are the bludgeon." He tapped his hand against the Bay of Naples. "Italy! We will roll over this little island in a few weeks but we need to work out how to capture Italy. Now the coast between Amalfi and Agropoli is somewhere I would like you to explore. It is my baby." He tapped his new crown and star. He was now a full colonel. "I am part of the planning for the invasion of Italy. So I want you to find out as much as you can about this coast."

"Wouldn't aerial photographs be of more use sir?"

"No Lieutenant Jorgenson!" I noticed how he emphasised the Lieutenant. "Aerial photographs only tell us so much besides I want you to not only look but do some sabotage while you are there. Your team seems to have a talent for this."

"Won't that tip them off, sir? That we are up to something?"

"I have other units doing the same thing closer to Reggio. But it is the Salerno coast that is our real target!"

Alan and I exchanged looks. Hugo was busy writing things down. The Colonel lit another cigarette and Hugo asked, "What is the time scale for this, sir?"

"You have until the middle of August. Thanks to our rapid advance we have plenty of diesel for the E-Boat. Sadly, we didn't manage to capture any of the boats but there spares for the engines."

Alan's eyes lit up. "Where sir?"

"The E-Boat base," He waved a hand. "Over there on the other side of the harbour. The MTB and Air Rescue boats are using its facilities."

Alan said, "Sir, if you will excuse me then I will pop over before all the good stuff is taken."

Before the Colonel could object he was away like a March hare! "Extraordinary! What a rude man! It is no wonder he didn't get his promotion.

"He should have had a promotion sir, he is a damned good officer and we could not operate without him."

"Really Harsker? You do surprise me. I thought it was he hanging on to your shirt tail. Well... We have more important things to discuss. We have plenty of German and Italian made explosives and timers. I believe they are as good as ours. We want you to use them whenever possible. There is a rift between our allies and we wish to exploit it."

"Sir, do we have flexibility about where we go to first and the order in which we examine the coastal sites?" Hugo had been doing what he did best; thinking.

"Of course but what difference does it make?"

"Well, sir, if the Italians see a pattern to all this they could trap us. We have to use surprise and do the unexpected."

"Good thinking, Lieutenant. Well whatever you think best but I want a daily report from you. None of this swanning off to your little hidey hole. I want a tighter handle on you this time. Understood?"

"Yes sir."

"I need as much detail about this coast as possible. We have a short time to plan and I want the same success we had in Sicily. Now whatever you want just ask! You have proved yourselves to be resourceful and I will help in any way I can."

"There is one thing sir. It has been bothering me since Sicily. The Italians moved units to protect the two targets we had selected. I think there is a spy in Valetta."

He smiled. It was the dead smile of a crocodile, "There was, Captain Harsker, there were three of them. They have been shot. It was another reason for our move. There is just the Lieutenant left from the staff I had in Valetta."

I could not help wondering if we had been the bait to draw out the spies. I would not put it past the wily Colonel.

We spent another hour while he went through the sort of information he needed and the type of sabotage we should engage in. When we left I felt physically sick from the smoke he had blown at us. "Come on Hugo! Let's get a beer."

"Shouldn't we get to the boat?"

I laughed, "If you think that Alan will leave the yard until he has everything he can pinch then you don't know him."

"Perhaps there is so much there that he can't take it all."

"Perhaps." I spied a bar just thirty yards away from the building. "In which case we shall stay here in this Piazza and have a few beers until he sends someone for us."

The beer was cold. That was about all that you could say for it. However it was welcome for it was a hot day and likely to get hotter.

"Well sir, you must be pleased with the promotion."

"Hugo, it is still Tom. You can sir me all you like in front of other units but it doesn't change me. I had no superior thoughts before and I still don't. As far as I am concerned you and Alan are still the same rank. It is a few bob more a week and that is all."

"I thought you would be more excited."

"You mean the slippery slope to senior rank? Looking for the next promotion like the little General there? That isn't for me. I could have stayed in OTC but I joined as a private. I have never sought promotion. If it comes, then it comes."

"I thought that having such a high-ranking father would make you more ambitious."

"You obviously don't know my dad. He is not bothered about such things either. His best friends are still the pilots he served with in the Great War. He knows high ranking officers but they aren't his friends."

We ordered another few beers and a pizza. We had just finished it when Scouse appeared, "Hey up sir! You know how to look after yourself and no mistake. Lieutenant Jorgenson sent me for you. I have a jeep around the corner."

"Where are we off to?"

"The boat. He said as how there was too much stuff to leave so we are using the E-Boat base just like we are supposed to."

I paid the bill and stood, somewhat unsteadily. It had been some time since I had had so many beers in such a short space of time and the sun was hot. We followed Scouse along the blazingly hot streets of Augusta.

"And congratulations sir! The Lieutenant told us about the promotion and we are all made up for yer. You deserve it and that's no error."

"Thanks Fletcher but it won't change me."

"Oh we know that sir but still. I bet your mam and dad will be dead chuffed like."

I smiled, "Dad will be pleased but Mum, well she will worry about me getting into even more danger. Mums are like that."

"Ay, y'are right an all there, sir. Here we are, sir."

I saw that the jeep looked brand new. "Where did you get this Fletcher?"

"It was lying around sir with no one using it. I'll take it back when we have finished with it. It was Freddie what started it. He is a whizz with motors is Freddie Boy!"

Considering he had only just arrived Fletcher seemed confident in the streets of the ancient town. He honked his horn and waved his arms like a resident. He whirled us to a stop close to a building with a wire fence around it. Private Emerson raised the barrier on the gate and we entered the compound. He parked the jeep out of sight in a partly damaged building. He gave me an innocent look, "It'll keep it out of the sun sir and stop it getting too hot."

"I think it is hot enough already, Fletcher!"

When we emerged from the half broken back door I saw that there was a small dock with the E-Boat and four other launches. The *'Lady Luck'* looked deserted. "Where are they Emerson?"

"In the stores, sir. It is like a gold mine in there."

Every sailor and Commando was in there. Alan was shouting orders and organising them. He was like a child in a sweet store. He saw us and waved us over. "I could rebuild *'Lady Luck'* three times with all of this stuff. Hugo, any chance of getting a couple of pongoes to act as guards? We don't want to lose this gear."

"Remember what Colonel Fleming said, Hugo."

"Right, sir, I'll get on to it. Have you set my radio up yet?"

Scouse nodded, "That was the first thing I did, sir. We have a nice little cubby hole for you. Just follow me."

"Well, Tom, what does that bastard want from us this time? Our organs?"

"Pretty much carte blanche to find out all that we can from a thirty mile stretch of coast. Hugo is going to devise a plan. The downside is that the Colonel wants a daily update on what we do and we have to have it all finished by the middle of August."

"Three weeks then."

He led me away from the men who were working under the supervision of Petty Officer Leslie. "The biggest problem is going to be getting there and back. It is the best part of two hundred and fifty miles there and the same back. We have to go through the straits which I am guessing will be heavily protected."

"How long to cruise that distance?"

"Seven hours or eight."

"So we are talking two-day missions."

"If we want to sleep then yes."

"Better make it three days. That means seven missions at the most so we tell him six. I will get Hugo to plan six trips."

"He won't get his daily reports! We daren't use the radio."

I smiled, "He will get a daily report. Hugo is a clever chap. After the first mission we will have an idea what to expect. What the Colonel doesn't know will not hurt us." I shook my head, "That's your trouble, Alan, you don't know how to play people. Use the Colonel's weaknesses against him."

"By the way, do I call you sir? I realise I forgot."

"Don't you start! It is still Tom. Now where do we sleep?"

"There are barracks here. It was a full squadron of E-Boats who were based here. I think we might have run into them. The MTBs have been moved to a better berths so we just share it with Air Sea Rescue. There is bags of room."

"Good, well I had better go and get cleaned up. I will need to find the quarter masters. I need a new uniform. This one makes me look like a beggar."

"And I will get back to Aladdin's cave!"

I found Hugo. He had arranged for some sentries. "I need a new uniform."

"Then we need the paperwork. Quartermasters give nothing away without everything in triplicate. Let's get new uniforms for us all." He flourished a rubber stamp.

"Where did you get this?"

"Colonel Fleming's office. He had two. We only needed one!"

I shook my head, "Hugo I think we are becoming a bad influence on you."

"When I think of the risks you chaps take then filching a rubber stamp seems a harmless enough act." He looked around and saw Fletcher and Emerson. "You two, over here. I have work for you."

Chapter 15

We were heading north. It had not taken Hugo long to plan our raids. We had eliminated Amalfi as a target immediately. A battalion of Commandos could scale those cliffs but no one else. The Colonel, however, overruled us. We were ordered to investigate the mountain passes to Naples. Vietri Sul Mare looked equally daunting from the aerial photographs. Hugo left those elements until later. We were heading for the southern end of Salerno. It was closer to our base and looked easier to attack.

We were forced to leave our base in daylight in order to get to the mainland with some hours of darkness left. It meant we would have to travel back in daylight and that would be even riskier. We had taken out the German uniforms once more. When we had finished our task then we would become a ship of the Kriegsmarine once more. We had also chosen to taken on the task of sabotage at the airfield too. It was a major target and, until the mainland was invaded, then a relatively soft target. They would fear an attack from the air, not from the ground. There was just the one airfield and damage to it could save lives later on.

As we passed Mount Etna and Messina we heard the shelling and gunfire from the west. The Germans and Italians were being forced back to the toe of Italy but the mountainous area around the volcano suited the defenders and we were having to capture the island inch by bloody inch. As we passed Reggio we saw trains heading up the coast again; their smoke and the flames from their boilers marked their passage. They had repaired the damage we had done. Hugo had told us that the damaged rail line had stopped them reinforcing Sicily. The operation had been a success.

Once we passed through the straits unharmed we breathed a sigh of relief. Alan had split his crew into two watches and one was sent below to sleep. My men and I also took the opportunity to rest. It would be a long twenty-four hours. Alan left Midshipman Higgins and Bill Leslie in charge and he went below decks when we did. He paused at the door to his cabin, "You know that this is the trickiest operation, Tom?"

I nodded, "We have to get to Montecorvino Airfield and back. That won't be easy. But on the positive side they won't be expecting us. If we left this until later in the week then we might have a reception committee. It's a risk but a smaller one than it might be."

As I lay down I reflected on Alan's words. The sea was his domain and he feared nothing upon it. He knew his boat was faster than anything else on the water and he could always run. For us it was down to our skill and the courage of my men. Besides the aerial photographs had shown that the end of the runway was just three quarters of a mile from the sea and that it ran east north east to west south west. The end would be the least guarded part and I was confident that we could damage it. The nearby mountains and the heavy anti aircraft had prevented the RAF and USAAF from doing too much damage. It was to be hoped that our small group could. I fell asleep as I always did on such missions: I thought about the operation. I was soon asleep.

I only slept for two hours. When I awoke we were in the Tyrrhenian Sea. It was inky black and we had the radar array up. We had been told that there was a new system becoming available which would not need to be deployed and stored. As soon as we had finished with this task then the E-Boat was scheduled for a refit. I popped my head into the radar shack. "Anything?"

Leading Seaman Symons shook his head, "Just the usual coastal convoys. Mr Higgins has us well out to sea." He pointed to a squiggly line. "That is the coast of Italy sir. That bump is just south of Agropoli. We'll be at the landing site in under two hours sir."

"Thanks. I will wake the lads."

I shook Sergeant Poulson awake, "Right Polly, rise and shine."

He was awake in an instant, "Right sir."

I went to the bridge. Midshipman Higgins shuffled to one side as Tosh handed me a mug of tea and a corned beef sandwich. It was navy style. Thickly cut bread and corned beef and layered with mustard. It brought tears to your eyes. "Thanks Tosh!"

Bill Leslie nodded to the sky, "Going to be another red-hot day, sir."

My mouth was too full to answer and I nodded.

The Midshipman said, "Every day is hot out here." He glanced at the compass, nervously.

Petty Officer Leslie said, "Don't worry sir. We are on course."

"I know Petty Officer but this is an important mission."

I washed the cloying bread from my mouth with the hot sweet tea. "Every operation is important, Middy, and they are all risky. The day that we stop taking them all seriously is the day we die because we will make a mistake."

"Captain Harsker, I have been meaning to ask you, when you are behind the enemy lines do you never worry about being captured or killed?"

"We could all get killed and I have been captured. If you are dead then there is nothing to worry about. If you are captured then at least you are alive and so long as I am alive then I will find a way to escape."

He nodded. Bill Leslie said, "It's almost time to change the watch sir."

"Thanks." He turned, "Tosh, go and give the skipper a shake and then rouse the starboard watch."

I said, "I will go and get ready too." I pointed to the east where we could just make out the coast.

We were only taking three Bergens with us. Hay, Shepherd and Beaumont would all carry the explosives. The rest of us had either our Colts or our Thompsons. The Italians and, we presumed the Germans, had cleared all the houses which lay in the flight path in and out of the airfield. We could land unseen. Gordy would take four men to scout out the beach north of the airfield while the rest of us would sabotage the airfield itself. After our experience at Dieppe the main purpose was to see what the sand was like and to ensure that the beach was not mined. If they had put in concrete obstacles then the invasion would be in trouble.

After we have blacked up I led my men on deck. Alan nodded towards the coast. "We have made good time. Thirty more minutes and you will be ashore. I will get in as close as I can and anchor. It we have to leave I will just cut the cables." His teeth flashed in the dark, "Thanks to the Kriegsmarine we have spares."

The spares meant we had four dinghies now. We could get in and out easier. We crouched at the side as Alan cut the engines a little and we edged in slowly to the beach. The surf was gentle and misleading; it could hide rocks or anything. Alan waved his arm and his men slipped the dinghies over the side. We were practised in this now and we boarded without fuss. Alan had done well. We were less than thirty yards from the beach and were soon ashore.

Sergeant Poulson was ashore first and he located the airfield. Although three quarters of a mile away the windsock and the control tower marked its position. I pointed to Gordy and he and his men headed north. We jogged inland across the narrow beach. We soon found the road. We saw the demolished buildings along the side. They helped us as they gave us cover. Our rubber soled shoes made no sounds on the road. The night was not totally silent. We could hear noise from ahead. The airfield was preparing for the new day. In the distant hangars air crew were readying aircraft. As we neared the fence Polly waved us to the ground. We dived to the side of the road.

I heard German. They were too far away to make out the words but they were sentries patrolling the perimeter. Their voices drew closer and then faded. I rose and waved the men forward.

We soon reached the fence. It was a wire one and had been recently erected. Scouse, Emerson and Corporal Hewitt had their wire cutters out while Sergeant Poulson and I stood guard. The two sentries had moved five hundred yards down the perimeter. Unless they turned around they would not see us. I took in the airfield. The hangars were a hundred yards to our right. We would have to follow the sentries to avoid the open ground. I glanced to my left. I saw no more guards. The three wire cutters snipped through the wire. Ironically the new wire helped us. It cut easier than rusted wire. The three of them worked as a team and cut a large hole in the wire. We just needed to be in.

Once inside I pointed to the runway. Shepherd and Corporal Hewitt ran in that direction. They would damage the middle of the runaway. I was thankful that there was no moon. They would be exposed in the middle of the runaway. The rest of us ran towards the hangar. When the two sentries turned the corner, at the far end of the field, there was a chance that they might see us. I took out my Colt. I would have to be ready if that was the case. As we ran across the grass I saw a large tank. Parked close by were two fuel bowsers. It was too good a target to miss. I tapped Beaumont on the shoulder and pointed to it. Sergeant Poulson nodded and went with him.

I led the other two towards the hangar. We could hear someone singing inside. It was an Italian voice. Then a German shouted to him to shut up. I guessed that the garrison would be German but the mechanics would be Italian. We reached the wall. It was now up to Lance Sergeant Hay. He would have to decide the best place to set off the charges. We wanted maximum damage. I saw him hurry to a pipe which came from the ground and went into the hangar. It was services of some kind. He took off his Bergen. Fred Emerson helped him and I walked along to the end of the hangar.

I saw that the two sentries had stopped their patrol and were heading for the hangar. They must have been due a break for I saw the glow from their cigarettes. I hoped that there was a back door into the hangar. If they were heading for the front then they would have to come past me. I lay on the ground and held my Colt two handed. They were a hundred yards from the end of the hangar. I was willing them to turn right and go into some unseen door but they did not. They kept on coming. I heard them talking. It was the usual complaints about their allies and their superiors. As much as I might have wanted to just incapacitate them I could not take the chance. Six other men's lives depended upon me. I took a bead on the nearest one. They kept coming.

Then Emerson dropped something. It did not make much of a noise but it made a sound. The sentries' heads whipped around. They were just twenty yards from me. I fired four shots two at each. I hit one in the side of the head and the other, as he turned, full in the face. They fell to the ground. The Italian had begun singing again in the hangar and any noise their fall made was masked.

I ran to Bill and made the hurry up sign. He nodded. We were on the clock now. If this was their break then their absence would be noted. Someone would investigate. As I looked east I saw the first glow of dawn. We had not long. Bill finished and stood. I waved them back to the fence. I watched while they ran and then followed. When I reached the fence all of my men were all there. We had barely made it through the wire when I heard a shout. A floodlight illuminated the area next to the hangar.

"Go!"

The klaxon sounded and I saw men rush in from the hangar. More guards appeared and a searchlight mounted on a half track played around the perimeter. It was a matter of time before it spotted the hole. We were a hundred yards from the severed section of wire when I heard the sound of the halftrack approaching the hole.

"Right lads! It is a foot race!" We were lucky that we had little equipment to carry. The road we were on was straight and I caught sight of the sea in the distance. Behind me the half track's machine gunner opened fire. As the half track was bouncing across the broken fence it was an inaccurate burst. It would, however, alert the *'Lady Luck'* to our plight. I stopped and risked a glance back. The half track was two hundred yards away. I took out a grenade, pulled the pin, threw it and ran as hard as I could in the opposite direction. The chances that the grenade would do any damage were slight but, at the speed the half track was approaching it would distract the driver.

I had run so hard that I outran the blast. The beach was now visible. It was less than three hundred yards away. The rest of my men were thirty yards ahead of me. I stopped again. The half track had turned to avoid any more grenades. I began running again but this time I ran to the right and the half-demolished buildings. It was not a second too soon as the machine gun on the half track opened up and shredded the space I had just occupied. I kept to the right and heard the ship's Oerlikon as it duelled with the half track. The cannon shells tore into the engine of the German vehicle. I risked a look over my shoulder and saw smoke coming from the engine but, behind it were more. I had a hundred yards to go and the sun was now rising from the east. There was the first of the explosions from the airfield. I had no idea which one it was although as it did not sound large I suspected it was the one on the airfield. Bullets zipped around me and I dived to the ground as some chipped the remnants of a wall. It was fortunate that I did as the fuel on the airfield exploded and the concussion would have knocked me from my feet. I stayed on the ground, a little stunned, as dust and other debris floated down. A second explosion and a third came almost five seconds later. Then there were more smaller explosions.

"Come on, sir!"

Corporal Hewitt's voice sounded urgent. I staggered to my feet and lurched the last few yards to the beach. My men grabbed me and helped me towards the rubber dinghies. Every gun on the boat was firing. I did not hear too many in return. We paddled out to the boat and climbed up the net to the side. As I rolled on my side I saw that the airfield was ablaze. German vehicles littered the road.

"Hold on!"

The E-Boat spun away from the beach. As I rose I saw that we had no flag flying yet. "Captain Harsker, get your men below. We are about to become German."

I noticed that he was heading north west towards the distant island of Capri. It was a clever ploy. Once he turned south again it would appear that we had come from Naples and, by then we would be flying the German flag and our men wearing German uniforms.

"Right lads, below decks."

Once there I took off my battledress and my khaki trousers. We had the German uniforms we had taken from Sicily. I donned mine. Alan might need a German speaker. I grabbed the cup of tea Tosh handed me and swallowed it down. It was too hot and burned my mouth but I needed the rush of sugar! As I clambered out of the hatch Alan swung the boat on his new course and I had to cling on to the guard rail. I looked up and saw the swastika flying. The boat began to slow as we pretended to be German. I glanced over to the east and saw the cliffs at Amalfi. They were even more intimidating close up. I saw a truck going along the cliff road and it looked tiny.

Dawn had finally broken and Martindale, the lookout, shouted, "Aircraft at three o'clock."

Alan shouted, "Remember we are German. Keep away from the guns. We are just a patrol boat from Sorrento." Our aerial photographs had shown that they had moved a squadron of E-Boats to Sorrento. The RAF had bombed the facility and damaged a couple.

Wacker's voice came from below, "Sir, it's the flight commander. He wants to know who we are?"

"Tell him, Schnellboote 175 from the Augusta flotilla now operating out of Sorrento. Ask what the fuss is all about. Keep your voice calm!"

A few minutes later he said, "They are looking for British Commandos on an MTB. They have asked us to search west. They are heading south."

"Tell him we are glad to cooperate with the Luftwaffe!"

I looked at Alan, "MTB?"

"They didn't get a good look at us and the ones who might have seen us we hit with the cannon. They saw your chaps and put two and two together. A fast boat carrying Commandos sounds like an MTB or a launch." He put the wheel hard over and headed west at top speed. It would delay our return but it would give us a degree of authenticity.

"How far will you head west?"

"We will head for Palermo and approach our base from the west. It will add eighty miles or so to our voyage but we will be safer." He turned to Bill Leslie, "Bill give the captain one of your pipes." He handed me one without question. "Tom, go up forrard and pretend to be smoking a pipe. If their fighters come over us they will take you for someone off duty. Wave if they come over."

"Righto." I went and sat with my back to the Oerlikon. I put the pipe between my teeth. It tasted disgusting. I had no idea how Bill could smoke it. After a while, when no one had flown over, I took it out. Taff was back on his Oerlikon and half an hour later he said, "Ey up, sir. The fighters are back."

I stood and pretended to be cleaning out the pipe. I walked to the fo'c'sle. I heard the sound of the fighter engines from the south and I turned and waved. One of them waggled his wings. I strolled slowly back to the bridge. When I reached it, Alan grinned, "They have asked us to sail as far as Santa Stephano. Apparently, it is still in German hands. They say they saw a pair of MTBs there. They are low on fuel and have asked us to investigate. Suits us."

"Have I finished with this then?" I held up the pipe.

"Of course!"

"Here you are Bill. It has persuaded me never to take up the pipe!"

"Your loss, sir! Very relaxing it is; especially with a pint!"

We passed the German port in the late afternoon. Alan had not wanted to attract attention by going too fast. We would not reach Augusta until after dark. As soon as we had passed the German front line we switched flags and uniforms. We became a

Royal Navy vessel once more. At the same time Wacker sent a coded message to Hugo to tell him that the operation had been a success and that we were on our way home.

My men had taken advantage of the last part of the voyage to sleep. The exception was Gordy. After I had finished writing up the first draft of my report I went to the galley and found him making a pot of tea. "Tea sir?"

"Thanks. How did it go up the beach Gordy?" We went into the mess and found two unoccupied seats.

"It will be a piece of cake. There are neither mines nor wire. It is shallow and the road runs along it. The high ground is so far inland that they would not be able to use machine guns effectively. If our job is to find a site to invade then we can stay home. We have found it!"

"The trouble is we need a wide front. We will have to come back but I don't think we will have to tackle such a big target."

He laughed, "It didn't half go up! Was that the fuel dump?"

"I guess so. We obviously didn't manage to damage the airfield enough although they were just fighters who took off. Perhaps larger aircraft will struggle to use it." He nodded. "Did your lads do well?"

"They all did. This is a good team, sir. We have been in plenty before but I can't think of a weak link here. Just so long as the brass leave us alone and don't interfere."

After a little more chit chat about times past and friends lost we both fell asleep. A Commando can sleep on a clothes line. We were awoken by the E-Boat gently bumping into the harbour wall. "Right lads, grab your gear. We have the morning off but we may be needed again tomorrow afternoon. Give any unexpended explosives to Lance Sergeant Hay. Well done!"

"Thank you, sir."

Hugo had a beaming smile on his face as Alan and I walked down the gangplank. "Major Fleming just sent the photographs over! Spectacular! But I am afraid he wants a report tonight, before you go to bed."

I smiled and flourished my report. "It is done but I can tell you what you wanted to know in a couple of sentences. Amalfi is a no go. Only Commandos could get up those cliffs and into the high country. The land south of Salerno is perfect for invasion. You could go tomorrow and almost walk in."

He nodded and Alan said, "But of course Major Bloody Fleming would rather risk the boat and Tom's men to check every inch of it."

"Sorry."

"How about this then Hugo. We go the day after tomorrow and examine the southern side." I had a sudden idea, "Could you get me a camera, a good one and some film?"

"Of course. The Germans left some of their Leica cameras around and we can get the film, Why?"

"They say a photograph is worth a thousand words. Aeroplanes take photographs from a great height. We can do it from ground level, the way the soldiers will see it. We can sail down the coast, flying the German flag and photograph the whole of it. We don't need to go ashore at all."

"What about the sabotage?"

"We have already taken out the best target. The only other place to attack is a port and we found out at Dieppe how stupid that was." I could see he was not convinced. "Listen, get me the camera and the film. I will persuade Major Fleming!"

"Right. You know I will do anything to help. I will take this directly to the Major and get you your camera."

Chapter 16

I slept late. I didn't get up until seven. I felt every bump and blow I had suffered the day before. I wandered to the small bar which was opposite the dock and bought myself a coffee and a pastry. It was indulgent but it was such a lovely morning I thought I would forget the war for a while. The Italian who served me was effusively friendly. I had not known what to expect. I had little Italian but I used the bits I knew like the numbers, please and thank you. It turned out that, like most waiters, his English was good.

"You English are gentlemen. You try to speak our language. I like that. The Germans... they are pigs and they leave no tip! Tell me signior, will they be back?"

"I doubt it but you never know."

"I think we are all a little unhappy with Il Duce. He has made us dance to the Austrian Corporal's tune!"

Another customer came in and I was left to enjoy my warm, sweet pastry and my strong, black coffee. I felt as though the war did not exist. If I had had an English newspaper then the world would have been perfect.

I saw Hugo arrive with his arms full. I waved the waiter over and paid the bill. I left him the tip he had hinted at. It never hurt to have the locals on your side. I followed Hugo into the yard. He turned, "Ah there you are. I have your camera and Major Fleming thinks it is a good idea. However, he still wants the whole of the coastline examining."

I took the camera from him and held it up. "And we will do!" I held out my hand, "Film?"

He handed me a bag. "There are ten rolls. A couple are fast films. You can take photographs in poor light."

I went to the waterside and found a seat. It was a Leica IIIa. I had heard of this one. It was a good camera and had a fast shutter speed of one thousandth of a second as well as a one second speed. It had interchangeable lens although the one with which it was fitted, the 50mm, was more than adequate. The letters D.R.P, Deutsches Reichspatent, showed that it was a genuine Leica and not a copy. I looked through the shutter. The camera felt solid in my hands and it was compact. It would be perfect. After clicking and winding on a couple of times I went indoors to load the film in a shaded area. It would be trial and error but I enjoyed photography and this time it might save the lives of some of my men. If I could take a photograph from ground level it would give a better view of what the soldiers might expect.

We left the following afternoon. There had been a breakthrough on the northern side of the island and we thought we might be able to sneak through the straits while the Germans rushed reinforcements to fight the Americans. Monty and the 8th Army were still stuck around Etna. The British had the harder terrain. Despite all of Major Fleming's efforts things had evened themselves out. Once again we sailed without a flag. We had explosives but I was not certain that we would need them. We were going to photograph Agropoli when we passed it and then land at Paestum. The aerial photographs of Paestum showed no military targets although there was a military presence and so I hoped it might be a cakewalk. The machine guns and the explosives were in case it was not.

We managed to get through the straits unseen. It was daylight but we flew no flags and we did not hurry. This time we were not going as far north and had more time. We kept to the centre of the straits and saw no other vessels. We had heard that, thanks to allied bombers, the Italians and Germans were using the cover of darkness to resupply Sicily. We ran up the Swastika once we passed the straits. The sun was dipping in the west as we passed Agropoli. It was perfect for taking photographs. The light was from behind me. Alan took us in as close as he dared and I clicked away. Agropoli was defended. I saw 88mm and machine guns. There was an old citadel and a harbour. Both would be fiercely defended. Wacker had to fend off questions from the shore as we passed but he and Alan had concocted a story of engine failure near to Sicily and the need to get to Naples. We were believed, apparently. The slow speed of the E-Boat seemed to confirm some damage.

My men and I went below decks, as darkness fell, to prepare. As it became night we gained speed and headed to Paestum. The aerial photographs had suggested empty beaches with scrubland close behind. They were accurate. We slowed so that the engines were barely turning over and listened. There was no sign of life close to us. We stopped and lowered the dinghies. This time the seamen who rowed us in would stay with the dinghies; we wanted a swift departure. They were armed with our spare Tommy guns. I was using my Colt as was Polly and Gordy.

The first thing we did was to examine the beach. It was not mined. We headed across the narrow belt of sand towards the scrubland and found wire but it was not barbed. I think it was there to deter people from using the beach. We moved in a long line across the scrubland. We examined the ground but it was solid. It had not been mined either. As we neared its edge we heard vehicles using the coast road. I waved my hand and we dropped to the ground. Crawling forward we saw houses and shops ahead. We had arrived at a busy part of the town. This was no military target. There were people enjoying the warm summer evening. I saw a busy cafe bar with both German and Italian soldiers fraternising with pretty young girls.

I waved my men to the left and we moved parallel to the road. After a while the shops and bars ceased and it became more residential. These were substantial houses. I guessed that, before the war, they had been summer homes for the rich of Rome. Now they were shuttered or boarded. Then I saw an Italian flag and some armed sentries. It was a hotel, I could see the name had been painted out, and now it was a military building of some description. We had seen hotels from the air but the flag and the sentries had been hidden from view. I began to wonder if we might glean more valuable information here than by marching up and down the beach.

I crept forward to examine it from the safety of the shoreline. There were four Italian sentries: two at the main entrance and one at each end. They had rifles and were wearing soft hats. We waited a while and watched as a car pulled up and some senior officers arrived. This was a military target. I waved Scouse over, "Get back to the boat. Have the Lieutenant bring it down here. We may need a quick pick up."

He nodded and slipped away in the dark. The sound of the sea behind us would hide any noise we might make. I waved over my sergeants. "I want to take out these sentries. Let's see if we can capture some information; perhaps even a couple of senior officers."

They nodded. They were never surprised.

"Just incapacitate the sentries. Gordy take your section and come in from the rear. Polly you take the left. Bill, you come with me on the right."

We crept forward. Gordy and his men moved down the beach towards the quieter section we had just passed. Polly waited until the sentries' backs were turned and led his men across the quiet road. I was about to move when a bus came down the road from the south.

"When it passes rise and we will cross in its wake." I gambled that the sentries would either look, briefly, at the bus or be so disinterested that they ignored it completely. It was an old bus and seemed to take forever to reach us. As soon as the cab passed me I stood and walked towards the road. By the time it had passed I was striding across the centre of the road. I had my sap in my hand. Things happened really quickly. I pointed to the sentry at the end who was staring down the street. I hurried to the main entrance for I had seen that the sentry closest to Sergeant Poulson was down.

As I neared the entrance one of the sentries saw Sergeant Poulson and his men creeping along the wall. He said something and his companion turned. As they unslung their rifles I ran behind the first sentry and hit the back of his head. The other made the mistake of turning and Sergeant Poulson smacked him one too. I made the sign for them to tie them up and I tapped Hewitt on the shoulder. I took out my Colt and stepped into the lobby of the former hotel.

It was a grand entrance with a staircase ahead of me and a reception desk to my right. It looked like they were using the desk to give information to newly arrived officers. The recently arrived officers were waiting and talking. Corporal Hewitt cocked his Thomson. These were soldiers in front of us and they recognised the sound. The ones closest to us turned. I had my Colt levelled at them.

"Hands up!" I spoke in German.

There was a hubbub of noise as they all spoke. Next to the desk was a bust of Mussolini. I fired one shot. The bust cracked and shattered. The effect was instantaneous. Their hands went up. I heard the noise behind me of the four unconscious sentries being dropped to the ground and my men following me into the hall. I saw the resignation on the faces of some of the officers. One, a colonel by the insignia on his collar, said, in English, "You cannot get away with this!"

I ignored him. "Lance Sergeant Hay, tie up the officers. I want to take the six most senior back with us. Sergeant Poulson, upstairs and clear the rooms there. Check the luggage and the bags for papers. Just bring back anything that you can find. Corporal Hewitt keep an eye on them. Crowe, follow me."

Just then there was a noise from the service door under the stairs. Gordy and his men prodded forward the men who had been working in the kitchens. A couple had been knocked about and had bloody noses. Gordy knew how to get a man's attention.

We moved behind the desk. There was a private standing there and, hiding at his feet, a second man, a sergeant, with a pistol. I tut-tutted and gestured for him to rise. As he did so I took the Italian pistol and pocketed it. I gestured for them to join the others. There was a door behind the desk and I opened it. Obviously, during peacetime, it had been the manager's office. Now it looked to be the admin office of the headquarters. There were filing cabinets. "Hewitt grab all the papers that you can see. Don't try to read them; just grab them. I will find a bag for you."

I went out of a second door. It led to a toilet and hanging from the back of the door were two army rucksacks. I found nothing else of interest and I emptied the two bags. I rejoined the Corporal who had a large pile of papers. "Put them in here. Join me out front when you are done."

When I rejoined my men in the former lobby I saw that there were about fifteen enlisted men and twelve officers. Six stood apart, watched by the eagle-eyed Lance Sergeant Hay. I saw that the colonel who had spoken English was with them. I also spied a General. He had tried to hide himself when I had addressed them all. I made sure I was close to the Colonel when I said, "Lance Sergeant, have your section take these to the beach. If they give you any trouble then wound them, quietly!"

"Yes sir." Bill was a clever chap and he put his Colt in the back of the General while saying to the Colonel. "Right gentlemen, move!"

I heard a murmur of disapproval from the other officers who were seated on the ground. I fired a shot close to the legs of a truculent looking Major. Splinters of wood spattered into his legs. "Silence or we will shoot. If you behave then you will all live and be able to tell your children and grandchildren this tale."

Some must have understood English for I saw a couple whisper to their fellows.

Sergeant Poulson came down the stairs behind four men whose hands were in the air. There were also a couple of women. I guessed, from their clothes, that they were local prostitutes. They did not look put out or worried by the guns.

"Tie them up."

One of the women said, "Us too, Tommy?"

I smiled, "I fear I must. We don't want you going for help do we but my men will be gentle."

She nodded, "Have you any nylons for us?"

"Had we known we would have seen two such beauties then we would but I fear we have not. Next time, perhaps."

She nodded, "Of course." They sat, not on the floor with the soldiers, but on the comfortable sofa. I admired her style.

Hewitt came out. I saw that he was struggling with the two heavy rucksacks. "Emerson, grab one of those bags and help Doc. You two, head back to the beach. We will be along soon."

I waited until the women had been tied up. "Sergeant Barker, move the sofa and the ladies away from the door, if you please." Gordy had no idea why but he and Smith moved it. They rejoined me. "Outside, I will join you in a moment." When I was alone I said slowly and carefully. "I know that you will get out of the bonds in a short time. I should warn you that I intend to booby trap the front doors from the outside. It is why I have moved the ladies away from the blast area. Do not try to leave by the front door. The back doors will be safer." Only a couple of those before me seemed to understand the words. I said to the woman, "Could you translate please."

She nodded and did so then she said, "You are a gentleman, Englishman."

"I try!"

Once outside I slammed the doors shut and rammed a rifle between the ornate handles to hold it shut. "Back to the boat." I had no intention of using a booby trap. It was simply not worth it. We did not have far to go to get to the boat.

"Won't they try to escape, sir?"

"Yes but by then we should have gone."

We hurried across the road, back over the scrub to the beach. I saw the reassuring shape of the E-Boat. Corporal Hewitt, Emerson and Scouse stood on guard. "They took the Eyeties and the rucksacks on board sir. We are waiting for the dinghies to come back for us."

We were still in enemy territory and we made a half circle facing the land. It all seemed quiet. I had delayed the escape of those in the former hotel so that they would not know which direction we had taken. I had thought of booby traps but this was a residential area. I did not want innocent civilians dying. I heard the splash of paddles behind me. It was the dinghies.

As we boarded the E-Boat I looked at my watch. It was just after midnight. We had finished earlier than we had expected. I went to the bridge, "Home James and don't spare the horses!"

"Course for home, Midshipman Higgins. Petty Officer Leslie, take it easy until we are away from the shore. Let's not advertise our presence eh."

They both said, "Sir!"

He turned to me, "You have been busy, Tom."

"It was too good an opportunity to miss. The papers might be useless but I think they will be gold. Intelligence will love the opportunity to grill senior officers and it saves us hanging around."

"If we go at full speed then we can be home by six. We might get through this without anyone noticing us."

"Where did you put our prisoners?"

"I am afraid you and your lads have lost your mess."

"It is a nice night. We will sleep on the deck. I will go and arrange the sentry rota." I descended to the mess. It was crowded. There was a lot of noise, Shut up!"

Gordy banged on the table to silence the Italians. "You heard the Captain!"

"Sergeant Poulson, I want two men on this door and one on the galley door. Use Thompsons. I want one sergeant on duty too. Two hours on. We will sleep on the deck. It is quite pleasant up there."

"Right sir. Hay, Emerson, Smith. You have the first watch. Wake me in two hours."

"Right Sarge."

By the time I reached the deck we were heading south and going at almost full speed. It was not economical but it was necessary. I rejoined Alan. "I think we may be pursued." He cocked his head to the side, "We have a General and two bags full of papers. They won't sit and twiddle their thumbs."

"Right, Middy, have the guns crews closed up and get the cook to whistle up some cocoa and sandwiches. We may not have time later on."

"Sir!"

"Let's hope they are slow to start the chase. At least we are safe from aerial attack."

"What time is dawn?"

"At this time of year about five, maybe a little later, but we will be visible from four or so. Still we are faster than anything that they have in the water." He smiled at me, "You have done well. Are you going to get your head down too?"

"No. I thought I would keep my men company. Besides, until we get home this is not a successful operation."

"Cheerful blighter!"

As I left Bill Leslie said, "Just like my mum; she always said, *'don't count your chickens'*!" He paused, "Or in this case Eyetie generals!"

I went down to the mess. The Italians looked despondent. The one who could speak English looked up at me. "This is an E-Boat."

"Is it?" I said innocently. "I hadn't noticed."

"We thought there was something wrong when the airfield was raided the other day and we could not find you." He gave a sly smile, "The Germans suspect, you know! They will catch you."

"Well you had better hope it is on our next trip otherwise you will meet the same fate as us!"

The realisation of his position hit him. The general asked him something and he gave a long answer. The general waved a fist at me. Fred Emerson went towards the General and said, "Now then, we'll have none of that. You touch the Captain and I will give you a good hiding!"

"It's all right Emerson. I can take a few empty threats. I'll go and make a brew."

Jimmy Smith said, "But sir, you are an officer!"

"And I can make a pot of tea. I joined up as a private, Smith. I have just been lucky."

The Colonel said, as I passed, "It is true you have been promoted from the ranks?"

"I'm afraid so, Colonel. Awful isn't it?" I think he was offended that he been captured by a common soldier. I made a pot of tea and brought out enough cups for the Italians too.

Emerson and Smith came over and took the teapot, milk and cups from me. "Lieutenant Jorgenson asked if you could go on deck sir. We'll dole out the tea."

"What's up, Alan?"

"Wacker has picked up a lot of radio traffic and Paestum was mentioned. And about ten minutes since Symons spotted a line of boats moving quickly north west of Messina."

"E-Boats?"

"That is my guess."

I told him what the Colonel had told me. "If the Germans are suspicious they may remember that we went along the north coast of Sicily to get home."

"That makes sense but I had not planned on going that way home this time. I was going to risk the straits again anyway. We should just make it before dawn. We have plenty of go-go juice. Let's ride our luck."

"When do we hit the straits?"

"In an hour or so. I'll give you a shout if we hear anything else."

As I entered the mess I was handed a cup of tea.

"If it is a bit stewed, sir, I'll make a fresh pot."

"No thanks Emerson. This tastes like Sergeant Major Dean tea. It reminds me of home!"

The Italians were asleep by the time we changed the watch. I filled Sergeant Poulson in on what had transpired. He nodded. "You should get some sleep, sir."

"No, I am fine."

"Scouse go and make a brew. See if there is any corned dog left."

Private Crowe said, "I have something even better! I forgot about these. Hang on a mo' Scouse."

He disappeared and then returned with his Bergen. He drew a long salami from it. "The Sarge and me found these in the kitchen. He has a bagful too. Do you fry them?"

I held one next to the light. "No, you eat them raw. Stick some marge on the bread and cut a slice of it. You'll enjoy it."

He grinned, "Too right I will. My dad always said, *'stolen sweets taste best'.*

"True. You father was quoting Colley Cibber an eighteenth-century writer and philosopher."

"I don't think so sir, my dad worked down a mine in Nottinghamshire!"

The three of them enjoyed the new taste. The Italians were all asleep or else I would have offered them some too. I found myself, despite my words, dozing. Tosh came into the mess, "Sir, Captain wants you. Trouble."

"Sergeant best wake the lands and have them stand too. Leave Emerson and Fletcher watching these prisoners."

When I got on deck there was a great deal of action. I hurried to the bridge. Alan pointed to the darkness of the north east. "Symons spotted three E-Boats they are following us." I nodded. We could outrun three E-Boats that far astern. There was obviously something else. "And he saw two more up ahead. They were not moving."

"It is a trap."

"Indeed, a trap and we have walked or rather sailed right into it. German radar must be getting better. They must have spotted us and sent the three E-Boats to cut off our escape. The three behind us stop us going around the north and these two will blast us as we pass."

"What's your plan?"

"Use our speed, our extra firepower and your men to blast our way through them. If we can get by these two we have a chance. It is less than seventy miles from Messina to our base. I have had Wacker signal Hugo and ask for help. There is little point in maintaining radio silence now."

"I'll go and sort out my lads."

I went to the mess and grabbed my Thomson. "You two lads sit tight. There are five E-Boats after us. If you have any bother with these six then use your sap." I handed Scouse my Colt with the silencer. "Threaten them with this if you have to."

"Right sir."

I went on deck. It was deceiving for the night looked peaceful and the seas empty. I glanced in the radar shack and saw the dots as they flashed up. They had us surrounded. Whichever way we moved at least two of them could cut off our retreat. They were the same boat as us and two to one were not good odds in such a fight. I had no doubt that there would be shore batteries waiting to join in. The Thompsons and our grenades might be the only difference.

I went to the bridge. "It looks hopeless."

Alan smiled, he had lit a cheroot, "Not as bad as the Germans think. We know that every E-Boat is an enemy. In the dark they may hesitate until they are certain we are the enemy. And we have more speed. If we get into a race we can out run them. *'Nils Desperandum'*; that was my old school motto."

"Sir, the ones from the north are closing with us."

"How about those to the south?"

"Still waiting."

"How far between the boats?"

"I think it is about two boat lengths."

Alan smacked the bridge. "Then we have them. Petty Officer Leslie, I intend to sail between them. Try to get as close to the one on the starboard side as you can."

"Right sir." Bill shouted to Symons, "Keep giving us distances to the starboard boat."

"Right Coxswain."

"Have you got someone who can use the grenade launcher?"

"I do indeed."

"When we get close to the starboard E-Boat the bigger weapons will be useless. Use grenades and charges. If we get rid of that one we have a chance."

I found my men. They were waiting towards the stern. "Crowe get the new grenade launcher. You are our secret weapon. The rest of you get as many charges and grenades as you can. We are going to close with one E-Boat and try to destroy it. We have to hit them and hit them hard!"

"Right sir!"

My men were always happiest when they had something to do. They enjoyed fighting against ridiculous odds. The fact that there were five against one did not bother them in the least.

"A mile, Coxswain! Ten degrees more to starboard."

"Thanks Sparks!"

"Gun crews hold your fire until I give the order."

Crowe had returned with the grenade launcher. It was a new version and I hoped that it would be more robust than the one which had jammed in Sicily. Crowe, I want you to launch one as soon as you see them. They will not see a flash and have no idea where we are firing from. Even a close hit will scare them witless. Shepherd you load for him. It will save time."

"Half a mile and you are bob on, Coxswain! Any closer and you would take a lick of paint off him."

Alan shouted, "How far away are the ones to the north?"

"Less than a mile and closing."

"Right, stand by. Full speed."

Crowe shouted, "I can see him!" He pulled the trigger and the grenade flew into the dark. Ken Shepherd had one reloaded. The German began to fire but the lack of muzzle flashes meant he was firing blind. The second boat began to fire too. They were wasting ammunition. There was an explosion and a water splash. It was short. The second one rose as bullets from the second German hit our hull. It was like a game of dare.

Crowe got lucky and the second grenade exploded in the air over the E-Boat. The crew of the forward gun were struck by shrapnel. We could all see the boat now for there was a fire.

Crowe firing another grenade at a lower trajectory. It exploded in front of the bridge and completed the work of the first one.

"All guns fire!"

The ships who were following us could not fire for fear of hitting their own and the E-Boat to port could only use small arms. They were doing damage. I heard cries for the SBA.

My men opened fire at the rapidly approaching E-Boat. I emptied my magazine and began to throw grenades. There was little chance to aim. We just threw them as far as we could. Symons was right. We almost stuck the bow of the E-Boat. I saw Gordy cheekily roll two primed grenades over the canted bow. And then we had passed it. The Pom-Pom at the rear had an unobstructed view of the E-Boat and he sent shell after shell into the hull. The grenades rippled and exploded along the length of the E-Boat. Perhaps one had found its way below decks. All I knew was that the whole E-Boat seemed to rise out of the water in one enormous explosion. The force of the blast hit us. As it settled in the water I knew it was sinking.

It was then the shells and the bullets from the other E-Boats began to hit us. I heard cries and shouts from the Pom-Pom crew as they were hit. Our stern was also struck as well as the side of the hull.

Alan shouted, "Taff! Get your men from the Oerlikon and fire the Pom-Pom."

"Crowe keep sending the grenades aft. We might get lucky!"

Beaumont suddenly disappeared below decks. He returned a few minutes later. He had his Bergen. He quickly emptied it and lined it with his oil skin. Then he put in some explosives with a timer. He closed the Bergen and tied a long piece of parachute cord to it. He went to the stern and threw it over. I saw him look at his watch and then release it. He dived to the deck.

I saw two E-Boats. They were less than a hundred yards behind us and their shells were pounding the stern. Sooner or later they would get lucky and hit the rudder or the engine room and then we were dead. Suddenly Beaumont's improvised charge went off. It explode between the two E-Boats. One of them swerved alarmingly to starboard while the other began to slow.

Gordy shouted, "Well done that man! Get the rest of the Bergens up. We can all try that!"

There were now just three E-Boats pursuing us and they were almost keeping pace. Bill was having to veer from side to side to make us a hard target. Our superior speed merely kept us the same distance. We were not out pacing them as we would in a straight race. More shells and bullets riddled the air and smashed into the *'Lady Luck'*. I took the chance to go to the bridge. I saw Alan slumped next to Bill Leslie.

"Corporal Hewitt!" I knelt next to him. "Where are you hit?"

"I think I copped one in my back. Tell Higgins he is..." Then he passed out.

"Midshipman Higgins!"

Bill Leslie did not take his eyes off the bow but he said, "He copped one too sir. I reckon you are the new skipper." I must have hesitated for he said, "You can do it, sir."

I nodded, "Start heading for the coast. We should soon reach our lines."

"Righto sir."

"Symons how far to the British lines and our ships?"

"Almost forty miles sir." At this speed that meant we had to buy at least thirty minutes. It would almost be daylight by then.

"How many E-Boats are left?"

"Just three, sir but they are keeping pace with us."

Hewitt came up. "Take Mr Jorgenson below. He is hit in the back."

"Right sir. It is pretty bad back there sir. The three Germans are making us look like a colander."

"Do your best. Sergeant Poulson I want all the Bergens launching at once. Gordy and Beaumont are sorting them. Spread them out."

"Sir!"

Even as I looked aft I felt shells hitting the engine room again. An oily stoker rushed up. He looked at me in confusion. Bill said, "Tell the officer what the problem is, Harry the Gas."

"Sir, the Chief says we have to shut down one engine soon or we will seize up."

"Ask him to keep it going as long as he can."

"Yes sir." He grinned, "It's a lot cooler with all the new holes though, Coxswain!"

As he left I said, "Harry the Gas?"

"Yes sir, he was a gas fitter in civvy street."

"Wacker get on to Lieutenant Ferguson. Tell him if we don't get help in the next twenty minutes then we are dead men!"

"Sir!"

I looked aft and saw that my men were ready. They were lying down to avoid the machine gun bullets. I heard Gordy's voice boom out, "Now!"

The eight bags were thrown out in a wide pattern.

"Release and duck!"

This time the explosions were spread out over a wide area and the three boats all took evasive action. Bullets stopped hitting the hull. Symons voice came up a moment or two later. "Sir, one of the E-Boats has stopped. There are just two."

That gave me hope until Harry the Gas ran up. "Sir, we have to stop the engine now. The Chief says you will have to make do with just the one."

"Okay, tell him to let me know when we can have more power. Symons, how far to the coast?"

"Two miles sir but it is held by Jerry."

"I know." I turned to Bill. "When I shout I want you to turn to starboard. Head directly for the coast. Hold that course for a mile; no more and then run parallel to the rocks. Get Symons to let you know when we have to turn."

He nodded, "What do you plan to do, sir?"

"The only thing we can do; use the firepower of the Thompsons to try to take out an E-Boat. They must be low on ammo. Crowe might get lucky again." I shrugged, "I'll be back!"

The boat was like a charnel house. I saw that Gordy, Shepherd and Scouse all had wounds. They were still upright but that was about all. Taff and his gun crew were still firing.

"I am going to turn to starboard. It will bring the end E-Boat close to us. I want Crowe and Shepherd to send every grenade we have at it and the rest of us will use our Thompsons. Taff, you concentrate on the bridge."

Taff nodded, "What then sir?"

"We are going to head for the rocks on the coast and see who blinks first, us or the other E-Boats. Ready?"

They chorused, "Yes, sir."

"Now Coxswain!" Even though I was expecting it I was taken aback by the turn. The starboard E-Boat saw our move late and made a jerky turn. It threw his gunners. Our men were ready and the noise was so loud that I could not have shouted an order even had I wished to. The grenades cleared the decks and the machine guns ended the lives of the wounded. Taff's Pom-Pom tore through the side of the bridge. I saw the helmsman and the captain fall. The E-Boat continued its turn. With a dead man at the helm it would sail in circles.

I had bought us some time for the other two boats were out of position and had to readjust to catch us up. I raced to the bridge. "Well done, Bill."

He nodded to the bow, "All I see, sir, is Mount bloody Etna!"

"Five hundred yards, Coxswain."

"Don't worry, we have radar and they don't. In half an hour when it is dawn they would see this. It is our only chance."

As if to confirm it the nearest E-Boat opened up and I heard shouts from the stern.

"Two hundred and fifty yards!"

"Turn!" I could see him struggling with the wheel and I helped him to turn it. The boat almost fought us and I saw a wall of rock looming ahead of us and the white of breakers on rocks. I wondered if we would make it. Miraculously we turned. I glanced astern and saw that the E-Boat had seen our turn late. As I saw his bow come around he suddenly stopped as he struck something. He was not going to turn in time.

Harry the Gas ran up, "Sir, the chief is dead and there is a bloody great oil leak. What do I do?"

"Your best." There might have only been one German left but we were as good as dead in the water. I had tried every trick I knew and we had still come up short.

Just then Wacker's triumphant voice came up, "Sir that was the captain of "*H.M. S Daedelus*". They are half a mile away."

"Tell him we need a tow and there is still one Jerry on our tail."

The last E-Boat had been out of position but she saw our predicament and she was hurtling towards our peppered stern. Tosh ran to us. "Sir, we are taking on water. We are hit below the waterline."

I looked helplessly at Bill Leslie. He said, "Get the crew on the pumps. If the engines pack up there are hand pumps. Go, son, get to it!"

The E-Boat got one shot off before a pair of geysers erupted in either side of her. The destroyer had fired a ranging shot. The E-Boat turned and then I heard the sound of four, four and a half inch shells being fired. It only took one of them and the E-Boat exploded in a fireball.

"You can slow down now, Bill. Well done!"

"No sir, well done to you. The Lieutenant couldn't have handled it any better."

Wacker shouted, "*'Daedelus'* is asking us to be ready to take a tow."

"Taff and Tosh get to the fo'c'sle. Prepare to receive a line."

I sank down to my knees. "You all right sir?"

"Just tired, Petty Officer Leslie, just tired. It has been a long night."

Part 3

Italy

Chapter 17

We barely made port. We were seriously damaged so much so that we issued life jackets to the whole crew. I genuinely feared that we would sink. Everyone who could manned a pump. The crew were almost as badly hurt too. Twelve crewmen were dead. Alan and the Midshipman were both in serious need of a hospital but the E-Boat would need months of repairs. Even if we had wanted to continue our operation we could not. Colonel Fleming and Hugo met us at the dock along with ambulances and red caps. Alan was too drugged to speak when he went ashore and Bill Leslie was left in charge. I left him on the bridge. I shook his hand. Neither of us said anything. We didn't need to.

The prisoners looked white as they were taken off. It must have been terrifying for them below decks not knowing if they would live or die. Colonel Fleming looked as though all his dreams had come true. I thought, for a brief moment, that he would kiss me but he just pumped my hand. "What a coup! A general, a senior officer and two bags full of papers. I could never have hoped for such success. Well done!"

And then he was gone.

Hugo smiled, "And that is another first: praise from him." He looked at the *'Lady Luck'*. I had sailed home in her and yet I could not believe that she was still afloat. Water spat from her pumps and from those the naval engineers had brought. Hugo pointed at the blood running from her scuppers. "And I do not know how you did it. "

I shrugged, "You deal with one problem at a time. If we hadn't had such good men then we wouldn't have made it. None of them let us down. They all did their duty and more. It was a privilege to lead them."

Hugo said, "Come on, sir, breakfast. You have earned it."

"Fine but we will eat with the chaps."

The Germans had a fine mess and we went there. My men and the survivors of the *'Lady Luck'* were there. Cooks were ladling out food. The men who were seated, eating their food, made to stand. "Stand easy. Keep your seats. We are all messmates tonight."

I was the only officer who had survived without injury. As I walked to the end of the line there were nods, smiles and grins. I saw some of the sailors nudge each other. Bill Leslie was at the back of the queue. We joined him. "You can go to the front, sir, the lads won't mind."

"But I would, Bill. I meant what I said we are all messmates tonight. You can't come through something like that and expect privilege of rank." He nodded. "Do we know how the Lieutenant and the Middy are?"

"No, sir. The SBA went with then and your Corporal. The Skipper was breathing; I heard that much. You now I didn't even know he had been hit until you spoke. I had to keep my eyes forrard."

"It shows how lucky you were. The bridge has good protection from the front but the back is open."

We had reached the front of the queue. I picked up the plate and the cooks began to ladle food on to it. I would eat and I would clear my plate but I was not hungry. I realised that I would have to write letters to the families of the dead.

"Bill, when you have a minute, after this, I will need some help."

"Anything sir."

"I have letters to write. The Lieutenant can't do it."

"Letters? Oh, right. Yes sir I'll help you. I wouldn't be much good at that. I don't have the words."

"It is not a task I enjoy and I sometimes wish that I didn't have the words either but we owe it to the dead to tell their families how they died."

We had reached an empty table and we sat down. "And the Colonel will want a report too, sir."

My eyes flashed as I hissed, "And what the hell else does he need to know, Lieutenant? He has the officers and he has the papers! That should be enough!"

Bill's voice sounded soothing, "Easy sir. The Lieutenant is right and what about all those photographs you took. He will want to see our holiday snaps too eh?"

I saw the twinkle in the Petty Officer's eyes. Unlike Hugo, Bill was a warrior and he knew how to use humour in such a situation. I smiled, "I suppose we could have bought some holiday postcards."

"A stick of Italian rock eh, sir?"

Hugo looked puzzled, "The Italians don't eat rock."

For some reason that made Bill and I laugh until we cried. As I say humour is the best release valve in the world. We laughed at something silly and we did not go, as some did, crazy.

It was dark by the time the three of us had written the letters and finished all the paperwork. The E-Boat had been taken away. We did not know that would be the last time we would see her. The engineers later told us that they had decided that her working life was over and she could not be saved. The *'Lady'* had given her life for us. I knew that had she not held together for as long as she had then we would all be in the Tyrrhenian Sea.

"I suppose I will be reassigned again, sir."

I tapped his stripes, "At least this time you go with rank. Do you want to stay in Combined Operations?"

"I think so, sir. You feel like you are doing a bit."

I looked pointedly at Hugo. The Lieutenant nodded, "I will see the Colonel. I am sure he will endorse any such transfer."

"I'll go and see the lads. See who else wants to stay." He stood, "I'll do it now, sirs. Strike while the iron is hot."

After he had gone Hugo lit a cigarette, "You know you chaps have a unique relationship. You appear to be a service unto yourselves."

"I think that is what Churchill thought when he first came up with the idea. I know that Lord Lovat and Lord Mountbatten think so. I have spoken with them." I knew that like Dad in the RFC, I could not envisage fighting in another force. "Which begs the question, what happens to us? The *'Dragonfly'*?"

Hugo frowned, "Perhaps, but she is in Greek waters now. You may get some time off."

I laughed, "You have a dry sense of humour Hugo. I am betting that the Colonel has plans for us already." I put the future from my mind. "We need to get to the hospital and see how my chaps are."

"I will go and ring." He came back ten minutes later with a grin on his face. "They are on their way back sir. Apparently, they discharged themselves. They appear to have borrowed an ambulance. The chap on the other end asked if we could send it back to them."

"Of course."

I felt like a parent waiting for naughty children who were late out as I stood at the gate watching for the ambulance. I had Emerson and Hay with the jeep which we had still retained. Emerson would return the ambulance. The ambulance screeched to a noisy halt before me. The three of them tumbled out. Gordy had a bandage across one eye. Scouse had his left arm in a sling and I could not see Shepherd's wounds. They saluted.

Gordy said, "Detachment reporting for duty, sir."

I could smell the Grappa on their breath. I turned, "Fred, take the ambulance back. Hay go with him."

"Sir."

I waited until the ambulance and the jeep had left before I said, "And you three, what am I going to do with you? You will be lucky if they don't press charges."

Scouse grinned, "Oh they won't do that sir. We were bloody awful patients. They were glad to get rid of us."

"Anyway, sir we wanted to get back to the *'Lady'*."

"I am afraid that the *'Lady'* has sailed her last voyage. She is being broken up." All their good humour disappeared. They had all become sailors and were deeply attached to their vessel.

Gordy shook his head, "I hadn't been with her as long as you lads but she was a lucky ship. I shall miss her."

Scouse said, "They took the two officers back to Valetta, sir. They were badly wounded. I mean, really badly." He shook his head, "What'll happen to the crew sir? I mean will we sail with them again?"

"I am not certain. They are all good sailors and want to stay in Combined Ops but you know how these things work."

"It's just a shame sir. We worked well together. Me and Wacker understood each other."

It took more than a couple of days to tie up all our loose ends and then all hell broke loose. We had a breakthrough on the fourteenth of August. The Germans and Italians started to pull back from Sicily towards the mainland. At the same time, we were finally free of Colonel Fleming. Hugo told me that as a result of the intelligence we had gathered he was being flown back to London to be part of the planning team for a new operation. My relief was short lived. Rather than being returned to England and Number Four Commando we discovered that we were to be attached to Number Two Commando for the invasion of Italy. Major General Laycock had been impressed by our success. He had specifically asked for us. It also meant the departure of Lieutenant Ferguson.

"Sorry about this, sir but I have been assigned to the staff of Colonel Fleming." He shook his head, "He said I might be promoted. I would rather work with you and your chaps. You made a difference and it has been an honour to serve with you."

"And you too, Hugo. I know the lads will miss you. You are a damned good officer and you deserve better than Colonel Fleming."

"Who knows, our paths may well cross again."

"I hope so."

It was a mark of the respect that my men had for him that they all insisted on shaking his hand. I could see that the quietly spoken Lieutenant was touched. This was the first unit he had been part of and now he was leaving. After he had gone and with the crew of the *'Lady'* transferred we rattled around the base. Hugo had been gone less than half a day when a lorry arrived driven by a Commando from Number Two Brigade.

He saluted smartly, "Captain Harsker I am here to transport you and your section to San Agata. Major General Laycock requests your presence."

I had been expecting it. "Right Sergeant Poulson, get your gear in the back of the lorry."

I climbed in the cab. "How far is it Sergeant?"

"Eighty or so miles but it will take all afternoon to reach it sir. You might as well get your head down."

Polly banged on the cab, "All aboard, sir."

The sergeant put it into gear and we began to drive. "No, Sergeant, I shall stay awake. I have been all around this island. I shall be interested to go through it and see what the land is like."

We drove in silence for a while and then he said, "A lot of the lads are keen to see you and your lot sir. They have heard a lot about you." He smiled, "Some say you should have a V.C. like your old man."

"My dad will tell you that getting fruit salad is all a matter of luck. I have seen braver men than me who deserved medals. A V.C. doesn't matter if you are dead."

"It does to your family."

I smiled, "Have you ever noticed that most of the men who get V.C.s and the like have no families. That should tell you something."

He nodded, "Anyway most of us are happy to have you with us. I have heard that we and the Rangers have the hardest task. We have Amalfi to take."

I must have shown my surprise, "Amalfi? I have been there. I recommended that we do not attack it. It is high cliffs and narrow gorges."

"Ah well, sir, some bright spark called Colonel Fleming came up with a plan to take it. Apparently, he recommended that you and your section lead the attack. It is why you are attached to us for this operation."

I closed my eyes. Colonel Fleming still continued to haunt us. Even though he had departed we still had the slippery touch of his tentacles to contend with. The journey was over recently conquered ground. We passed damaged vehicles and crudely marked graves. We were retaking Europe. I still remembered the horror of the retreat across Belgium when we had lost the war for Europe. I would lose no sleep over the dead Germans but I said a silent thanks to the dead Americans, British and Canadians who had fallen to help us secure Sicily. It was now obvious that the battle for Sicily was over. By the second week of August it would be completely in our hands. Already there were rumours of an Italian surrender. I hoped so. The war would end that much quicker. The fall of Mussolini at the end of July was the first of the bricks to tumble. The rest would surely follow.

"Here we are sir." I must have dozed off. I found myself at a vast field of tents. "It is a bit rough and ready sir but it is only temporary. The General said there will be a briefing tomorrow at 0800. A jeep will pick you up."

"Thanks Sergeant. I am sorry I was such a miserable passenger."

"After what you have been through sir, it is to be understood."

I went to the rear, "Right, chaps. Here is our new home."

The bags were thrown down. I banged on the side when the last of my men had left the vehicle. It sped off. It was new to us. I could not remember the last time I had been in such a large camp. Gordy said, "Hang on here, sir and I will go and suss it out! Bill come with me."

Sergeant Poulson joined me. "Back to the real army then sir?"

"Perhaps. Colonel Fleming recommended us."

Polly gave a knowing look, "Then it might be more of the same."

Half an hour later Bill Hay appeared, "I have found our tents, sir. Sergeant Barker has gone to make sure there is some grub left for us."

Our tents were at the end of a row and close to a drainage ditch. We had endured worse. I had a tent to myself. The rest of the men were three to a tent. It was adequate. We dumped our gear and followed Bill to the mess tent. We were the only ones left. That proved to be an advantage as they had been expecting more of us and had prepared plenty of food. Those omnivores amongst the men ate well. They worked on the premise that you never knew what was around the corner so when you could eat, as Gordy often said, *'fill yer boots*!'

I was up early. The nap in the cab had taken the edge of my need for sleep. I was one of the first in the mess tent and the only officer. I was waiting, ready for the jeep when it arrived.

Headquarters was the town hall. I saw that it had been recently used by the Germans. Their discarded signs lay everywhere. The fighting here had been so recent that they had not even moved some of the damaged vehicles. The inevitable red caps stood on guard outside. The private who had brought me had seemed a little in awe of me. Having spoken to the sergeant I realised that our exploits had become the subject of gossip. I hoped the officers I met would be less impressed.

I was one of the first to arrive and I was shown to what looked to have been a ballroom. A major, assisted by a young lieutenant, was busy sorting papers and maps into piles. Without looking up the Major said, "There is coffee by the door. Just help yourself."

"Thank you, sir." I poured myself a cup and sipped it. It was hot and it was real coffee. I suspected the Americans had provided the coffee. When I was pouring it a second major entered. This time he was a Commando. I recognised his flash. I gestured to the coffee.

"Thanks." He sat next to me. He smiled as he drank. "I had forgotten what real coffee tasted like." He held out his hand, "Siddons, Second Commando."

"Harsker, Four Commando."

"By Jove I am in the presence of a celebrity. You are the chap who has been causing such a stir behind the lines. My chaps were singing your praises after the landings. Jack Durrant was most impressed and he knows his business. Well done, sir. I am glad you are on this one. I can tell you."

"You and your chaps will know more about attacking beaches. We have an easy job. We just sneak in, have a footle around and then toddle off home."

He shook his head, "No false modesty, old boy. We both know that what you do is damned dangerous. You are the chaps that Old Adolf wants to string up by the bollocks!"

The room was filling up with Commandos and Royal Marine Commandos too. General Laycock arrived and the Lieutenant closed the door and placed his chair in front of it. We were not going to be disturbed. The Major stood next to him with a pointer. He took a sheet off the easel and revealed a map of the bay of Salerno. The General nodded to him and began, "Gentlemen, today we begin the preparation for Operation Avalanche; the invasion of mainland Italy!"

There was a hubbub of conversation. The Major snapped, "Come, gentlemen, we are not schoolboys!"

I saw a smile on the face of Lucky Laycock, "This is Major Taylor. He is seconded to us from the Guards and works directly under Colonel Fleming whom I know some of you know."

That was all I needed to know. Already I did not like the Major.

"You represent the Commandos who will be working in close cooperation with the American Rangers led by Colonel Darby. Now we have been given the task of attacking what are deemed to be impossible targets: Amalfi and Vietri Sul Mare."

"We know this because Colonel Fleming sent in Captain Harsker of Number Four Commando to inspect the landing sites and Captain Harsker informed the Colonel that infantry could not take either place. He was quite right." He held out a hand towards me, "You were quite right, Captain Harsker. We have examined the aerial photographs and the ones you took. Excellent photography by the way. We believe that Commandos and Rangers can, indeed, take them both."

I was suddenly aware of heads swivelled in my direction.

"Our target is the Molina Pass just a mile north of Vietri Sul Mare. We are to hold it and, if possible, put pressure on Salerno. We will be going in first before the main attack further south. Thanks to the papers and the officers Captain Harsker captured in Paestum we know a great deal about the defences of this area. You may not be aware but the provisional Italian Government has just signed an armistice. Now I believe this means that Italy will sue for peace and there will be a hiatus while the Germans take over the positions occupied at present by the Italians. Gentlemen we attack on the morning of the ninth of September!"

"The ninth! That is a week away!"

The captain four seats away could not contain himself. It made Major Siddons laugh out loud, "Damned fool. We are Commandos. We go in at a moment's notice. I bet your chaps are always ready."

I nodded. "Sometimes less than that. I worked for Colonel Fleming,"

"You poor sod. I met him once. Awful man. Stank like an ashtray!"

Major Taylor snapped, "Focus, gentlemen!"

"Let us look at the attack in detail. Lieutenant."

The Lieutenant gave out folders with maps, times and other vital information.

"We leave here on the eighth. It is one hundred and eighty miles to our destination. It will take us ten to eleven hours to reach our destination. The Air Force will ensure that we arrive unmolested. We will land at dawn. We have *'H.M.S. Ledbury'* for close support. Some of you know her from the Sicily invasion. We will be travelling in Landing Craft. The exception will be Captain Harsker and his team. They will be travelling on ML 220. His team will land one hour ahead of the main force under cover of darkness. Their task will be to seize and hold the beach close to the main road north. It means that when we land we should have minimal opposition. It is imperative that Captain Harsker's team captures the beach. If he does so then we can easily capture the pass."

Major Siddons said from the side of his mouth, "No pressure then."

The rest of the briefing concerned the weaponry and the logistics of support. I remembered both St. Nazaire and Dieppe. I prayed that this one did not result in the number of deaths which those two raids had. We broke for lunch to allow us the chance to ask questions. I was talking with Major Siddons when Major Taylor approached. I had not noticed that he was much smaller than the rest of us. He had a neatly trimmed and waxed moustache. I detected the smell of eau de cologne. This was not an officer who had experienced the rigours of war.

"Captain Harsker, Colonel Fleming has spoken highly of you." He frowned, "However I am less than impressed by your appearance. I want you to have a haircut and shave before our next meeting. And I would have expected a clean uniform at the very least! There are standards."

"Why, sir?"

"Why do we have standards? What a stupid question!"

"No, sir, why do I need to shave and have a haircut."

"You need to set an example."

"Who to?"

"Why, your men of course."

"You mean my men will follow me to hell and back if I have a haircut, a shave and clean uniform?"

"Of course!"

"Then I can see you have never led men into action, Major!"

He reddened, "That sounds like insubordination to me."

I had had enough of this and I took the bull by the horns. "Then you have led men into action, Major. Where?"

"I..."

He got no further for Major General Laycock had heard the last interchange. "Captain Harsker, Major Taylor does not need to explain to you his record. Suffice it to say he is very experienced in the planning of operations such as this!"

"Sorry sir."

I saw the Major begin to preen himself at what he took to be a compliment.

"However Major, the Captain is quite right. His appearance will not detract in the slightest from his section. I have seen them in action and they are as big a bunch of pirates as their leader. Captain Harsker's men will never stand guard outside Buckingham Palace but it is the likes of men like that which ensure that you can."

The Major was suitably deflated

We worked for an hour after lunch and then we were sent back to our units. We had each given a list to the flag lieutenant of anything which we might need for the operation. I just asked for explosives and ammunition. My men were my biggest asset.

During the afternoon I sought out Major General Laycock. "Sir can I ask you something?"

"Of course Captain Harsker. I owe you that much at least."

"When this is over could my men and I go back to join Number Four Commando? No disrespect sir but if we are going to have to do this sort of thing then I would rather do it with my own brigade."

He smiled, "I fully understand and the answer is yes. We are using your expertise here but we are going to have to develop our own version of you. Besides, between you and me I think Colonel Fleming has plans for you. And those plans involve France, not Italy. Your skills there will be quite useful I would imagine. Just get through this in one piece and you can go home, Captain Harsker." I nodded, "One thing though. Try to put on a decent uniform eh? Until we leave. You have enough fruit salad on your battle dress to make even Major Taylor think twice about making snide comments. Just a word to the wise."

Later, as we left sharing a jeep, Major Siddons said, "You have made an enemy of that one. Mind you I wouldn't lose any sleep over it. The man is a martinet. They should have had a Commando." He glanced down and saw the Luger and the Colt. "Unorthodox weapons, Harsker."

"Yes sir. Sometimes by using the Luger we can confuse the enemy for a few seconds. Often that is all that we need. It can be the difference between winning and losing."

Chapter 18

My men had had an easy day while I received my briefing and I did not begrudge them that. They were all together when I arrived. There was a rocky headland which overlooked the sea and I took them there. It was quiet and there would be no one to eavesdrop. They sat around me and waited. Gordy broke the silence, "Well sir, where to?"

"Near to Salerno. We are going to hold the mountain pass which leads to Naples."

Scouse grinned, "Great. I have never invaded before! We goin' in with all these lads, then sir?"

"No, Fletcher. We go in an hour before them and hold the beach head. Then we join Number Two Commando and hold Molina Pass."

Sergeant Poulson rubbed his chin. "Sir, I saw the place you are talking about on our last little jaunt. The mountains rise straight above it."

"I know but I have seen the aerial photographs and read the intelligence we gathered at Paestum. There is just a company of infantry at Vietri Sul Mare. The odds are that there will just be a platoon, at most, on guard." I stood, "Look, it doesn't matter how many men are there or what the dangers are we get this job done and then we can go home to Falmouth and the Brigade. We get to eat Mrs Bailey's dinners again."

"Then let's get on with it, sir!" Scouse rubbed his hands together. He enjoyed his food. They had their carrot and they would not let me down.

The next morning I left the sergeants to gather the equipment while I went to speak with the captain of the motor launch. I wore the best uniform I had with me. I didn't like advertising my medals but if they kept Major Taylor off my back then that would be a good thing. ML 220 was the type I had been on before. Lightly armed they were fast and they had plenty of room. Lieutenant Williams looked like all such captains; young enough to still be at school. The crew were all equally young but I liked them immediately. They had an easy-going attitude which appealed to me.

The fraternity of the small boats was close and the first thing he said was, "Sorry to hear about Alan Jorgenson. He is a good egg."

I nodded, "The last I heard he was still hanging on. A shame about our E-Boat though. It was very handy."

"What are they like sir? The rumour is that you captained her when Alan was hit."

"I had a good crew and I just made a couple of decisions. It was nothing but as for the E-Boat, I have nothing but respect for them. They are one hell of a boat. They can catch anything we have and out gun them too. Still we shouldn't need to worry about them. We have destroyers with us for most of the way. Now I am not being funny but have you done this sort of thing before?"

"No, sir."

"Then here is what we will need: four rubber dinghies already inflated and two of your men in each boat to paddle us ashore. Trust me it is better for you. This way you can skedaddle off quicker."

"What if you need picking up again, sir?"

"Then we will have failed. Don't worry about that. My men and I can look after ourselves and we have two Brigades of Commandos following us. For us this is going in mob handed. We are used to being alone behind the lines and for some time too."

Once I was satisfied that he knew what he was doing I left for our camp. I had to pass the American camp. I recognised the

Ranger flash on some of the uniforms. I was just turning to head back to our own camp when a couple of officers approached me, "Say, sir, are you one of those British Commandos?"

His companion said, "Dwight, look at his shoulder flash! Of course he is. And take a look at those medals!"

Soon I had a crowd around me. I tried to leave but they would not let me. I was rescued when a voice shouted, "Ten shun!"

"What in God's name is going on here?"

"Sorry Colonel Darby but this is a British Commando and just look at his medals."

Colonel Darby shook his head, "Sorry about this, Captain. My men are keen to emulate you guys. Can I make up for it with a drink?"

"Of course sir."

He led me to his tent. "What is your name?"

"Captain Tom Harsker, Number Four Commando."

He stopped suddenly, "Say you are the guy who said Amalfi couldn't be taken by regular infantry."

"Sorry about that, sir."

"Nothing to be sorry about. I have seen the photographs and you are right." He gestured for me to sit and poured me a glass of an amber liquor. I sniffed it. It was Bourbon. "It seems to me I have heard your name before. Didn't you rescue a General from behind enemy lines? And weren't you the one who captured that Italian Intelligence?"

"Guilty on all counts, sir."

He shook me by the hand, "No wonder they gave you these medals. It is an honour to meet you. My Rangers are just starting but we aim to be as good as you one of these days."

"You do yourself a disservice sir. If you and your men can take Amalfi then you are superior to us Commandos."

"You Brits! I can't get over this god damn modesty. What is wrong with being good and letting others know?"

I shrugged, "I don't know, sir. I guess it is the way we are."

"Well Captain Harsker..." he stopped mid sentence, "Harsker. You are related to that World War One Ace, aren't you?"

"My father."

"Jeez Louise it must run in your family." He poured me a second glass.

We spoke for some time how about he had been inspired to become a Ranger after seeing the Commandos train. I told him about some of our operations. I looked at my watch. "I am sorry sir. But I have a section to prepare."

"Quite right, Captain." He leaned over and said, "Listen, son, if you ever need anything then let me know."

I nodded and rose. "And good luck at Amalfi. One tip, sir. German grenades are not to be sniffed at. If your men can capture them they are great for making booby traps." I patted my Luger, "We are not shy about taking what we can from the Germans. Some of their weapons are better than ours. That's why we use Colts and Thompsons!"

He nodded, "I learned from you guys in Carrickfergus. I am still learning. Don't be a stranger, Captain."

By the time I had reached our camp I had decided upon a course of action. Talking with Colonel Darby had reminded me that we had not trained as Commandos since we had landed in North Africa. When we invaded we might be in action for weeks.

"Right, Sergeant Poulson. I want everyone in full kit with Bergens and Thompson. Twenty minutes."

"Right sir!"

I went to my tent and packed my Bergen. I put in spare ammunition and grenades. I had to test myself too. I looked at the map. I could see a ten-mile run up into the hills and back down. It would test me and it would test my men.

I was aware, as I inspected them, that three had been recently wounded. Today would give me a better idea of their combat readiness. If they fell behind then they were not ready to attack Vietri Sul Mare. Sergeant Poulson, take the rear."

"Sir!"

Our lack of fitness became apparent just a mile into the run as we began to ascend the steep hills. I could feel my chest burning. I pushed on through. The further we went on the more I could feel the strain in my calves and thighs. They had lost their hardness. We had had months where we had been taken to war by boat. My head began to pound and I could not suck in enough air. As we reached the half way point and turned I was tempted to give them five minutes rest and then I realised that would be a mistake. The enemy would not give them a rest. It was a hot day and I could feel the sweat dripping down my back. My uniform was a winter one and it was wool. I was suffering. Although this was a circular route I saw the end of the line as they ascended the peak. There was a slight gap to the last men but nothing to worry about. I decided to push them on the downhill section. It would test the ones with wounds to breaking point. If they survived this then they could come on the mission.

It was late in the afternoon as I put in a power surge down the last half mile to the camp. Number Two Commando were resting outside their tents and they clapped us in. I powered the last hundred yards. I stopped and turned. Scouse was almost in my footsteps. His wound had not hampered him. Gordy too had run through the pain. I saw that it was Fred Emerson and Jimmy Smith who were struggling. My section stood before me, chests heaving as they gasped for breath.

I looked at my watch to see how long it took. I nodded, "Right chaps. We are not fit. That is my fault. Sorry. Tomorrow morning we do exactly the same run but we will do it five minutes quicker. Tomorrow afternoon we run in our shorts to the sea. We will have a swimming race. We have less than seven days to become the Commandos we once were."

They nodded. Fred Emerson said, "Sorry I held you up sir. I'll have to knock the fags on the head!"

Gordy shook his head, "It makes no odds Freddie. You just have to bite the bullet and take the pain. Don't worry sir, we'll get there. We won't let you down."

After three days things improved. The extra and more varied exercise regime paid off. Emerson and Smith no longer lagged behind. On the fourth day, with just a couple of days before the off I took them on a longer more extended route. As we came towards a rise I heard the sound of gunfire and explosions. Our training kicked in and we all hit the ground and began to crawl up to the ridge line. The Germans and Italians had all left the island in the middle of August but there had been rumours of Italian resistance.

As I peered over the top I relaxed. It was the Rangers engaging in a mock attack. I waved my men to their feet and we walked towards them. I heard a whistle and an officer waved his arms and shouted, "Cease fire!"

I saw Colonel Darby take off his helmet and walk towards me. He held out his hand, "Captain Harsker! Perfect timing. We were just going to take a break."

"We wondered what the firing was all about."

"I think you and me are the only two who are still pushing before this invasion. We have seen you out twice a day. It puts us to shame."

"No sir, us. We have been in action since the end of last year but we didn't train like we used to. We are getting close now." I noticed some men carrying long tubes. "Excuse me, sir, what are those? Short Bangalore torpedoes?"

"No, Captain. They are anti-tank rocket launchers; M1A1 firing the M6A1 rocket. The guys nicknamed them the bazooka! A little bit like the Boys anti-tank rifle but more powerful. These can stop a Mark III." He waved over a sergeant, "Sergeant Willis give the Commandos a demonstration of the capability of this weapon."

"Yes sir!"

We followed them down the slope to a Panzer III which had been knocked out during the invasion. It had thrown a track and its gun had been sabotaged by the crew but other than that it was whole. Colonel Darby said, "We were saving this for later on but you guys might as well enjoy the show too."

The Sergeant and his loader stopped a hundred yards from the tank. He knelt down with the tube on his shoulder and the loader loaded it and then tapped the Sergeant on the helmet.

Colonel Darby said, "Stand clear of the rear of the weapon and kneel!"

We all complied and the Colonel said, "Whenever you are ready, Willis."

There was a whoosh and the projectile hit the turret. The turret exploded. There was an audible gasp from my men. "Impressive."

"The effective range is a hundred and twenty yards. That and the fact that the operator has to kneel makes it risky; especially with the machine guns on the tanks. However, this baby can penetrate three inches of armour. The front of those tanks is just two inches thick and the sides just over an inch. So long as the tank isn't one of the new Panthers then we can take them. The Panther has an angled front and three-point one-inch armour."

"Fantastic sir. You guys are lucky. We just have a grenade launcher. We just give them a headache."

I saw the sergeant laugh. Colonel Darby turned to the Major who was with him. "Say, Sam, didn't we see a few of these lying in the docks the other day?"

"Yes sir. They are ear marked for the 46th Texas Division."

Colonel Darby nodded, "Those Texas boys are tough enough. They wouldn't miss one. Sergeant Willis I have a little extra training for you and your squad."

"Yes sir."

"Let's see how sneaky you can be. I want you to get a launcher and a case of ammunition for our British cousins. Call it lend lease on a local level."

"Yes sir. Just the one sir?" He grinned, "We could do with a couple more ourselves."

Colonel Darby smiled, "Use your discretion Sergeant!"

I saw my pilferers nodding. The Sergeant was a man after their own heart. "Thank you, Colonel. We had better continue our run. We have less than three days to go."

I was woken at midnight by Sergeant Poulson. "Sir, care to see this?" I followed him to his tent. There, outside were two crates marked 46th Texas. "Father Christmas has come early!"

"Did you hear them bring it?"

"No sir. I got up for a leak."

"Right, let's get rid of the evidence. Open the crates, quietly, we don't want Number Two to hear. Put the weapon in one tent and the ammo in another. Put the broken crates in my tent. If anyone comes looking then I will carry the can."

We had been using a campfire to make an early morning brew and I rose at four to light the fire. I used the incriminating stencilled sections of the crates first and soon had a healthy blaze going. The men rose early as the smell of the burning wood woke them. We put a brew on and Sergeant Poulson told them of the gift.

I nodded to Polly's tent, "We have a rocket launcher and now we need a crew. You all heard what the American colonel said, it is risky for you have to get close. Any volunteers?" Every hand went up. "My choice then. Lance Sergeant Hay you are explosives and we need you for that. That leaves Sergeant Poulson and Sergeant Barker. Gordy you take the bazooka, Smith, you are the loader." I saw the disappointment on the faces of the rest. "You will all need to know how to fire it in case anything happens to our two heroes. After the run this morning we come back here and sneak the weapon down to the launch. It is time we practised loading the dinghies and we might as well do that out of sight. You can try a rocket out, Sergeant."

"Yes sir."

We broke our running record that morning by six minutes. They were all keen. To disguise the bazooka, we used two Bergens. The bazooka was just over four and a half feet long. Two Bergens hid it. The ammunition was spread amongst the other Bergens. Number Two Commando were used to our weird behaviour and we made it to the harbour without any questions.

Lieutenant Williams was keen to practise with the dinghies. He and his men had been preparing for the attack and were now just waiting for their chance. "We need a quiet bay. Can you find one Lieutenant?"

"I think so, sir."

We headed off. Once we were at sea I said, "We need to store some of our equipment on board if that is all right with you."

"Of course, sir."

"However, it is, er, secret equipment. We would appreciate it if your chaps didn't talk about it." I tapped my nose.

He grinned and nodded, knowingly, "Quite!"

The practice proved useful. My men knew what to do but the crew were a little awkward the first couple of times they launched us into the dinghies. Some of them were wary of pushing an officer. After the second run I said, "Look lads, the key to this is to get us ashore as quickly as you can. If that means pushing me around a bit then do it! I am not fragile, ask these lads."

They gradually overcame their fear and soon were as adept as the crew of the *'Lady Luck'* had been. On the way back, I asked the Lieutenant to cruise slowly around the island on our way to the harbour. I spied what I needed and asked him to head in to shore. There was a damaged Italian truck on the beach. It lay below a cliff. I guessed the driver had been killed and it had landed on this inaccessible piece of sand. Storms and strong tides would soon destroy it but, for now, it made a perfect target.

"If you could anchor a hundred yards from shore, Lieutenant."

"Yes sir."

I could see that he was intrigued, "Sergeant Barker, go and fetch your toy."

The crew of the ML gathered close to the bridge as Barker and Smith set up the launcher. This was the first time they had used one and they were being both careful and slow. I knew that in action they would be just as careful but much faster. They would have a moment or two only to hit a tank before they were gunned down by the crew. Smith tapped Gordy on the head and there was a whoosh. The truck must have had some fuel on board for it exploded like a Roman candle. Both the crew and my men cheered.

Gordy beamed, "That'll do for me, sir!"

"Good, now go and store it somewhere safe."

As we headed back Lieutenant Williams said, "An interesting weapon, sir. What do you call it?"

"Secret, Lieutenant Williams, secret!"

We had one last briefing on the seventh of September. There we were issued passwords and call signs. I made sure that, when I attended, I had a decent uniform and I combed my hair. I did not wish to incur the wrath of Major Taylor. After the main briefing was over Major Taylor and Major General Laycock took me to one side.

"Is everything going to plan for you, Captain?"

"Yes sir."

"Once you have secured the pass I want you and your team to act as forward scouts and push on to Salerno."

"You will be with us, General?"

He smiled, "They have yet to put me behind a desk. I will be there. That is why you have been issued radios. I need you to keep me informed about the enemy. Speed is of the essence."

"Right sir."

Major Taylor said, "There was a report the other day of some ordnance being stolen from the docks and then a truck being blown up on a beach. Do you know anything about that, Captain?"

"The truck? Yes sir. That was us. We were practising for the operation. The ordnance? No idea sir? Black marketeers?"

I saw a wry grin on the General's face as Major Taylor said, "What on earth would black marketeers need with four rocket launchers? The commander of the Texas Division is not a happy chappie!"

"Well he wouldn't be. Is that all sir?"

Major General Laycock saluted, "Yes Captain and good luck. I can see I have picked the right man for the job. I like a man with initiative. I shall be sorry when you go back to your unit."

Scouse had his new radio. It was lighter than the ones we had used previously. He was adjusting the straps. I gave him the sheet with the call signs. "Learn them then destroy them. Shepherd is your back up. Tell him too."

"Right sir."

He read them and grinned, "Who came up with these sir? Not that Major Taylor?"

"No Scouse, I rather think that Major General Laycock devised them. They have his sense of humour."

Sergeant Poulson asked, "Why, what is our call sign?"

"Rocket!"

Chapter 19

Our convoy left at six. We were the smallest vessel. We were even dwarfed by the landing craft which could carry a whole company. There were destroyers which raced around like sheepdogs keeping boats in line and seeking enemy submarines. There were cruisers, and as we headed north east, I saw four battleships. In the air I saw a couple of Sunderlands too. They could stay in the air for hours. Normally such a voyage would have had me in a state of high nervous energy but, as the smallest target, I felt safe enough to sleep.

Sergeant Poulson woke me at midnight. It was an inky black sky. This was not like the invasion of Sicily; there was neither wind nor rain. Major Siddons had told me that they had planned on using the Airborne Brigade again but the disaster of Sicily had made them cancel it at the last minute. This time it was the proximity of the mountains which had deterred their use. We were coming in from the sea. I blacked up and went on deck. As I did so I saw a light flashing from a destroyer. I took a swallow from my cup of tea as the launch replied.

Lieutenant Williams said, "That is our signal. We are to detach now."

We had changed the original plans. I did not doubt that Major Taylor would be unhappy but we were the ones going ashore. The original plan had been for us to land on the beach itself. I did not fancy that as the aerial photographs had shown both wire and machine guns. Instead we were going to land at the sea wall which protected the harbour. That way we could approach the beach unseen. We would destroy the wire but from the safety of the secured side. There would be sentries at the end of the sea wall but I had my Colt.

"How long to landing?"

"We should be off Vietri in three hours."

I nodded, "I would have the men who are paddling us in black up too. White faces show up at night. Either that or balaclavas."

"Not much call for those in the Med sir, but thanks for the advice. We are learning every day. We will soon be used to it."

I said, "I am afraid not, Lieutenant. The day that you think you have it all is the day you die. We are still learning and we have been doing this for three years. You know it all when you retire or they stick you in the ground. And so far I don't know of any Commandos who have retired."

I went below to make sure that we were all ready. "Three hours chaps. We are now detached so I would get on deck as soon as you are ready." I picked up my Bergen and my Thompson and went back on deck. The worry was our detachment. The launch had no radar and there was radio silence. Should a wandering E-Boat find us then the first we would know would be the crack of cannon shells into our hull. I did not want to worry the Lieutenant even more and so I kept my counsel. Having my men on deck was an extra precaution. Their ears and eyes would give warning of any danger.

Time passed slowly but it did pass and we remained unmolested. A seaman found me, "Sir," he whispered, "Skipper says could you join him on the bridge."

When I reached him the young officer pointed north. "Not long now sir."

The great mass of Italy could be seen as a darker part of the night. "Take it steady. Keep a constant speed and let's pray we hit the right spot."

Had I been with Alan I would have been confident of the correct landfall. He was a superb navigator. The Lieutenant was an unknown quantity. I went back to my men. "Better get to the boats. We will be landing soon." Our constant practice meant that they knew the sailors who would paddle them in and they all went to their stations. I was the exception. I went to the bows to watch the coast as we approached. There was a lookout there. "See anything?"

"Just the coast sir. It could be Blackpool." He paused, "Except there's no tower here!"

I caught a flash of light which reappeared a moment later. I pointed. "That's a road. There is a car ignoring blackout. Watch for the lights again and see if you can pick anything out."

The mere act of focussing on the car brought everything into perspective. He jabbed his finger forward. "There sir, five points off the starboard bow; it looks like the sea wall."

"Good eyes, lookout. Go and tell the skipper."

I now saw the breakers, small though they were, at the base of the sea wall which arced around the front of the small harbour. The lookout returned and I patted him on the shoulder as I returned to my men.

"Less than half a mile to go!"

I took out my Colt and fitted the silencer. I had my Thompson strapped to my Bergen. Its time would come. We knew we had arrived when we stopped and the Lieutenant allowed the stern to drift around. It made launching easier and escape quicker. We quickly lowered the dinghies and we began the slow steady paddle towards the sea wall. Four of us did not paddle. Each of us crouched in the front of the dinghy with a ready Colt. I could not see any sentries but that did not mean that they were not there. We had instructed the sailors to wait by the wall in case they needed to take us closer. We had to play this part by ear. We paddled towards the beach side of the wall. The wall itself was twenty feet high. Made of huge blocks of stone we could scale it, even without ropes. Emerson and Crowe had the ropes in case they were needed.

As we edged closer I heard voices and they were German. The sound of the sea stopped me from making out their words but they were Germans and the speakers were smoking. The smell of their tobacco drifted over to me. Jamming my Colt into the shoulder straps of my Bergen I stepped on to the slippery rocks.

My rubber soled shoes managed to find purchase on the weed covered stones. I moved to the wall and began to ascend. There were four of us and that would be enough to overcome however many men we found. I put my hands on to the top of the wall. They had been blacked up too. I eased my head up. There were three sentries. I glanced down the wall. The fourth was marching toward the town. He was a couple of hundred yards away. I saw that Sergeant Poulson and Lance Sergeant Hay were in position and I nodded.

Drawing my gun, I stepped up and pointed my Colt at the Germans. I hissed, in German, "Keep still and you will live!"

One said, "Kommando!" and raised his gun. The phut from Bill Hay's pistol pitched him to the sea below. He hit the rocks first and made barely a splash.

I walked to the other side and saw a ladder. "Sergeant, tell the sailors to go around the other side we have three prisoners for them. Bill, take their weapons from them."

He nodded.

I spoke German, "You two climb down the ladder, now." I waved the Colt at them. They had seen one of their comrades die and they complied.

"Sir, the other Jerry."

I glanced around. The last sentry was walking towards us. His head was down and his rifle was slung over his shoulder. Levelling my Colt, I walked towards him. I was thirty yards from him when he lifted his head. "Hands up or you will be shot." He hesitated and I fired a bullet a yard from his foot. His hands came up. I turned, "Bill, when the prisoners are secured, follow us. The rest of you, on me!"

I walked down the sea wall. I kept my Colt in my hand. For the time being we needed silence. I risked a glance at my watch. It was fifty minutes until the invasion. We had to move quickly. My deviation from the plan had been the right one. These sentries might have seen us and raised the alarm. As I neared the end of the wall I saw a machine gun post just below me. If was fifty yards away and facing the sea. They would not see us. There were two men in it. That was our first target. I waved my hand to lead my men beyond them so that we could make our approach from the road. It was the direction which would arouse the least suspicion. Once past them I signed for Polly and Scouse to follow me and for Gordy to take the rest along the road. They all knew what to do: eliminate the opposition.

I walked up behind the two Germans. They were talking about a local Italian girl who was free with her favours. They laughed. Our approach had been silent. I put the gun to the back of one German's head, "Hands up or you die!"

His hands came up. The second looked at me, and the gun and he obeyed too.

"Take off your helmets!" They looked at me uncomprehendingly. "Now!"

As they did so Fletcher and Poulson hit them with their saps. "This will be our headquarters. Scouse set up the radio and tell them where we are." I saw the telephone cables which I assumed ran to the Headquarters building. I took my dagger and cut them. I moved down the beach leaving those two to tie them up. The next machine gun post had been dealt with. I could see another but it was two hundred yards down the beach. I waved Gordy over, "Take four men and clear the wire."

I was left with Bill Hay, Fred Emerson and Roger Beaumont. I waved them back to the road. We were silent as we walked down. I could see that there were three more machine gun posts but the next one had four men. We approached from the road. This time we were unlucky. One of them turned and saw us. As he opened his mouth to shout I shot him twice. As he fell the other three turned around. Their fatal error was to try to swing their gun around. Four silenced shots killed them. I changed the clip in my Colt as we headed for the last two. I glanced at my watch. The landing craft would be less than half a mile out. Soon they would be either seen or heard and we had still two machine gun posts to deal with.

The klaxon from the building a hundred yards to the right alerted us. The German radar had picked up the ships. We raced towards the nearest machine gun. Bill and I shot them but the last machine gun knew we were coming and they fired a burst. It was early and it was wild. We dived into the machine gun emplacement. Freddie swung the already cocked gun around and fired in the direction of the other Germans. His was a more measured burst and both fell dead.

"Hay, take Beaumont and man the last gun. Swing them around to face the land."

I turned to Emerson. "It looks like you and me on this gun. You happy about that?"

He grinned, "Yes sir! Let the bastards come. I have a full mag and my Thompson."

"I will use my Thompson. Give me a shout if you have a problem." I laid out half a dozen grenades. Turning around I grabbed a couple of potato mashers from the dead Germans. There was nothing I enjoyed more than using German weapons against Germans.

The German weapons above us were intended for ships at sea. They were bigger guns. We were the defence against infantry. I heard a German voice shout, "There are a handful only! Destroy them!"

I shouted, "Here they come! Our lads will be here soon! Hang on chaps!"

There were only a handful of voices but the 'Yes sir!' from my left and right put steel into my spine. This was my section and we could take whatever the Germans threw at us. Four captured German machine guns fired as the rest of the company designated to defend the beach attacked us. They stood no chance. We had four machineguns and seven Thompsons. It was a wall of steel thorough which they tried to attack. I just emptied my Thompson.

"Reloading sir!"

As soon as I heard Emerson I hurled first one, then a second and finally a third grenade. "Grenade!"

Fred and I threw ourselves into the sand. The shrapnel tore into the advancing Germans. I peered over the sandbags. I was grateful that the Germans had prepared their defences well. There were bags to the rear. I sprayed the bodies which littered the ground to our front. The one or two cries told me that I had hit their wounded. I heard the cracks of hand grenades to my left and right. My section was doing what it was trained to do. Behind me I heard the sound of engines as the landing craft powered into the beach. I knew we had not cleared the wire behind us but, closer to the sea wall, we had.

I saw a German rise to throw a grenade. My burst cut him in two and he fell back. His grenade scythed though his companions. I reloaded my clip and took the pin from a grenade. Our weak spot was the unmanned gun to my right. I saw eight Germans run towards it.

"Fred, you are on your own!" I paused only to pick up my last two grenades.

I ran towards the Germans. I hurled the grenade and then threw myself to the ground. I emptied the Thompson blindly and then drew my Luger. The grenade went off and I heard screams and cries. When the sand settled I held my Luger two handed. Less than twenty feet from me was a German Major. I fired three shots into his head and then shot the two men on either side of him. I took a potato masher from my battle dress. I could hear the Landing Craft. They were within shouting distance. We just had to hold on a little longer. I threw the German grenade as high as I could. I was lucky. I dived to the ground. It exploded in the air; the concussion washed over me. I rose and fired the last of my bullets at the Germans I could see.

I stood and loaded another clip into my Thompson. I ran, screaming, at the Germans. I swung the Thompson from side to side. I had no doubt that the Germans would have seen our weak spot and sent the last of their defenders to it. My machinegun tore through the Germans who were less than twenty feet from me. My gun clicked empty and I drew my Colt. I had reloaded it. It was bizarre; I fired the silenced weapon and Germans fell wondering what had killed them. I took out another grenade and running forward, threw it as far as I could. I dropped into the sand. The explosion was so close that I felt the shrapnel whip through the air just above my head. I rolled on to my back and changed the magazine on my Thompson.

I stood and saw Germans cowering. I shouted, in German, "Surrender! Now!"

Slowly, at first, hands came up and the shell-shocked survivors stood. I didn't know what to do. There were fifty men in front of me. Then Bill Hay and Gordy Barker were next to me and their Thompsons were pointing at the Germans.

"On your knees!"

They all dropped. I heard a cheer from behind me and Number Two Commando raced ashore. Major Siddons appeared next to me. "Thanks, old chap! Do you mind if we do a bit now or do you want to win the war all by yourself?"

I turned and smiled, "Be my guest!"

As he passed me he said, quietly, "Bloody magnificent! Worth a V.C. at the very least! " Then he shouted, "Come on Number Two Commando! Let's get into this war! Captain Dawkins secure the prisoners!" With a roar the Commandos raced up the beach passing the stunned Germans. Overhead the RAF began to attack the gun positions higher up the valley.

I patted Fred on the shoulder. Come one, Emerson, let's get the others. This time we don't get to go home on the *'Lady Luck'*."

I waved my hand for Hay and Beaumont to join me. Both were exultant as they approached me. We marched down the beach towards the others. I saw the line of landing craft lined up on the beach. More were already coming in, heading for the gaps on the beach. When I saw Sergeant Poulson leading the rest of my section towards me I couldn't help the smile on my face. We had taken the beach and not lost a single man.

Gordy Barker shook his head, "You haven't changed have you, sir? You could have been killed in that mad charge! If we had done anything like that we would have been on jankers and no mistake."

"Well I wasn't killed, Mother Riley, so you can stop worrying! Now let's catch up with Number Two."

I heard firing and the sound of grenades from up ahead. I had reloaded my Thompson. Scouse had his radio, Gordy had the bazooka and Smith the rockets. The three of them were behind the rest of us. I knew it galled Gordy but their time would come.

There were a handful of dead Germans at the crossroads in the main street. Some Commandos emerged from the railway station with ten more German prisoners. We headed up the hill towards the pass. I began to run. Major Siddons had moved quickly. There was a danger he could move too far and become isolated. A hundred yards from the pass itself we found the Major and his men. They were taking shelter in the ditches at the side of the road.

I dropped next to him. "Problem, Major?"

He nodded, "An armoured car up ahead. He has us pinned down and we have no armour." He pointed to the steep valley sides. "I have sent Sergeant Perkins with a section to work their way around the flank. We need armour really."

I smiled, "No, sir. You need Number Four Commando." I turned and whistled. "Sergeant Barker, Private Smith, get your bag of tricks ready. There is an armoured car ahead."

"Right sir!"

"How far up the road is it?"

"A hundred yards. If you get to the bend then they use their machine gun." He looked at Gordy, "What is your sergeant doing?"

"Using a present we got from the Rangers." The two of them ran up. Smith had two rockets ready. I turned to Emerson, "You and me will go to the bend, fire a burst and take cover in the ditch on the left. That will give you the chance to hit it with the rocket."

"Sir."

I dropped my Bergen as did Freddie. We ran up the road to the bend. Through the trees I could see the armoured car and the men next to it. What we were about to do was not as risky as it sounded. A moving target is hard to hit especially if it is firing back at you. We had just twenty feet to cover. "Right Emerson, on three, one, two, three!"

We burst across the road spraying our Thompsons wildly. I threw myself into the ditch as bullets from the armoured car shredded the trees and branches above my head. Emerson lay on top of me. He rolled off and we both reloaded. I held the gun above my head and fired blindly up the road. Emerson did the same. We drew more fire and then I heard the whoosh of the rocket and the armoured car exploded in a ball of fire. I jumped to my feet and ran up the road, firing from the hip as I did so. Fred was next to me shouting obscenities at the Germans. Once again, our firepower cowed them and the survivors stood, dazed with their hands in the air. I saw the charred corpses of the armoured car crew. I suspected they had been dead before they burned but the acrid smell of burned human bodies was not pleasant.

Sergeant Poulson and my men reached me before Major Siddons. "Scouse, radio the General and tell him the pass is secured and we are moving on to our next objective."

Major Siddons shook his head at the sight of the dead Germans. "A handy weapon. I can see you are more resourceful than us."

"It is handy, sir but the problem is you have to kneel less than a hundred yards from the enemy. That was why we had the diversion. I have radioed Headquarters, sir. Target number two now?" I took my bag from Polly.

"Yes, and you had better stay with us. I think we will need that little metal tube of yours before too long." He turned as the Captain he had left on the beach marched up with a company of Commandos. "Good timing Captain Dawkins. Take charge here. Clear the road and hold it. When Captain Durrant arrives, he can reinforce you. Two companies should be enough. I will take the rest of the Brigade and support the Colonel's attack on Salerno."

"Sir."

He pumped his arm twice and we followed him down the steep and twisting road to our left. "Sergeant Macgregor, take four men and go on point."

"Aye sir."

We saw Salerno as we rounded a bend in the road. The bay was full of tiny dots as the forty sixth division landed. There was heavy firing from the beach. Suddenly we heard firing from ahead. Sergeant Macgregor, limping, and his men hurried back. "Sir, tanks and armoured cars! Six of them!"

"Gordy get the bazooka ready. How many rockets do you have left Smith?"

"Eight."

"Gordy use them wisely, there are six targets coming up."

I took out the German grenades I had taken from the beach. Major Siddons shouted, "Take cover. Set up those Bren guns! Get your grenades ready."

I heard the crack of a German gun as the first of the Mark III tanks opened fire. He was firing blind as he came up the hill. The shell shattered the trees above our heads and we were showered with branches and debris. I saw that Gordy was ready. I knelt next to him with my Thompson ready. The Panzer emerged around the bend and began to spray the road with its machine gun. The Major's men were lying down. They returned fire and threw grenades. I fired at the driver's visor. Gordy fired his rocket launcher. A flame shot out from the rear of the tube and the rocket hit the tank just above the track.

"Bugger!" The turret could still traverse and the tank could fire. As it turned to swat this irritating insect Smith tapped Gordy on the shoulder. This time the rocket hit the turret. It must have ignited ammunition for the turret and tank lifted off the ground as it exploded.

"Come on!"

The Major led the charge down the road. The smoke from the burning tank gave some cover. Gordy hefted the tube on his back. "Only six rockets left Sarge."

"I had better use them a bit better next time then."

I turned to Private Crowe. "Get the grenade launcher ready."

We moved as close as we dared to the burning tank. Gordy took shelter behind a large rock which covered most of his body. His head and shoulders, however, were still exposed. Machine guns fired from the tanks and armoured cars which now covered the road. Behind them were infantry and they were digging in. The tanks' shells now had targets and they fired at Number Two Commandos as they took cover. Two of the men who had been with Sergeant Macgregor raced forward and hurled grenades beneath the leading armoured car. It exploded but one of the men was wounded. I saw him being helped back up the road.

Gordy aimed at the middle of the three tanks. It was a hundred and fifty yards away. He hit the front armour. The rocket exploded but the tank appeared undamaged. "Gordy, the turret!"

"Sir!"

"Crowe start lobbing grenades at those grenadiers." The Panzer Grenadiers were moving forward to tackle our attack.

"Sir."

Bullets from the small arms were sweeping through the trees above our heads. As the first grenade exploded in the air the fire diminished and Gordy fired another rocket. This time he hit the turret which stuck. It could not traverse.

"We have to get closer sir."

I nodded and shouted, "Covering fire!"

Brens, rifles and Tommy guns erupted and a wall of bullets flew down the hill. My section ran in front of Gordy past the tank to the road on the left. One of the tanks fired blindly but the burning tank protected us. The tank's machine gun clattered off the wrecked panzer.

We dropped into the ditch some eighty yards from the nearest tank. I could see the eyes of the driver. The turret began to turn. I fired at the slit and emptied my magazine. Gordy needed time to aim. The driver's face disappeared. I heard the whoosh of the rocket and I dived to the ground as the German machine gun fired at where I had been. The rocket struck the side of the tank and exploded.

"Come on!"

I pulled a grenade out and ran towards the third of the three tanks which had blocked the road. Polly sprayed his Tommy gun as did Hewitt. The stunned German infantry fell as I jumped on the side of the tank. The hatch was open and I dropped a grenade in and closed the hatch. Bullets zipped above my head but I appeared to have a charmed life. I barely had time to throw myself to the ground before it went off. It did not do much damage to the tank but the crew were all hit as the shrapnel clattered around the confined space. John Hewitt opened the smoking hatch and sprayed the inside with his Tommy gun.

I heard another whoosh and saw the last armoured car explode. The surviving infantry ran down the hill to Salerno. "Well done Gordy. Smith, you had better save those last rounds in case we meet any more tanks."

Major Siddons had been on the radio and he came over, "It looks like the Rangers have also secured their objectives. However, the rest of the invasion is not going so well. The other infantry are held up on the beaches. It looks like the Germans have taken over the Italian positions. The Italian Government has surrendered."

I nodded, "So what is the plan, sir?"

He grinned, "It looks like the Commandos take Salerno! Lieutenant Johnson, take your company. You are the point!"

"Yes sir."

"Harsker you and your tank busters can stay with me!"

"Yes sir." I was being restrained. I turned and checked that all of my men had survived. I smiled as I saw them taking the German grenades and pistols. We wasted nothing. Number Two Commando, in contrast, was just checking if the Germans had any souvenirs like watches.

Chapter 20

As we walked down the road to Salerno I examined the papers I had taken from one of the dead tank commanders. It had been the Sixteenth Panzer Reconnaissance Battalion. I wondered how many other armoured units we might face. The country here did not suit armour. The roads were narrow, steep and twisted. The suburbs of Salerno nestled between the mountains and the port. We were on the mountain road above them. We could see down the coast. The naval bombardment appeared to be the only thing which was keeping the army on the beach. It was strange to think that a month ago it had been peaceful. The Germans had reacted quickly. This would not be as easy as the generals had thought.

Gunfire and the sound of grenades ahead alerted us to our own little war. "Right, lads, it looks like Lieutenant Johnson has run into a bit of bother. Captain McQueen take the right flank. Captain Harsker can your lads scramble aorund in the rocks to the left?"

"Will do."

The narrow road twisted and turned as it descended towards Salerno. We had seen a sign, Via Valle, it was well named. The road followed the contours of the valley. To the right was an area of woods. Captain McQueen was heading for them. We had the slightly harder task of using the steep ground to the left. There were stunted trees but it had a severe slope. It would be hard to keep our feet.

"Gordy, you Smith and Scouse are Tail End Charlie. Bill take the left. Sergeant Poulson take the right."

We left the road and climbed up the slope. Soon the road disappeared from my view but I saw Sergeant Poulson raise his Thompson and fire a short burst. He could see enemies. I peered through the foliage. I was now the point of our arrow. I had managed to find the line of least resistance and I made good time. Hewitt and Beaumont flanked me. I caught a glimpse below me of grey and I dropped to my knees and aimed my Thompson. It was a sandbagged machine gun. We were slightly above it. I put my Thompson down and took out two of the German grenades. I smashed the porcelain caps on them, pulled the cords and threw them high. We dropped to the ground. I heard the German machine gunner shout, "Grenade," just before they exploded. I jumped up and sprayed the emplacement. The crew were dead, dying or wounded.

"Come on!"

We made our way down the slope. To our right I heard Sergeant Poulson and his men as they fired at the infantry who had lost their machine gun support. To my left Bill and his men had continued on and were now above us and in front of us. The road twisted back on itself and I saw Germans heading back to the town. We had outflanked them. We had paid a price. I saw that some of Lieutenant Johnson's men had been either wounded or killed at the ambush. I whistled to Bill and waved for him to come down. The enemy were now in full flight towards the town. There would be street fighting soon. I would need all of my men close to hand.

Major Siddons joined us. He had binoculars in his hand. "We have been told to capture Salerno as soon as we can. If we can hold it then the navy can use the port to bring in more men and supplies. I would like you to take your section and capture the port, Tom. I know you don't have enough men but with Dawkins guarding the pass and Johnson's men hit hard I am shorthanded. We can take the town if you can take the port."

"Right sir. That is fine." I held out my hand, "Good luck!"

"And you. If we get out of this alive I am putting you in for a commendation."

I shook my head, "Just getting out in one piece will do me sir." I waved my arm in a circle above my head, pumped the air and pointed to the Via Porto below us. It looked deceptively quiet but I knew there would be defences. Our only advantage was that we were attacking from the landward side and the defences would be seaward. We moved through the woods, passing Captain McQueen and his men. I pointed to the road, "The Major wants you and your chaps to join him and take the town. We are off to capture the port."

"Good luck with that, old boy! Rather you than me."

We spread out in a line with Gordy, Scouse and Smith just behind. We moved from the woods through the backs of some houses. They had been shelled by naval fire and still smoked. It hid us from view. There was a Piazza in front of us. I pointed to Hay, Poulson and Beaumont and made the sign to follow. We sprinted across the open ground. There was the crack of a rifle. We kept running. Then a fusillade of shots hit the ground behind us. It was a German ambush. They had a sniper or snipers in a high building.

I heard Gordy shout, "Open fire!"

The Thompsons rattled away and I heard a cry from ahead of us. We kept running and I saw a body hanging from an upstairs window. Four Germans erupted from the door. We just reacted. My gun was up and firing before I even knew they were there. It was instinct. They were mere feet away from us. They fell dead. Bill went to the building, pulled a grenade and threw it inside. We flattened ourselves against the wall. As the dust flew out a dazed German staggered out and Beaumont shot him dead. I whistled.

"Polly, take Beaumont and check the road."

The Via Porto was just ahead of us. Did they have a roadblock? Were there more men hiding in buildings? We had to proceed carefully. The two of them disappeared and Gordy and the rest joined us.

"Sorry about that sir. We were looking down and not at the buildings. My fault."

"No harm done. Let's go."

We caught up with Sergeant Poulson, "The road looks clear, sir. If you use your glasses you might see some guns, yonder."

I took off my Bergen and took out my binoculars. He was right. There was an eighty-eight and it was firing towards the beaches. It was a good two hundred yards from us. As I scanned the nearby ground I saw, fifty yards to the right, a fuel or gas tank of some description and pipes leading from it. There was also a large warehouse type building behind the guns.

"Gordy, see that fuel tank?" He peered ahead and nodded. "The Colonel said these babies have a range of four hundred yards. That tank will be half inch steel. Do you reckon you can give the German gun the hot foot?"

"I can try sir."

He knelt and Smith loaded. We had one more rocket left after this. Smith tapped him on the head. There was a whoosh and the tank exploded showering the contents, I guessed it was petrol, over a huge area. It ignited the ammunition in the gun pit and the gun exploded. It then set off a dozen smaller explosions and the port was filled with thick black smoke.

"Well done Gordy. Right chaps. Let's take advantage of the confusion!"

We ran to the road and then down it. The wind blew the smoke towards the sea. It effectively hid us. I was looking for the dock gates. There would be guards there. If we held the gates then we controlled the port. Sergeant Poulson saw the gate and the guards first. He gave a burst from his Thompson as Emerson hurled a grenade, "Grenade!" We hit the ground as the Mills bomb exploded and the guard hut at the gate was destroyed.

We were on our feet in an instant and racing through the now open gate. We were in! There was an office just inside the gate and three armed men ran out. Crowe and Bill Hay opened fire and cut them down. I pointed to the office. "You two check that out." I saw the huge warehouse type building to our right. It looked to be three stories tall but there were no windows. I guessed it housed material when it was landed at the port. I hoped it might contain something which we could use.

I heard the double crack of two German artillery pieces and the distinctive sound of an Oerlikon followed by what sounded like a tank gun. "The rest of you, come with me. We have to take out those guns."

The smoke from the fire was still helping us and we ran towards the sea. The crack of shells grew louder. I waved Sergeant Poulson to the right. As we came through the smoke I saw that they had two eighty-eight-millimetre guns, an Oerlikon and an embedded Italian tank. The four of them were firing at the troops on the beaches south of Salerno.

"Gordy take out the tank." I waved to the others and we sprayed the sandbagged emplacements. They had infantry with them. Our first shots made them duck behind the sandbags. A grenade came over. It landed at my feet. I knelt down, picked it up and threw it back. I barely made the ground before it exploded in the air. It showered the gun crew and the infantry.

I saw the Oerlikon swing around to fire at us. The gun layer was winding as fast as he could. Private Beaumont calmly shot the two men with a short burst from his Thompson. As Sergeant Poulson overwhelmed the last eighty-eight there was a whoosh as Gordy Barker fired his final rocket. The tank exploded in a spectacular fireball which knocked us all to the ground.

"Gordy, go to the left and make sure there are no hidden surprises." I ran to Sergeant Poulson, "Sergeant take your men to the sea wall and make sure we are safe. Scouse, send the signal, harbour taken."

Even as I was congratulating myself there was a rattle of rifle fire and Roger Beaumont fell to the ground and Ken Shepherd followed him a shot later. There were still Germans left alive.

"Signal sent, sir!"

"Doc see to the lads. Scouse, Freddie, come with me." Bill Hay and Crowe ran to me. I pointed to the large building which lay at the rear of the docks. That was the only place left where there could be Germans. There were no windows but it had a roof.

I emptied my magazine at the parapet as I saw a German helmet. I ditched my Thompson and drew my Colt as I ran to the door of the building. "Crowe, Emerson, check if there is a rear entrance. You two with me."

The door was locked. Bill Hay shot the lock out with his Colt and then kicked it open. He slammed it shut again and threw himself against the wall. "Grenade!"

The door was blown out. Scouse put his Tommy gun around the door and sprayed his bullets in a hundred and eighty-degree arc. I ran in and hit the far wall with my shoulder. There was a staircase going up. I heard the sound of a Colt and Crowe and Emerson burst through the back door. They had blown the lock too. I pointed up and they nodded.

I took one side of the staircase and Scouse the other. Bill Hay looked up the stairwell to the top. We were almost at the first floor when he opened up with his Thompson. I heard a cry from above us. When I reached the first floor I pointed to Scouse's gun. He fired in all four corners of the huge building. It appeared to be filled with crates.

I waved the others up and we began to ascend the last flight of stairs. A pair of potato mashers were thrown down. Scouse had very quick reflexes and he kicked them over the side. We threw ourselves away from the stairwell and the two grenades went off below us on the ground floor. Bill Hay emptied another magazine at the floor above. "I have had enough of these bastards sir! Let's finish them."

"They are going nowhere and they have used three grenades already." Let's do it the same as before. Fred and Bill, you two cover us. Alan, you come up the middle. Scouse, take the right."
I held my Colt in one hand and my Luger in the other. I felt like Tom Mix! I watched for any movement. I saw a hand and fired the Luger. I hit the doorway and splinters flew. I heard a cry. I took the stairs two at a time and did not pause at the top. I threw myself through the opening. As I landed I saw a German officer just ten

fcct away. I fircd thc Colt and a holc appcared in his middle as he was thrown backwards.

I heard Colts, Thompsons and German rifles as the gun fight erupted. I turned and fired at the machine gun which was thirty feet away. My two guns knocked the gunners over the side. Their cries as they fell told me they were still alive; right up until they hit the concrete. I stood and saw that there had been a platoon up here. We had taken out a third of them already. Alan Crowe spun around as he was hit and I put two bullets into the German who had shot him.

Bill Hay was like a man possessed. He was firing his Thompson from the hip and running at the Germans. Scouse also had the wild look in his eyes that told me he had almost lost it. Fred Emerson, in contrast was kneeling and calmly firing his Colt at the Germans. I shouted, "Hands up and surrender or we will shoot you all!"

An officer of the Waffen S.S. raised his Walther. I fired three bullets from my Luger and all three smacked into his face. He fell backwards.

"Are there any more heroes?" I pointed with my Colt. "There is a fleet out there with more men that you can imagine. Surrender now or I will let my men loose on you."

I think it was the look in the eyes of Scouse and Bill Hay which convinced them. The ten survivors dropped their weapons and held up their hands. "Bill, Scouse, disarm them."

I ran to Crowe, "Where did they hit you?"

He held up his Thompson. The stock had been shattered. "The gun saved my life, sir. It just knocked the wind out of me."

"You are one lucky boy, Private Crowe."

"I know sir!"

I reloaded both of my pistols as I examined the roof. They were using it to direct artillery. There was a radio in the corner. The operator had been shot. I went over to it in case it still worked. If it had then we might have made use of it but the last burst which had killed the operator had destroyed the radio.

The prisoners were lined up. I saw that half of them were Waffen S.S. It was unusual for them to surrender. I said, quietly, "Did you search them properly, Bill?"

"I think so, sir. Why?"

"These are Waffen S.S. These are the hard lads. Emerson, Crowe, we will divide these men into two." I walked over and tapped the five who were not Waffen S.S. on the shoulders. I said in German, "You go with these men. Do not try anything. They are Commandos." They nodded. "Take these down to Sergeant Poulson and have him wait by the doors for these others."

The five who were left did not look like men who were anticipating spending time in a prison camp. I pointed my gun at them. "Take off your boots."

There was a tough looking sergeant. He reminded me of Brian Donleavy in *'Beau Geste'*, "Why? We have surrendered."

I went closer to him, keeping my Colt pointed at his middle. "Because I told you to and I know what the S.S. is like. I met some in Belgium. Do it or I will shoot you... in the foot of course!"

Scouse had put his silencer on his Colt and he fired a round between the Sergeant's legs. The German nodded and said, "Do it! Our time will come."

As he bent down to untie his boots I knew what was coming. I had already taken a step back when he launched himself at me. I stepped to the side and brought the Colt down on the back of his neck. One of the others produced a knife and was about to lunge at Bill Hay when Scouse shot him. The German Sergeant shook his head. I brought my knee up sharply and his head cracked back. This time he did not get up. I pointed the gun at the three survivors. "Boots! Now!"

They complied.

"Now take off his boots and carry him down the stairs. One false move and you will be shot!"

With three of us watching them and encumbered by the body of the sergeant they were in no position to cause trouble.

When we reached the bottom I said, "Fletcher go and radio the fleet. Tell them we have taken out their fire control!"

Sergeant Poulson said, "Did you have trouble, sir?"

"Yes, Sergeant. I want these four men searching. Hold them down if you have to."

With guns surrounding them we soon found the knives they had hidden in their boots. Scouse and Bill took one each. They were the Hitler Youth daggers. "A nice souvenir my German friend."

We made our way to the dock for I could see the destroyer with the General aboard heading for us. There were also the two landing craft with the reserve force of Commandos. Major General Laycock was the first one off. He grinned as he strode towards me. "Well done, Captain Harsker, Major Siddons has just confirmed that Salerno is in our hands. The rest of the beach heads might be in jeopardy but we have Salerno, we have the port and thanks to the Commandos and Rangers we have the passes to Naples. Congratulations! We now have a toehold in Europe and, believe me, it will take something to shake us free!"

I pointed to the four Waffen S.S. prisoners. I would have these watched carefully, sir. They are cunning customers."

"I have met the S.S. before. We know how to deal with them." He turned, "Major Reed. Take charge of these prisoners and then set your team to manning the perimeter. What we have we hold."

"Yes sir."

"And you, Captain, can have the trip back to Falmouth you asked for. I am sorry to lose you but I am a man of my word. You have done all that I asked of you and more. Major Siddons is putting you in for a gong!"

I shrugged, "I was just doing my duty, sir."

"And you do it very well too. The destroyer is heading back to Valetta. Get aboard her and you can fly back to Gib and then England. The Lieutenant Commander has your orders."

I could not help myself. My face lit up into the biggest smile ever. "Thank you sir!"

Epilogue

In the event we did not leave until the next morning. The destroyer was taking the intelligence we had captured back to Malta so that it could be sent to England. In effect we were the guards for the papers. The ship's doctor saw to our wounded men. The two of them, Beaumont and Shepherd, had slight wounds. They were not going to risk being separated from us. We assured the doctor that Corporal Hewitt could be their nurse until we reached England. We had a night in Valetta before the Sunderland took us, first to Gibraltar and then to Southampton. By then we knew that the invasion had been a huge success. They had pushed on beyond Naples and were heading north. For the first time it felt like we were winning.

I had time to write my reports. I recommended Bill Hay and Scouse Fletcher for promotion. I also put in Hay, Fletcher and Emerson in for the Conspicuous Gallantry Medal. They had deserved it. To be honest they all deserved something.

I spent some time speaking with Roger Beaumont. He was the youngest of my men but he had impressed me. "Why didn't you try to be an officer, Roger? I am certain that you would have thought about it at University."

He smiled, "Blame yourself, sir. I went to Manchester University and I was told about this undergraduate who packed in the OTC, joined up and won the Military Cross. I thought if you could do it then why not me? I am happy I made that choice sir.

This team is all that I want and, perhaps, one day I might be a corporal or even a sergeant. I still have a lot to learn and neither of us believes that this war will end any time soon, do we, sir?"

"No Roger. You are right. Well if you ever need any advice, feel free to speak with me. You have made me feel responsible for you."

When we landed at Southampton there was a lorry waiting for us and a grinning Reg Dean. He looked fit to burst. "Welcome home lads! It has been quiet without you! Get in the back of the lorry."

They began to throw their bags and guns on board. Reg turned to me, "And you sir, promoted to Captain. No more than you deserve."

"Thank you Reg. That means a lot."

He grinned, "Aye sir but there is more. You have been put forward for the V.C. and General Laycock himself has endorsed it. Well done sir! You'll soon have the same medals as your dad. What a family!"

As I climbed into the cab I reflected that I had joined up as a private so that I would not be compared with Dad and yet here I was in the same league as him. Fate!

The End

Glossary

Abwehr- German Intelligence
Bisht- Arab cloak
Butchers- Look (Cockney slang Butcher's Hook- Look)

Butties- sandwiches (slang)

Chah- tea (slang)

Comforter- the lining for the helmet; a sort of woollen hat

Corned dog- Corned Beef (slang)

Ercs- aircraftsman (slang- from Cockney)

Fruit salad- medal ribbons (slang)

Gash- spare (slang)

Gauloise- French cigarette

Gib- Gibraltar (slang)

Glasshouse- Military prison

Goon- Guard in a POW camp (slang)- comes from a 1930s Popeye cartoon

Jankers- field punishment

Jimmy the One- First Lieutenant on a warship

Killick- leading hand (Navy) (slang)

LRDG- Long Range Desert group (Commandos operating from the desert behind enemy lines.)

Marge- Margarine (butter substitute- slang)

MGB- Motor Gun Boat

Mickey- *'taking the mickey'*, making fun of (slang)

Micks- Irishmen (slang)

MTB- Motor Torpedo Boat

ML- Motor Launch

Narked- annoyed (slang)

Neaters- undiluted naval rum (slang)

Oik- worthless person (slang)

Oppo/oppos- pals/comrades (slang)

Pom-pom- Quick Firing 2lb (40mm) Maxim cannon

Pongo (es)- soldier (slang)

Potato mashers- German Hand Grenades (slang)

PTI- Physical Training Instructor

QM- Quarter Master (stores)

Recce- Reconnoitre (slang)

SBA- Sick Bay Attendant

Schnellboote -German for E-Boat (literally translated as fast boat)

Schtum -keep quiet (German)

Scragging - roughing someone up (slang)

Scrumpy- farm cider

Shooting brake- an estate car

SOE- Special Operations Executive (agents sent behind enemy lines)

SP- Starting price (slang)- what's going on

Snug- a small lounge in a pub (slang)

Sprogs- children or young soldiers (slang)

Squaddy- ordinary soldier (slang)

Stag- sentry duty (slang)

Stand your corner- get a round of drinks in (slang)

Subbie- Sub-lieutenant (slang)

Tatties- potatoes (slang)

Thobe- Arab garment

Tommy (Atkins)- Ordinary British soldier

Two penn'orth- two pennies worth (slang for opinion)

Wavy Navy- Royal Naval Reserve (slang)

WVS- Women's Voluntary Service

Maps

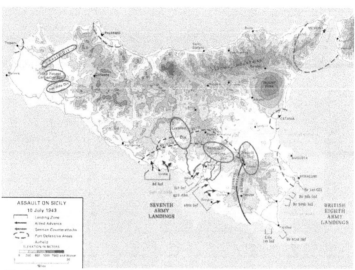

Operation Husky courtesy of Wikipedia

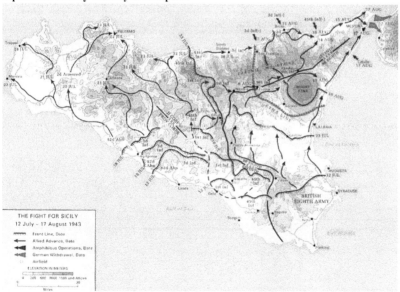

Map courtesy of Wikipedia

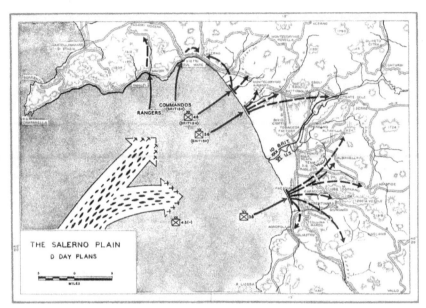

Maps courtesy of Wikipedia

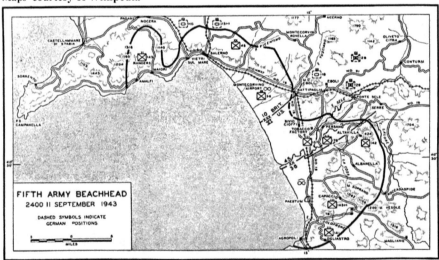

Historical note

The first person I would like to thank for this particular book and series is my Dad. He was in the Royal Navy but served in Combined Operations. He was at Dieppe, D-Day and Walcheren. His boat: LCA 523 was the one which took in the French Commandos on D-Day. He was proud that his ships had taken in Bill Millens and Lord Lovat. I wish that, before he died I had learned more in detail about life in Combined Operations but like many heroes he was reluctant to speak of the war. He is the character in the book called Bill Leslie. Dad ended the war as Leading Seaman- I promoted him! I reckon he deserved it.

I went to Normandy in 1994, with my Dad, to Sword beach and he took me through that day on June 6th 1944. He also told me about the raid on Dieppe. He had taken the Canadians in. We even found the grave of his cousin George Hogan who died on D-Day. As far as I know we were the only members of the family ever to do so. Sadly, that was Dad's only visit but we planted forget-me-nots on the grave of George. Wally Friedmann is a real Canadian who served in WW2 with my Uncle Ted. The description is perfect- I lived with Wally and his family for three months in 1972. He was a real gentleman. As far as I now he did not serve with the Saskatchewan regiment, he came from Ontario. As I keep saying, it is my story and my imagination. God bless, Wally.

I would also like to thank Roger who is my railway expert. The train Tom and the Major catch from Paddington to Oswestry ran until 1961. The details of the livery, the compartments and the engine are all, hopefully accurate. I would certainly not argue with Roger! Thanks also to John Dinsdale, another railway buff and a scientist. It was he who advised on the use of explosives. Not the sort of thing to Google these days!

I used a number of books in the research. The list is at the end of this historical section. However, the best book, by far, was the actual Commando handbook which was reprinted in 2012. All of the details about hand to hand, explosives, esprit de corps etc were taken directly from it. The advice about salt, oatmeal and water is taken from the book. It even says that taking too much salt is not a bad thing! I shall use the book as a Bible for the rest of the series. The Commandos were expected to find their own accommodation. Some even saved the money for lodgings and slept rough. That did not mean that standards of discipline and presentation were neglected; they were not.

The 1st Loyal Lancashire existed as a regiment. They were in the BEF and they were the rearguard. All the rest is the work of the author's imagination. The use of booby traps using grenades was common. The details of the German potato masher grenade are also accurate. The Germans used the grenade as an early warning system by hanging them from fences so that an intruder would move the grenade and it would explode. The Mills bomb had first been used in the Great War. It threw shrapnel for up to one hundred yards. When thrown the thrower had to take cover too. However, my Uncle Norman, who survived Dunkirk was demonstrating a grenade with an instructor kneeling next to him. It was a faulty grenade and exploded in my uncle's hand. Both he and the Sergeant survived. My uncle just lost his hand. I am guessing that my uncle's hand prevented the grenade fragmenting as much as it was intended. Rifle grenades were used from 1915 onwards and enabled a grenade to be thrown much further than by hand

During the retreat the British tank, the Matilda was superior to the German Panzers. It was slow but it was so heavily armoured that it could only be stopped by using the 88 anti aircraft guns. Had there been more of them and had they been used in greater numbers then who knows what the outcome might have been. What they did succeed in doing, however, was making the German High Command believe that we had more tanks than they actually encountered. The Germans thought that the 17 Matildas they fought were many times that number. They halted at Arras for reinforcements. That enabled the Navy to take off over 300,000 men from the beaches.

Although we view Dunkirk as a disaster now, at the time it was seen as a setback. An invasion force set off to reinforce the French a week after Dunkirk. It was recalled. Equally there were many units cut off behind enemy lines. The Highland Division was one such force. 10,000 men were captured. The fate of many of those captured in the early days of the war was to be sent to work in factories making weapons which would be used against England.

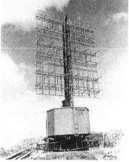

Freya, the German Radar.

Germany had radar stations and they were accurate. They also had large naval guns at Cape Gris Nez as well as railway guns. They made the Channel dangerous although they only actually sank a handful of ships during the whole of the war. They did however make Southend and Kent dangerous places to live.

Commando dagger

The first Commando raids were a shambles. Churchill himself took action and appointed Sir Roger Keyes to bring some order to what the Germans called thugs and killers. Major Foster and his troop reflect that change.

The parachute training for Commandos was taken from this link http://www.bbc.co.uk/history/ww2peopleswar/stories/72/a3530972.shtml. Thank you to Thomas Davies. The Number 2 Commandos were trained as a battalion and became the Airborne Division eventually. The SOE also trained at Ringway but they were secreted away at an Edwardian House, Bowden. As a vaguely related fact 43 out of 57 SOE agents sent to France between June 1942 and Autumn 1943 were captured, 36 were executed!

The details about the Commando equipment are also accurate. They were issued with American weapons although some did use the Lee Enfield. When large numbers attacked the Lofoten Islands they used regular army issue. The Commandos appeared in dribs and drabs but 1940 was the year when they began their training. It was Lord Lovat who gave them a home in Scotland but that was not until 1941. I wanted my hero, Tom, to begin to fight early. His adventures will continue throughout the war.

The raid on German Headquarters is based on an attempt by Number 3 Commando to kill General Erwin Rommel. In a real life version of *'The Eagle Has Landed'* they almost succeeded. They went in by lorry. They failed in their mission. Commandos were used extensively in the early desert war but, sadly, many of them perished in Greece and Cyprus and Crete. Of 800 sent to Crete only 200 returned to Egypt. Churchill also compounded his mistake of supporting Greece by sending all 300 British tanks to the Western Desert and the Balkans. The map shows the area where Tom and the others fled. The Green Howards were not in that part of the desert at that time. The Germans did begin to reinforce their allies at the start of 1941.

Motor launch Courtesy of Wikipedia

Motor Gun Boat Courtesy of Wikipedia

E-Boat

Short Sunderland
Aeroplane photographs courtesy of Wikipedia

Fieseler Fi 156 Storch
Photographs courtesy of Wikipedia

The Dieppe raid was deemed, at the time, to be a fiasco. Many of the new Churchill tanks were lost and out of the 6000 men who were used on the raid only 2078 returned to England. 3,367 Canadians were killed. wounded or captured. On the face of it the words disaster and fiasco were rightly used. However, the losses at Dieppe meant that the planners for D-Day changed their approach. Instead of capturing a port, which would be too costly they would build their own port. Mulberry was born out of the blood of the Canadians. In the long run it saved thousands of lives. Three of the beaches on D-Day were assaulted with a fraction of the casualties from Dieppe. The Canadians made a sacrifice but it was not in vain.

S-160 Courtesy of Wikipedia

The E-Boats were far superior to the early MTBs and Motor Launches. It was not until the Fairmile boats were developed that the tide swung in the favour of the Royal Navy. Some MTBs were fitted with depth charges. Bill's improvisation is the sort of thing Combined Operations did. It could have ended in disaster but in this case it did not. There were stories of captured E-Boats being used by covert forces in World War II. I took the inspiration from S-160 which was used to land agents in the Low Countries and, after the war, was used against the Soviet Bloc. They were very fast, powerful and sturdy ships.

Sherman Tank- courtesy of Wikipedia

The first Sherman Tanks to be used in combat were in North Africa. 300 M4A1 and M4A2 tanks arrived in Egypt in September 1942. The war was not going well in the desert at that point and Rommel was on the point of breaking through to Suez. The battle of El Alamein did not take place until the end of October.

The Hitler order

Top Secret
Fuhrer H.Q. 18.10.42

1. For a long time now our opponents have been employing in their conduct of the war, methods which contravene the International Convention of Geneva. The members of the so-called Commandos behave in a particularly brutal and underhanded manner; and it has been established that those units recruit criminals not only from their own country but even former convicts set free in enemy territories. From captured orders it emerges that they are instructed not only to tie up prisoners, but also to kill out-of-hand unarmed captives who they think might prove an encumbrance to them, or hinder them in successfully

carrying out their aims. Orders have indeed been found in which the killing of prisoners has positively been demanded of them.

2. In this connection it has already been notified in an Appendix to Army Orders of 7.10.1942. that in future, Germany will adopt the same methods against these Sabotage units of the British and their Allies; i.e. that, whenever they appear, they shall be ruthlessly destroyed by the German troops.

3. I order, therefore:— From now on all men operating against German troops in so-called Commando raids in Europe or in Africa, are to be annihilated to the last man. This is to be carried out whether they be soldiers in uniform, or saboteurs, with or without arms; and whether fighting or seeking to escape; and it is equally immaterial whether they come into action from Ships and Aircraft, or whether they land by parachute. Even if these individuals on discovery make obvious their intention of giving themselves up as prisoners, no pardon is on any account to be given. On this matter a report is to be made on each case to Headquarters for the information of Higher Command.

4. Should individual members of these Commandos, such as agents, saboteurs etc., fall into the hands of the Armed Forces through any means – as, for example, through the Police in one of the Occupied Territories – they are to be instantly handed over to the SD

To hold them in military custody – for example in P.O.W. Camps, etc., – even if only as a temporary measure, is strictly forbidden.

5. This order does not apply to the treatment of those enemy soldiers who are taken prisoner or give themselves up in open battle, in the course of normal operations, large scale attacks; or in major assault landings or airborne operations. Neither does it apply to those who fall into our hands after a sea fight, nor to those enemy soldiers who, after air battle, seek to save their lives by parachute.

6. I will hold all Commanders and Officers responsible under Military Law for any omission to carry out this order, whether by failure in their duty to instruct their units accordingly, or if they themselves act contrary to it.

The order was accompanied by this letter from Field Marshal Jodl

The enclosed Order from the Fuhrer is forwarded in connection with destruction of enemy Terror and Sabotage-troops.

This order is intended for Commanders only and is in no circumstances to fall into Enemy hands.

Further distribution by receiving Headquarters is to be most strictly limited.

The Headquarters mentioned in the Distribution list are responsible that all parts of the Order, or extracts taken from it, which are issued are again withdrawn and, together with this copy, destroyed.

Chief of Staff of the Army

Jodl

FW 190 Courtesy of Wikipedia

The FW 190 had two 13mm machine guns with 475 rounds per gun. It also had two 20 mm cannon with 250 rounds per gun. It could carry up to 500 kg bombs. It usually had just one bomb in the centre of the aeroplane

Gabbiano class corvette Courtesy of Wikipedia

The Persefone was a real Gabbiano class Corvette. It brought Mussolini to Ponza under arrest after he was toppled from power.

Ju 88 courtesy of Wikipedia

Faith, Hope and Charity were the nicknames given to the three Gloster Sea Gladiators which, for a time, were Malta's only air defence. These ancient biplanes did sterling work. In actual fact there were more than three but it suited the propaganda of the period to ascribe the success against the Italian bombers to just three aeroplanes. They were based at the Sea Air Arm base, H.M.S. Falcon.

The Royal Navy rum ration was 54.6% proof. It was an eighth of a pint. Senior ratings (Petty Officers and above) received their rum neat while junior ratings had it diluted two to one. *'Up Spirits'* was normally between 11 and 12 each day.

Bristol Beaufighter- courtesy of Wikipedia

Mitchell Marauder B-26 courtesy of Wikipedia

Douglas C-47 Courtesy of Wikipedia

The Rangers under Colonel Darby were at Amalfi. The rocket launcher known as the bazooka was first used in North Africa. Italy was the first time it had a widespread use. It was limited to the Americans only at first but later was used by the Russians and the British. The Germans captured some and used them to make their own version, the Panzershreck.

M1A1 Rocket Launcher Courtesy of Wikipedia and the Smithsonian

The Commando attack at Vietri Sul Mare went according to plan and the only losses they suffered were when they attacked Salerno itself. Nine Commandos were killed and thirty-seven wounded. The Commandos were opposed by the 16th Panzer Reconnaissance Battalion which they defeated before capturing Salerno. It was an impressive feat for a brigade of Commandos. Following this and Lord Mountbatten's departure for the Far East Major General 'Lucky' Laycock was appointed commander of

Combined Operations. It was a position he occupied until the end of the war.

Reference Books used

- The Commando Pocket Manual 1949-45- Christopher Westhorp
- The Second World War Miscellany- Norman Ferguson
- Army Commandos 1940-45- Mike Chappell
- Military Slang- Lee Pemberton
- World War II- Donald Sommerville
- St Nazaire 1942-Ken Ford
- Dieppe 1942- Ken Ford
- The Historical Atlas of World War II-Swanston and Swanston
- The Battle of Britain- Hough and Richards
- The Hardest Day- Price

Griff Hosker March 2016

Other books

by

Griff Hosker

If you enjoyed reading this book, then why not read another one by the author?

Ancient History

The Sword of Cartimandua Series (Germania and Britannia 50A.D. – 128 A.D.)

Ulpius Felix- Roman Warrior (prequel)

Book 1 The Sword of Cartimandua

Book 2 The Horse Warriors

Book 3 Invasion Caledonia

Book 4 Roman Retreat

Book 5 Revolt of the Red Witch

Book 6 Druid's Gold

Book 7 Trajan's Hunters

Book 8 The Last Frontier

Book 9 Hero of Rome

Book 10 Roman Hawk

Book 11 Roman Treachery

Book 12 Roman Wall

Book 13 Roman Courage

The Aelfraed Series (Britain and Byzantium 1050 A.D. - 1085 A.D.

Book 1 Housecarl

Book 2 Outlaw

Book 3 Varangian

The Wolf Warrior series (Britain in the late 6th Century)

Book 1 Saxon Dawn

Book 2 Saxon Revenge

Book 3 Saxon England

Book 4 Saxon Blood

Book 5 Saxon Slayer

Book 6 Saxon Slaughter

Book 7 Saxon Bane

Book 8 Saxon Fall: Rise of the Warlord

Book 9 Saxon Throne

The Dragon Heart Series

Book 1 Viking Slave

Book 2 Viking Warrior

Book 3 Viking Jarl

Book 4 Viking Kingdom

Book 5 Viking Wolf

Book 6 Viking War

Book 7 Viking Sword

Book 8 Viking Wrath

Book 9 Viking Raid

Book 10 Viking Legend

Book 11 Viking Vengeance

Book 12 Viking Dragon

Book 13 Viking Treasure

Book 14 Viking Enemy

Book 15 Viking Witch

Bool 16 Viking Blood

Book 17 Viking Weregeld

Book 18 Viking Storm

The Norman Genesis Series

Rolf

Horseman

The Battle for a Home

Revenge of the Franks

The Land of the Northmen

Ragnvald Hrolfsson

Brothers in Blood

Lord of Rouen

The Anarchy Series England 1120-1180

The Napoleonic Horseman Series

Book 1 Chasseur a Cheval

Book 2 Napoleon's Guard

Book 3 British Light Dragoon

Book 4 Soldier Spy

Book 5 1808: The Road to Corunna

Waterloo

The Lucky Jack American Civil War series

Rebel Raiders

Confederate Rangers

The Road to Gettysburg

The British Ace Series

1914

1915 Fokker Scourge

1916 Angels over the Somme

1917 Eagles Fall

1918 We will remember them

From Arctic Snow to Desert Sand

Wings over Persia

Combined Operations series 1940-1945

Commando

Raider

Behind Enemy Lines

Dieppe

Toehold in Europe

Sword Beach

Breakout

The Battle for Antwerp

King Tiger

Beyond the Rhine

Other Books

Carnage at Cannes (a thriller)

Great Granny's Ghost (Aimed at 9-14-year-old young people)

Adventure at 63-Backpacking to Istanbul

For more information on all of the books then please visit the author's web site at http://www.griffhosker.com where there is a link to contact him.